HIDDEN IN TIME

Books in the *After Cilmeri* Series:

THE AFTER CILMERI SERIES

HIDDEN IN TIME

by

SARAH WOODBURY

To my sister

Cast of Characters

David/Dafydd – King of England
Lili – Queen of England
Meg/Marged – Queen of Wales
Llywelyn – King of Wales
Gwenllian – Princess of Wales
Elen – Meg's niece
Christopher – Meg's nephew; Elen's brother
Humphrey de Bohun – Earl of Hereford
William de Bohun – Humphrey's son
Goronwy – Llywelyn's friend
Tudur – Welsh lord; Llywelyn's steward
Dilys – Meg's steward
Edmund of Almain – Earl of Cornwall
Gilbert de Clare – Earl of Gloucester (deceased 1293)
Bogo de Clare – Gilbert's brother
Margaret de Clare – Gilbert's sister; Almain's wife

<u>Edward and Eleanor's Family</u>
Edward – King of England (deceased 1285)
Eleanor – Queen of England (deceased 1285)
Eleanor – Dowager Queen of England (deceased 1291)
*Edmund – Earl of Lancaster, Edward's younger brother
(deceased 1285)*

Daughter b. 1255 – deceased 1255
Katherine b. 1264 – deceased 1264
Joanna b. 1265 – deceased 1265
John b. 1266 – deceased 1271
Henry b. 1268 – deceased 1274
Eleanor b. 1269 – deceased 1288
Juliana b. 1271 – deceased 1271

Joan b. 1272
Alfonso b. 1273 – deceased 1284
Margaret b. 1275
Berengaria b. 1276 – deceased 1278
Daughter b. 1277 – deceased 1278
Mary b. 1278
Son b. 1280 – deceased
Elizabeth b. 1282
Edward II b. 1284 – deceased 1288

1

25 September 1295

St. Margaret's Convent

Day One

Lizzie

"This way, my lords." Abbess Helen's commanding voice sounded in the corridor outside the dormitory. The smooth wood of the floor was cool on Lizzie's cheek as she held herself still and breathless, listening. "All is well with the girls, I assure you. We've taken good care of them."

"We will need to see for ourselves." A man's voice answered in French, low and harsh.

"Are you sure they are who you say they are? I find it hard to believe they could have been here all this time, and we didn't know it." The abbess sounded more put out than worried. If these men had told her the sisters' real identities, she would feel affronted that she'd been lied to all this time.

"We are sure."

The vindictive part of Lizzie hoped the abbess was going over in her mind all the times she'd striped Lizzie's palm, deprived her of meals, or locked her in a closet. To be fair, Lizzie had sometimes deserved her punishments. Even more, that the abbess had been fooled wasn't her fault. While the old abbess had known the truth, she had died within a year of the girls' arrival at St. Margaret's.

With her demise, the only people who could attest that three princesses lived at St. Margaret's were Gilbert de Clare, the man who'd hidden them there, and the three princesses themselves.

Or so they had all thought until tonight.

Lizzie remembered well the urgency with which Earl Gilbert had spirited them away from their old convent of Amesbury after their grandmother's death. He had indelibly impressed upon each of the sisters the need for secrecy—a secrecy they'd maintained without exception all this time, even after Earl Gilbert had died too.

Maybe especially after.

Up until a few moments earlier, Lizzie had been curled up at the foot of her sister's bed. At the sound of the men's heavy footsteps coming up the stairs, she'd been startled upright, moving in an instant from almost asleep to wide awake. "That sounds—"

"—like men." Daisy had sat up too, pushing out of her face stray strands of light brown hair that had come loose from her long braid. "Go, Lizzie." Then she'd squeezed Lizzie's hand once, shooing her off the bed and onto the floor beneath it. "Hide."

"For once, do as you're told." This had come from Molly, Lizzie's other sister, who was almost exactly three years younger than

Daisy, as they were both born in March. That made her seventeen, Daisy twenty, and Lizzie thirteen. Unlike Daisy and Lizzie, Molly had entered the convent with some degree of willingness, having been promised to it from the age of six. All these years later, she barely remembered anything else.

In truth, Lizzie herself barely remembered anything of that former life, beyond a few vague memories. Her mother's scent, perhaps, though that could have come from another woman who cared for her. She didn't remember the funeral of her brother, Alfonso, when she was two years old. She did remember her parents' deaths in Lancaster the next year. She'd been three when they died, and her grandmother, the dowager queen Eleanor, had moved all the girls to the convent at Amesbury, to which she herself retired, in order to keep an eye on them.

Until someone finally explained to Lizzie where Lancaster was, she had thought it some far off, unreachable place, like France. Though Lizzie hadn't known anything about where her parents had died, her grandmother had made sure she'd known, from the moment she could listen and understand, *how* they'd died: Queen Marged had poisoned Lizzie's parents so David could take the throne from Lizzie's father without opposition.

Fear a tangible knot in her throat, Lizzie scooted away along the floor, under the adjacent beds and towards the far wall and a better hiding place. Even if these men were friends of Earl Gilbert instead of sent by the king, making Lizzie entirely wrong about what was happening, she didn't want to be punished (again) for being outside her own dormitory chamber at night. Her backside still hurt from the beating she'd received earlier that day for being late to the holy office.

Until the move to St. Margaret's, the sisters had always been known as *Margaret, Mary,* and *Elizabeth.* But the old abbess, within moments of their introduction, had dubbed them *Daisy, Molly,* and *Lizzie* respectively. This was partly because their given names belonged to nuns already living at the convent, but also to make the girls appear more common. Their years at Amesbury had taught them enough English to understand what she was saying to them and, with Gilbert de Clare nodding from the doorway, they'd acquiesced to their new identities.

Besides, it was only a confirmation of what Earl Gilbert had already told them in the carriage ride from Amesbury: from now on, nobody could know they were princesses. If that meant English pet names, so be it.

All this time, thanks to Earl Gilbert's foresight, the sisters had stayed safe from the king's men.

But somehow, after all these years, they'd been found.

2

Day One

Daisy

In the few moments of respite between when the abbess had spoken and when she'd flung wide the door so the men could peer into the dormitory, Lizzie had lifted herself into her favorite hiding place: the narrow window seat set in the far wall against which the door opened. A curtain hid her from view, but she would be able to see into the room through a narrow crack between the two halves of fabric.

Daisy let out a sigh of relief. She had feared someone looking under the beds and wanted her sister as far away from her and Molly as possible.

"Even if they are who you say they are, I'm sure I don't know why you need to move them in the middle of the night." As was often the case, Abbess Helen sounded impatient. She didn't like anything that disrupted the smooth running of her convent.

But Daisy knew why. It was on a night like this that Earl Gilbert had moved the sisters from Amesbury to St. Margaret's, fulfilling their grandmother's dying wish that he protect them from King David's wrath. Nighttime was for secrecy and clandestine action.

The rest of the world thought they'd been taken instead to a remote convent near Gloucester, one also under Earl Gilbert's protection. After the earl's death, the abbess there had put out that Daisy herself had been married to a foreign duke, Lizzie was in care somewhere in the north of England, and Molly had taken her final vows as a nun. Even from the grave, Earl Gilbert's concern had been to keep them safe.

"My lord Tudur has news of a threat against them."

The man's assurance had the opposite effect on Daisy than it had on Abbess Helen. Very likely, Lord Tudur had suddenly discovered their existence, perhaps in Earl Gilbert's papers, and was now determined to put an end to the three sisters once and for all. While Lord Tudur ruled at Chepstow, more than a hundred miles away in Wales, he had recently been appointed castellan of Kings Langley, a royal manor some seven miles from St. Margaret's. That proximity was the main reason Tudur had also taken over sponsorship of the abbey, the position having remained vacant since Earl Gilbert's death. With King David himself in France, they understood Kings Langley was currently occupied also by King Llywelyn, Queen Marged, and their children.

That connection practically stopped Daisy's heart: if Lord Tudur had sent men for them, it would be at the direct request of the king and queen.

Abbess Helen gave a tsk. "They're just girls."

By now, at least some of the other girls in the dormitory, a dozen in all, had to be awake and listening, though none were so bold as to sit up. Several pulled their blankets up over their heads. French was a second language for all of them, poorly spoken by most, so they might not understand what was being said. But to have men in the dormitory was so rare as to be unprecedented, and *that* they would know for certain.

"We don't understand it ourselves. We are just following orders." The speaker lifted the lantern he held, allowing Daisy to see his face more clearly. He was tall and broad, with a black beard and a piercing gaze, even from across the room. The combination was intimidating to Daisy, and she could understand why Abbess Helen had given way to him. Thankfully, neither man moved forward into the room, which would have been a greater violation of propriety, even had Abbess Helen let them.

She carried a lantern too, held low to the ground, so it gave out a narrow circle of light near her feet. The girls were allowed a single candle, which they carefully husbanded each evening and the stub of which Molly now lit, ensuring all eyes would turn towards it, rather than to Lizzie's dark corner. Molly had always been clever that way. Her hands weren't even shaking. Daisy was quite sure she wouldn't have been able to coax a flame.

While the men stayed by the door, the abbess processed across the room to reach the foot of Daisy's bed, ultimately looking down at the exact spot where Lizzie had been lying moments before. By now, even Mabel, who could sleep through anything and had the bed closest to the door for that reason, was awake. And while everyone knew better than to babble, some of the other girls were whispering amongst themselves.

Molly was already wrapping herself in her habit, which she put on directly over her nightdress, and coiling her long dark hair into a bun at the base of her neck. She was plain of face, more so than Lizzy or Daisy, but her brown eyes were penetrating. And such was her standing at the convent that she ventured a question, which was a relief to Daisy because it meant she didn't have to. "Is something the matter, Mother?"

She was speaking in English, the only language the sisters dared speak with each other in their guise of *not* being princesses. From the frustration in the men's faces, they didn't understand enough to follow what she'd said. Based upon their stillness and silence, the other girls in the room, however, were riveted.

"You both must rise and come with me."

Molly looked towards the door where the two men waited. "Who are those men?"

"They have been sent by Lord Tudur."

"What do they want?"

The abbess's face held a look that indicated she didn't want to answer, but this was Molly, her favorite. Thus, after a pause, she said, "To speak with you."

Molly nodded her acceptance, but Daisy found herself unsatisfied. "Why?"

"Daisy." The word came out clipped. "Do as you're told."

This was typical of the abbess. They were all to do as they were told, at every moment, and never ask why.

"Yes, Mother." Molly sent a hard look at her sister. "Daisy didn't mean to question your judgment."

But that was exactly what Daisy was wanting to do right now, and somehow, she didn't feel the need to stop herself from doing it. "It's just odd for strange men to want to speak to us in the middle of the night. You can't expect us not to wonder what they want."

"Daisy!" As the abbess had done a moment earlier, Molly admonished Daisy, trying to stop her from talking more. Cleverer than Daisy, and far more scholarly, Molly was a stickler for the rules and the least likely of the three sisters to break them. She was also often the one to enforce them—though, come to think on it, she'd never once tattled on Lizzie for sleeping at the foot of Daisy's bed.

"They are not strange, and it is not for you to wonder," the abbess said. "As I told you, they are here for your benefit, to keep you safe."

"Are you sure they were sent by Lord Tudur?" Daisy could feel the shock in the room, emanating not only from her sister, but also from the other girls. And maybe from the abbess too. Since the men had appeared in that corridor, and Daisy had sent Lizzie into hiding, she had felt almost lightheaded. And somehow, the questions just kept coming.

"Of course he sent them. Why would you think otherwise?"

"Then what about Lizzie?"

"She wasn't in her room. I assumed she was here." The abbess's tone deepened. "I know she sometimes sneaks about in the night. Have you seen her?"

"No, Mother." Daisy lied boldly.

Amazingly, not only did Molly not contradict Daisy, an astounding breach of her usual superior moral attitude, but neither did any other girl in the room, even those who'd seen Lizzie pull herself into the window seat. The closest girls could probably hear her breathing behind the curtain.

"Don't worry," Abbess Helen said. "We'll find her. She never goes far."

"We are just worried about her, Mother." Molly stepped in front of Daisy, trying to divert the abbess's wrath. "We wouldn't want to be separated."

And, because of Molly's intercession, all of a sudden Abbess Helen became conciliatory. This was still Molly after all, and even if Daisy had been uncharacteristically assertive, being awakened in the middle of the night meant allowances needed to be made. Particularly for newly discovered princesses. "Get dressed as quickly as you can and join us in my study."

"Yes, Mother." Together, Daisy and Molly bowed their heads, yet again the perfect exemplars of meekness and submissiveness.

Nodding to see their usual compliant attitude return, the abbess moved back towards the door. As she reached it, she motioned for the two men to precede her. "You shouldn't really be up here at all."

"We mean no disrespect." The black-bearded man spoke again, in French as before. "But we had to see for ourselves that they were here, especially with the youngest girl not where she was supposed to be." He loomed over the abbess, and his manner told Daisy he was glowering.

"As I said, she can't have gone far. We will find her." Abbess Helen pulled the door closed behind her, taking the lantern with her.

The moment they were gone, one of the other girls said, "What's going on? Is everything all right?"

"It's fine. Everything is fine," Daisy said, continuing to lie.

"What about Liz—"

Molly broke in before the girl could finish. "It seems these men are friends we didn't know we had. We'll clear everything up and return in no time. You should all go back to sleep." That she had cut off the girl's query indicated the depth of her concern that one of the men might still be in the corridor, listening, whether or not he understood English.

Daisy then lifted her chin so her voice would carry to the whole of the room, including Lizzie in her window seat. "If you see

Lizzie, tell her we love her, and we'll see her soon. She knows what to do. I'm sure it will be the right thing."

3

Day One

Lizzie

izzie had almost fallen out of the window seat to hear Daisy speak to Abbess Helen in such a fashion. Without a doubt, this was the first time in Lizzie's hearing that Daisy hadn't acquiesced immediately to everything Abbess Helen said. She'd asked *questions*. Maybe not enough and had settled for poor answers, but she'd *asked*.

With Daisy's last words, however, Lizzie pulled back, confused.

The right thing?

It was a message, a code meant for Lizzie, and exactly the kind of puzzle she normally liked. But in this case, she had no immediate idea of what Daisy meant for her to do.

Then Daisy and Molly left, leaving the dormitory door open behind them. Normally, doors were always kept closed to keep in the warmth generated by a dozen girls sleeping together. It was a small change, but one Lizzie interpreted as meaningful. They wanted her to follow them.

But as her sisters' footsteps faded down the passage, Lizzie remained frozen in position behind the curtain. Her legs simply wouldn't work properly, and the longer she stayed where she was, the faster she breathed.

And yet, any moment now, Abbess Helen was going to give Daisy and Molly to these men. Lizzie didn't know if she could do anything about it, but she had to try. Daisy was clearly counting on her to try.

The silence in the dormitory was so thick Lizzie could have cut it with a knife. The other girls were waiting for her, just as breathless perhaps as Lizzie herself. Then the light in the corridor dimmed and was gone, indicating one of the men had waited for Daisy and Molly to reach him and then led them away.

The knowledge that her sisters had known he was waiting, and even Molly had gone out of her way to ensure Lizzie wasn't ensnared too, had Lizzie swallowing hard. She'd been within a heartbeat of pulling aside the curtain and throwing herself at Daisy as she was on her way out the door. Even when Lizzie had been at her unhappiest, she had never doubted that Daisy loved her. It was Daisy who always knew how to make Lizzie feel better; Daisy whose bed she had slept on so many nights; Daisy who had quietly put herself between Lizzie and the abbess, as Molly had just done for Daisy, more times than Lizzie could count. But somehow, this time Daisy was counting on Lizzie.

To do what?

Lizzie hadn't the remotest idea, but whatever it was, it wouldn't happen if she stayed in the window seat. The longer she waited to move, the farther away Daisy and Molly would get, depending upon how quickly they sorted things out with Abbess Helen.

Bracing herself for the journey, as if leaving the window seat was the same as stepping off the top of a tower and falling—except unlike Queen Marged, she wouldn't be traveling to Avalon—Lizzie slipped from her hiding place and tiptoed across the floor, her bare feet making almost no noise. She knew the way well enough, even in the dark, to avoid the creaky floorboard directly in front of the door. Each of their visitors had stepped on it in turn when they'd entered the room, as had Daisy and Molly when they'd left it.

Again, Lizzie thought that had been deliberate, since they both knew how loud the sound would be. They wanted to remind Lizzie it was there, in case she could possibly have forgotten.

Lizzie peered around the frame of the door into the corridor. It was just as dark as she'd expected, which truly didn't fill her with confidence. Everything about tonight had been unprecedented, such that if Queen Marged herself had suddenly appeared in the corridor, like the tales said she could do when she returned from Avalon, Lizzie wouldn't have been surprised.

Then a whisper came from Mabel, the girl whose bed was closest to the door. "We don't like those men, Lizzie. Abbess Helen says they are here to take care of you, but something didn't feel right about them. We won't tell anyone, even her, that you were here."

In her years at St. Margaret's, Lizzie had been accused of exhibiting an abundance of unsavory character traits: she was lazy; she was stubborn; she was disrespectful and disobedient; she was impulsive. Even Daisy had never understood that, beneath it all, what Lizzie really felt was *anger.*

She was angry her parents were dead. She was angry Earl Gilbert had died. She was angry to be forced all the time to behave as if she didn't have a thought in her head that was her own. And she wasn't good at swallowing down her feelings. It was a wonder she hadn't been evicted from the convent long ago. Maybe she would have been if she'd had anywhere to go—and if she hadn't had two perfect sisters the abbess would prefer not to lose.

Molly had once asked Lizzie if she was exhausted by never doing as she was told. Lizzie had replied that it was quite the opposite. Doing as she was told, always fulfilling someone else's vision of her life, left Lizzie in inner turmoil, full of questions and thoughts she was unable to articulate. To not do so left her almost physically in pain at the effort of keeping her true self hidden. At the convent, everything she wanted to do or say was forbidden.

All that meant Lizzie had never felt like she had a place with these other girls. Now, however, Lizzie reached out, as earlier Daisy had done to her, and grasped Mabel's hand. "Thank you. You have always been kind to me. I know I haven't made it easy."

She sensed, more than heard, laughter in Mabel's voice as she replied: "We'll be praying for you, Lizzie. Take care of your sisters.

Even when you think you're completely alone, never forget that God is with you. As are we."

4

Day One

Daisy

While Daisy had been inside the convent, she had kept her many additional questions to herself. It had become clear to her, back in the dormitory, that the abbess had given all she could. That Daisy had been rebuffed without a slap to the face was something of a miracle.

Outside on the walk was a different matter. "Where are you taking us?"

The black-bearded man seemed to be in charge. "Some place safe. I already told your abbess that Lord Tudur is simply concerned for your well-being. We need to move you before someone else does."

Daisy found herself staring at his beard rather than into his eyes, which were an unreadable dark brown. She was quite sure icy blue wouldn't have been any better. Right then and there, she decided she was not content to be put off and halted abruptly just outside the convent's main gate. These men had the answers she wanted, if answers were to be had. "Our abbess has entrusted us to you, and we have come willingly, so you might as well tell us what place, exactly, is *safe*."

The man hesitated, and then his eyes flicked up and down, as if assessing the merits of throwing her over his shoulder and forcibly inserting her into the carriage. Daisy almost hoped he would. The abbess was watching them from the porch in front of the main door, and at that point even she might start to have second thoughts about releasing her girls to these men. Honestly, Daisy was shocked their abbess had allowed her and Molly to leave with these strangers at all, without even a chaperone or other woman to keep an eye on them.

The man's hesitation emboldened Daisy. Now was the only moment she had any leverage at all. Once she entered the carriage, she would be entirely at the men's mercy.

Instead, the man merely opened the carriage door and indicated they should get inside. Maddeningly, Molly obeyed his unspoken order, taking a seat on the bench that faced backwards. It wasn't Daisy's favorite way to ride, since the motion sometimes made her ill, but she certainly wasn't going to sit next to this man nor allow Molly to do so. Daisy wished as usual that she knew more about what was really going on inside her sister's head. Getting Molly to tell her what she was feeling was often like pulling teeth: painful and sometimes left a root behind.

In truth, she shouldn't have expected Molly not to do as the man said. Like Daisy, she had spent her life, long before the death of their parents, doing as others bid. Life at the convent was merely more of the same. Molly could be quite assertive within the range of things she knew. But, as earlier in the dormitory, she always remained carefully within the bounds her superiors set for her. Up until now, Daisy knew herself to have been even more compliant, which was saying something when she was comparing herself to Molly.

Thus was the fate of princesses and always had been. Sometimes Daisy found herself envying the girls from the village who came to the convent to learn to read and write. She didn't necessarily think they had any more choice about their lives than she did, but at least they could dance and sing and shout at the sky if they wanted to. Poor Lizzie spent half her life in that storage closet for doing exactly what everyone else viewed as normal. None at the convent had ever seen her misbehavior as a love of life. All they ever wanted to do was rein her in.

Daisy had learned how to rein herself in long ago. If she was being honest, their current predicament could be traced to the fact that she'd learned it too well. Born a middle sister, her tendency to acquiesce and deny she had any opinion had been a way to keep the peace among those born before and after her. Over the years, Daisy had carefully built walls around her own thoughts, stone by stone, until only she knew what was inside her own head. Thoughts were the one thing nobody else could ever control or take away from her. It was, of course, ironic that she had just lamented to herself about the way Molly had done the same thing.

Tonight wasn't about being a princess, however. It was about protecting herself and her sisters. In the walk from the dormitory, it was as if everything she knew and understood about the world had reached the same point. "Sir, you may have fooled the abbess, but you don't fool me. Lord Tudur didn't send you."

At these words, Molly let out a gasp of dismay. Daisy ignored her. She could even forgive her sister for making it. The light-headedness Daisy had felt before was gone, replaced by a cold certainty of what lay before her. If Molly was going to sit there and say nothing, and Lizzie was to be kept safe, that left only Daisy to do what must be done. Leaving the convent, though terrifying, was at the same time freeing, as if she had become a boat let loose from its moorings. The calm of this warm night was an illusion. They were really in the middle of a winter storm at sea, with wind and rain lashing her face. All of a sudden, she found herself saying the things that were piling up in her mind instead of keeping them inside as she usually did.

In truth, as she *always* did.

Daisy had hoped to elicit a genuine response by being provocative, but the man didn't even bother to come up with a more comprehensive lie. "Of course he did."

Molly leaned forward, looking out the carriage door. "Get in, Daisy."

Daisy ignored her again. They'd been waiting for men to find them since Earl Gilbert had put them here. Now, someone had not only found them, but had gone so far as to send men to fetch them. That they weren't dead meant that person wanted something from them. Lord Tudur was already married, so it couldn't be that he needed a royal bride like Earl Gilbert had wanted. "If he had been the one to send you, you would be Welsh. He wouldn't trust something this important to Normans."

Even as the man's eyes narrowed and he dismissed her concerns with a sweep of his arm, she knew she had guessed right. Wales was a separate country, but it shared a long border with England and, unlike in the immediate aftermath of Llywelyn being crowned King of Wales when the border had been closed to easy traffic, these days it was entirely uncontrolled. Welshmen had infiltrated every aspect of English life, every one of them singing David's praises and grateful he had elevated them from a conquered people to a member of the Confederated States of Britain.

With the death of her father, England (in many ways like Daisy herself), had been demoted to an equal participant, with the same rights and authority as every other member of the coalition. According to Daisy's grandmother, this was a humiliating comedown, and Daisy's father would be rolling over in his grave if he knew.

But at long last, Daisy had cracked the man's mask of courtesy, which had only ever been a façade. "You will get in the carriage now, or I will put you in it."

Daisy tried to stare him down, but with Molly making anxious noises from her seat inside the carriage, she knew she'd lost the battle. She thought about putting her nose in the air and behaving as if it had been her wish all along to do as he'd asked, but that would have been even more humiliating and likely would have amused the man.

As she settled herself on the seat beside her sister, Daisy's thoughts moved on to the next puzzle, which was the true identity of the person who'd sent for them and how he could have learned where they were. Lord Tudur—or the King and Queen of Wales—could be the ones to have discovered she and her sisters were at St. Margaret's instead of where they were supposed to be. But King David was surrounded by a host of ambitious and powerful men. It was perfectly possible one of them might have decided to curry favor by parading them before the king, one last triumph over a long-vanquished enemy. It would be petty, but in keeping with what she knew of the royal court.

Still, if true, Daisy was confused about the timing of this move. King David was in Normandy. Aquitaine had already voted to join the CSB, and now Normandy had petitioned to do so as well, in direct defiance of the wishes of the King of France. If the petition was approved, David would have to change the name of his coalition of states, because it wouldn't just be about Britain anymore. With Aquitaine, it already wasn't. She'd heard that Ireland, which had never wanted to be associated with Britain in the first place, had been pushing for a name change for some time.

She nudged Molly. "Maybe these men were sent by the King of France."

Molly swiveled to look at her. "Why on earth would he care about us? How would he even know where we were?"

"Earl Gilbert was allied with the brother of the French king."

Molly frowned. "I can't imagine what use we would be to him. We aren't leverage."

"Maybe we've been wrong about that, Molly. It isn't as if the world thinks we're dead."

Molly scoffed under her breath. "But has a single soul bothered to check to see if I'm really where I'm supposed to be? Or that you were really married to that duke? Nobody cares what happens to us. Likely, few gave any of us another thought once David was crowned king. With the possible exception of our prayers, we have no value whatsoever to anyone anymore."

"Then why are we in this carriage?"

For once, Molly didn't snort at her and instead gave Daisy a truth of a kind she rarely shared: "I am equally concerned about the answer to that question. In retrospect, I shouldn't have stopped you from asking about it just now, and we were right not to give Lizzie away. The more I think about it, the more I see that only Grandmother and Earl Gilbert ever gave a thought to our personal safety—though, considering the matter with current eyes, he likely didn't care about us at all either. We were pawns in his game against the king, a game he lost, just like everybody else who seeks to challenge David."

Daisy reached out a hand and placed it on top of Molly's. "Though I'm no less afraid of what happens next, I can be grateful you're here with me."

By way of reply, Molly clasped her hand around Daisy's.

Then the black-bearded man entered the carriage. As he settled himself in the seat opposite, the two girls held on to each other. With Molly's defense of Daisy back in the dormitory, her refusal to betray Lizzie, and now this, Daisy felt closer to her sister than she had in a very long time.

5

Day One

Lizzie

Her sisters were gone in a manner so much like *a lamb to the slaughter,* to take a phrase from Isaiah, as to make no difference. Because of it, however, Lizzie put aside her own fear and entered the corridor. Her first steps started her heart racing again, and she forced herself to tiptoe along the wall, stopping every few feet to make sure nobody was in front of her, waiting for her to reveal herself. Thankfully, all was empty and in darkness.

As Lizzie passed the stairwell, she could see a hint of light below her, indicating a lantern had been lit on the lower floor where the abbess had her quarters. Unlike at Amesbury, St. Margaret's was not wealthy enough for the abbess to merit her own suite of buildings.

Lizzie continued to creep along the darkened corridor, keeping her back to the wall and ready to run if anyone appeared. Given that it was past midnight, she had hours before the bell for morning prayers. Now that the excitement of her sisters' departure was over, everyone would be getting as much sleep as possible while they could.

At one time, St. Margaret's convent had been one of the poorest in Hertfordshire. Earl Gilbert had changed all that in the years before he'd moved the sisters to it, during which time the structure of the entire abbey had been reworked to include new buildings and a new wall around the abbey as a whole, while the old buildings had been refurbished.

Some of the latter work had been completed in something of an irregular fashion, perhaps in an attempt to avoid tearing down the old buildings entirely. Daisy had suggested too many minds had influenced the project. One of the results was what Lizzie affectionately called *doors to nowhere*.

In some places in the abbey, the remodeling had blocked these former doorways with stone, but it was still possible to make them out by the archways that had once formed the upper frame of the door. Even multiple layers of plaster or whitewash didn't hide them completely. There was one additional doorway Lizzie had discovered when she'd been shut in a storage closet as punishment for talking during dinner, when only prayers and readings were allowed. Not only had the doorway been left extant in the back wall, complete with the original wooden door and hinges, but it was a single story above the ground. The door had once opened onto a set of stairs that led towards the chapter house, but with Earl Gilbert's renovations, the chapter house was now a much larger building located on the other side of the newly created central cloister.

Lizzie guessed the masons had been told not to block the door because, in a fever of optimism, the abbess had speculated that someday they might want to expand further and build an addition onto the dormitory. If so, they would need a doorway into the older section, and leaving this doorway as it was would save them having to knock down a wall. Regardless, the thick oak door had been left in position, and a wardrobe placed in front of it to hide it.

A few hours of boredom in the closet had been more than enough time for Lizzie to explore every nook and cranny. Repeated visits had given her the opportunity to place squares of cloth under each corner of the wardrobe to allow it to slide nicely along the wooden floor without scratching it. She might even have chosen to do certain activities warranting punishment to make sure she had sufficient time and space to prepare the room as she pleased.

Many a night she'd lain in bed, hating her life, and been comforted by the fact of the door's existence. If there came a day when she couldn't stand another moment in the convent, she had a way out, even if it meant leaving her sisters behind.

She'd never considered the possibility that they would leave her behind first.

Even with the knowledge of the door's existence and how much she wanted to leave the convent, she hadn't used it often, just enough to familiarize herself with being outside alone after dark. It wasn't so much a fear of getting caught and punished that had prevented her from running wild at night. Rather, it was the fear of getting caught and not having the door as an outlet when it counted.

And always, in the back of her mind, had been the possibility of exactly what had happened tonight. Earl Gilbert had been quite clear that the sisters were in danger from King David and his men, who feared to leave any member of Lizzie's family alive to garner support from the people of England. According to Lizzie's grandmother, her son had been so beloved that it was only a matter of time before someone rose up—and the people of England with him—to challenge David.

That said, her grandmother had reserved her special ire for Queen Marged, whose arrival from Avalon had incited King Llywelyn to fight for the independence of Wales long after he should have given it up. To add insult to injury, she'd given him a son to ensure his line would continue, a son who'd then taken the throne from *her* son after Marged had murdered him. The dowager queen had been quite sure as well that David had murdered Lizzie's youngest brother, Edward. Maybe he'd murdered Alfonso too. It would be well in keeping with his character.

Earl Gilbert had promised to change all that, the living embodiment of what her grandmother had said was true. "Never mind the past, Elizabeth," he had told her when she'd asked him about those days. "What's done is done. Soon, we will all be back in Westminster where we belong, and Margaret will be Queen of England."

"Why don't you marry her now?"

"I will take the throne on my own merits first, because the people chose *me* to be their king."

Even if at the time she hadn't understood the distinction he was making, this plan had sounded lovely to Lizzie from start to finish. Queens and princesses didn't have to scrub pots until their hands were red and chapped. Her parents were dead, but that didn't mean she had to be miserable all the time ... *did it?* She didn't see why she should be punished because the king hated her family. The unfairness of it made her chafe all the more at her cloistered life. Daily, hourly, sometimes with every heartbeat, she longed for something beyond these walls, even if she didn't know exactly what that *something* might be. She knew only that there *had* to be more in her future than an endless round of work and prayer.

Unfortunately, David had killed Earl Gilbert too, despite the Earl having been chosen (as he'd wanted) by the barons to be the next King of England. When Lizzie's parents had died, she'd been too young to know what it meant. The day the news of Earl Gilbert's death had come to St. Margaret's, her grief had been profound, and she had known the convent would be her home forever.

Once the hidden door was open, Lizzie stood on the threshold, breathing in the fresh evening air and telling herself she was ready. She'd spent the last few years wanting more than anything to leave the convent, but now the moment had come, she was terrified.

Pulling in a deep breath through her nose, she eyed the distance to the old oak tree that had survived the remodeling of the dormitory block. Beyond was the exterior wall of the convent. By leaping the few feet to the tree, Lizzie would be able to scramble along a branch and drop over the wall to the other side. It wasn't a high wall anyway, since its purpose was merely to demarcate the borders of the convent and keep out unwanted animals—as well as (Lizzie secretly thought) men. Clearly, it had failed in the latter regard.

But still she hesitated, now with second and third thoughts. She was well aware that much of the time she acted hastily, without fully thinking through her actions. Certainly, she'd been told about this failing many times. Back in the dormitory, cautious voices in her head had told her to stay still, to trust Daisy, and they'd been right. This time, they were telling her she wasn't quite ready to go.

Up until that moment, as the breeze blew into her face and through her thin nightdress, she'd been entirely oblivious to what she was wearing. It was one thing to sneak into her sister's dormitory in the middle of the night without cloak or slippers. It was quite another to follow those same sisters into the night wearing nothing but what she'd worn to bed.

Turning back to the wardrobe, she opened it and found the same attire present as the last time she'd looked: mostly spare habits, but in the bottom at the very back was a small pile of clothing from when the last girl had joined the convent three months ago. Usually dresses worn into the convent by novices were given away to the indigent, since these were no longer needed by their original owners. But this particular dress must have been too worn. Or simply forgotten.

Lizzie grabbed the underdress and pulled it over her head, right over the top of her shift. The girl was larger than Lizzie, or had been, but once Lizzie put on the overdress too, she was able to wrap the accompanying belt around her waist in order to hold it all together. With the cloak, which she swung around her shoulders for good measure, she should be warm enough for traveling as far as she needed to go. Also available were stockings and boots, also too large for Lizzie, but not overly so. As a girl who'd spent many years wearing castoffs from other women, she was used to slopping about in too-big shoes.

Returning to the door, Lizzie could do nothing about the way the wardrobe remained skewed from its usual location, but she did manage to balance on the threshold in the doorway and at the last instant pull the door closed behind her. Unlike in the past, she wouldn't be needing to get back into the convent that way. Then, with her heart in her mouth, Lizzie flung herself into the tree.

There was no turning back now.

She made her way along the branch to the other side of the wall and, once she dropped to the ground, ran as quickly and silently as she could along the exterior of the convent towards the road. By the male voices ahead of her, making no attempt whatsoever to be quiet, all her dithering hadn't made her too late.

Turning the corner, she was in time to see her sisters being loaded into a carriage. She tried not to snort at how meekly Abbess Helen had given up her sisters, and they had acquiesced to it. Then she upbraided herself for judging them. She wasn't the one in captivity, and she was free because Daisy had done everything in her power to ensure it. *The right thing.* Lizzie still had no notion what that might be.

The original two men who'd come into the dormitory had been joined by two more. Creeping closer through the long grass that wet her skirts to her knees, Lizzie was able to overhear the tail end of a conversation two of them were having with each other. One had a black beard and the other barely a beard at all.

"You still couldn't find the other one?" Blackbeard said.

"I looked—"

Blackbeard made a cutting off motion, and his stare was so intense Lizzie imagined he could see right through his counterpart. She was thankful he wasn't looking in her direction. "This is a convent full of useless women! How far could she have gone? What did the mistress of novices say?"

"She said she didn't know."

"She's lying." He was very sure.

No-beard shook his head. "I don't think so."

Blackbeard scoffed. "Get back inside and search the place. The girl probably went to the latrine, and you missed her."

"I didn't miss her." No-beard pushed back. "I searched the convent, and the girl isn't here. Maybe she died, and they didn't want to tell us?"

Now Blackbeard grunted, as if he hadn't thought of that, and when he spoke next his tone was more conciliatory. "Find out, if you can." Lizzie thought he grimaced. "We can't wait for you. These two are restless enough, and the older one is asking too many questions."

"How am I to get back?"

Blackbeard's look could have been disbelieving. He definitely scoffed again. "It isn't far. Walk. Borrow one of the abbey's horses. I don't care."

"What if I have the girl with me?"

"She's a girl. She'll do as you say."

No-beard nodded and returned to the convent, while Blackbeard swung himself into the carriage with Molly and Daisy. The other two men sat together on the driving bench. Then the carriage started rolling forward. Lizzie watched its progress for a few moments, making sure it was going the way she expected (south), and then she crossed the road to enter the field where the convent's horses grazed, one of whom perhaps No-beard would soon be wanting to appropriate.

She hadn't had a plan when she leapt from the doorway other than to find out who the men were and where they were taking her sisters. She hadn't known how she was going to accomplish either task. However, by the time she crouched in the grass, heard the horses whickering in the field, and realized they were there for the taking, she began to feel as if God might actually be on her side tonight. From the men's conversation, she already knew where they were taking her sisters wasn't *far*.

Since the weather was so mild, the horses were spending the night in the pasture, and it was easy to find Herbert, her best friend in the world. She had learned to ride very young, as befitting her station as a princess. Her grandmother had made sure of that. Once at

St. Margaret's, any special lessons had stopped, but the convent did have horses, and she'd made a friend not only in Herbert but in one of the stable boys who'd cared for them for a time. He was gone now, called back to his family's farm to manage it after the death of his father. His name was Tim, and he'd even kissed her once, at the time engendering delight and shame in Lizzie in equal measure. These days, when she was having a difficult day, she hugged the memory close.

Herbert nudged her hand gently as she held it out to him. "I don't have anything for you, I'm sorry to say, and you aren't going to like roaming about in the middle of the night, but we have to go." She'd already collected the rope left around the gatepost, to make it easier to catch him if he ever went astray (which he never had, in her experience). Fitting him with it, she led him back through the gate onto the road. He was too big for her to mount without assistance, but she knew where there was a rock that would give her a leg up. Soon, she was riding bareback after her sisters' carriage.

This time, as she breathed in the night air, a joy rose up within her. The long days of summer had given her more stolen moments on her own than in previous years. She had thought it only her due, given what lay in store for her in a few weeks when she and her sisters had been finally supposed to make their vows to commit themselves fully to the convent. The very thought curdled Lizzie's stomach and, for a moment, she was overcome with relief and gratitude, odd as that might seem, to the men who'd taken her sisters.

Come what may, because of what they'd done, she was never going back.

6

Day One

Daisy

"What's going on out there?" The black-bearded man leaned forward to bang with his right fist above Molly's head.

They couldn't have traveled more than a mile or two and already the carriage had come to a stop. For a moment, Daisy dared hope they had reached their destination. If so, it would make it easier for Lizzie to follow them, if she'd managed to escape the convent on her own.

"A wheel is rolling funny," came the reply. "We don't want to risk it coming off."

Swearing under his breath, the black-bearded man opened the door to the carriage and got out.

The instant he was gone, Daisy gripped her sister's hand tighter. "Molly—"

Her sister looked at her warily. "What?" She sounded annoyed more than afraid, which was all to the good. Daisy was afraid enough for both of them.

But not so afraid she wasn't able to act. With Molly's hand still in hers, and without actually replying, Daisy pushed at the carriage door, which the black-bearded man had left slightly ajar. "Come on, Molly. We have to go."

Molly wasn't any less suspicious. "Go where? Are you mad?"

Daisy opened the door a little more and crouched in the entrance to the carriage. "I thought you said I was right, that you shouldn't have stopped me asking questions."

"That's true, but—"

Daisy looked back at her sister. "These men weren't sent by Lord Tudur."

"I know, but—"

"If you really thought everything was going to be all right, why didn't you tell them where Lizzie was?"

Molly had nothing to say to that, and while she considered her retort, Daisy tugged her off her seat. The wheel in question was the left front, which put it on the opposite side of the carriage from the door.

Four men had come to get them. One had remained behind at the convent, which left three to try to fix the wheel. All of them were huddled around it. Once Daisy was out of the carriage and ducking low, she could see their feet, which were illuminated by the lantern hanging from a hook near the driver's seat.

Blinking away the glare of lantern light and still holding Molly's hand, Daisy tiptoed away, her eyes on the wall that lined the road and separated it from the adjacent pasture, searching for a way to get over it. But just as she reached the rear of the carriage, one of their captors rounded the corner from the other side, and they ran smack into each other.

Daisy bounced off him, as surprised as he was. This was the third man, one of the two who had not entered the convent to fetch them but had waited at the carriage. He was small for a man, the same size as Daisy really, and probably weighed less. Thus, in that first instance, she got the better of the encounter. He staggered backwards, unbalanced more than Daisy, as well as surprised and discomfited.

Daisy saw when he recognized what had happened. She had been hoping to have escaped before any of the men realized she and Molly were gone, but they'd probably noticed the shifting of weight in the carriage when the girls had left it and sent this man to investigate.

He recovered a heartbeat after Daisy, opening his mouth to warn his companions of their escape. Before he could, Daisy punched him in the nose as hard as she could with the knuckles of her right hand.

It was a move Alfonso, her elder brother, dead these eleven years, had taught her when she was a girl and enthralled with all the interesting things he was learning. His world was sword fighting, wrestling, and hand-to-hand combat, each new skill added to his education over time to make him stronger and smarter in battle. She genuinely liked needlepoint and the camaraderie of women sitting around a tapestry as they created it, but since Daisy had been only a year younger than Alfonso, and neither had playmates of their own station most of the time, after his lessons he'd taught her what he knew.

Those had been happy days, all the more so in comparison to what had come after. The day Alfonso died everything good and fun in the world had disappeared. Her parents had lived another year, but even when they did visit, they were distracted by the new baby, Edward, her father's last living son and heir. And then her parents had been poisoned, and the five surviving daughters had gone to live at the convent at Amesbury with their grandmother.

In all these years, Daisy hadn't forgotten what she'd learned.

Stunned by the blow, the man stumbled backwards, blood blossoming from his nose. He attempted to stem the flow with both hands, and Daisy didn't wait to see what he decided to do next, since presumably that would be to finally shout for help, which was what she'd been trying to prevent. Dragging Molly behind her, she raced off, skirts clutched in her free hand to raise them above her ankles so she wouldn't trip. Now that they were away from the carriage and navigating by moonlight, she could see enough of the road to avoid the potholes and pits, many full of water from the day's rain.

After a few steps, Molly accepted her fate, and her feet pounded down the road alongside Daisy's. "I haven't run in years!"

Daisy herself was already so out of breath, her chest straining at the effort of the pace she'd set, that she didn't have the ability to reply.

"This way!" Molly saw opportunity before Daisy, swerving to the left and almost tugging Daisy's arm out of its socket as she headed for a tree that had grown up on the near side of the stone wall alongside which they'd been running. If they could climb into it, they could then drop over the wall into the field on the other side. While only four feet high, the stone wall had been built on the top of an embankment that added another three feet to its height. "Help me up!"

In response to her sister's plea, Daisy clasped her hands together to make a rest for Molly's foot, to boost her into the tree like she would if she were helping her onto the back of a horse.

The men came on behind them, their feet beat-beat-beating along with Daisy's racing heart. Then, as if summoned by an angel she resembled, a ray of moonlight illuminated Lizzie's face amidst the tree branches above them. Somehow she had reached this spot at the same time they had and entered the tree from the other side of the wall. In her surprise, Molly almost lost her grip on the branch she'd just grabbed.

Lizzie flung out a hand to help. "Hurry!"

But Daisy just stared up at her littlest sister. "No."

It was as if she was seeing Lizzie for the first time. Framed by the branches of the tree and wearing the ugliest dress Daisy had ever seen, one that accentuated the way the abbess had underfed her (and would have made anyone else look very homely indeed), she was beautiful.

In the convent, nobody ever looked at Lizzie closely, not even Daisy. But all of a sudden, Daisy knew that if Lizzie were caught, everyone would be looking at her, including the horrible men bearing down on them.

It didn't bear thinking about.

"What's wrong?" Molly looked down at her.

"Come back down here, Molly. There isn't time for both of us to get over this wall, and Lizzie needs to save herself, so she can ultimately save us." Daisy tugged on the back of Molly's dress.

"No!" Lizzie was practically upside down as she stretched a hand to her sisters.

Molly, for once, didn't question Daisy's judgment and dropped back to the ground. "Daisy's right, Lizzie. I might have been able to escape, but she wouldn't have, and I won't leave her. What's more, we can't risk you."

Daisy, glanced over her shoulder. The men still had a few yards to go. Probably their boots were no better for running on a dark road in the middle of the night than Daisy's thin shoes. "Hide yourself! They can't know you're here."

"Daisy—"

"Better yet, get help! You're our only hope!" She didn't dare make a motion that implied someone was in the tree and instead headed back to the center of the road with Molly, resolutely refusing to look back at Lizzie to make sure she did as she was bid. Lizzie was never one to obey orders, but as the men approached closer, she would be smart enough to realize they were outmatched. Or so Daisy hoped.

Molly held out both hands at her sides, letting the men see she wasn't going to fight them. Daisy stepped beside her.

All the men were breathing hard, which was a tiny bit comforting—or at least satisfying to know that Daisy had made them work for their prize. The black-bearded man slowed once he was within ten feet and walked the last few steps at a normal pace. "Did you really think you could outrun us?"

"You'll pay for what you did!" The man whose nose Daisy had bloodied grabbed her upper arm, unnecessarily roughly, and started hauling her towards the carriage.

"Don't hurt her, Leon," The black-bearded man said. "We don't get paid for damaged goods."

"I'm the one who's damaged. She broke my nose!"

"And you will be paid for your trouble." The black-bearded man had Molly by the upper arm too and was hustling her back to the carriage at a fast walk. "Do you think the earl cares about your nose? I assure you he does not."

Leon grumbled to himself, but his grip loosened slightly on Daisy's arm, enough so he might not be leaving more bruises on top of the ones he'd already made.

Daisy kept her head down, so none of the men could see her face. She didn't care so much about Leon's name as the identity they'd just given their benefactor: *the earl*. Perhaps in the heat of the moment, they had forgotten to pretend he was Lord Tudur. Tudur was a powerful lord, but not an earl, not yet anyway, though of course it would be an aspiration. Daisy had been right Lord Tudur hadn't sent them. It was a second small triumph—and an equally small consolation, truth be told, given the circumstances in which she and Molly found themselves.

Without further protest, she allowed herself to be returned to the carriage, all the while going over in her head the various earls they could mean. Her first glorious thought was that the earl in question was Edmund Crouchback, her father's brother and the Earl of Chester. Just the thought of him gave her a moment of rising excitement that he had somehow survived the carnage at Lancaster and had been in hiding all these years, coming out only now to rescue them.

She immediately dismissed the notion. It was so unlikely as to be impossible. Even if he'd had a long recovery from the poisoning that had killed her parents, it had been a tumultuous three years between her father's death and David's crowning as King of England. That had been plenty of time for any other worthy candidate to claim the throne or, at the very least, the regency. And he would have been one of the most worthy.

Other prominent earls she could identify included two more Edmunds: Edmund of Almain, Earl of Cornwall; and Edmund Mortimer, Earl of Montgomery. Others left over from her father's reign were Henry de Lacy, Earl of Lincoln; and John of Brittany, Earl of Richmond. And that wasn't even to mention certain of David's favorites like Nicholas de Carew, Alexander Callum, and Humphrey de Bohun. But if the earl in question was any of them, it seemed unlikely he would have resorted to collecting Daisy and her sisters in the middle of the night. All were allied with King David.

... or were they?

7

Day One

Lizzie

Lizzie knew, without having witnessed the exact order of events, how her sisters had escaped the carriage: Daisy had been the one to move first and, though Molly had initially resisted, she'd gone along with it rather than become separated from Daisy.

In that initial moment, Lizzie had been alight with happiness to see that her plan to rescue her sisters was going to work out almost before it had started. She'd been following the carriage, though staying fairly far back on the road in an attempt to remain hidden. From the conversation she'd overheard before the carriage's departure from the convent, she knew the men were looking for her too, and the last thing she wanted was to ride right into their hands.

Fortunately, it was a clear night with a bright moon. Though it had rained during the day, as it often did, the chill of autumn had not yet settled on the land. In the still night air, the noise from the carriage as the wheels bumped and jostled down the road carried clearly to where Lizzie was riding, and Lizzie had kept Herbert to the grass on the edge of the road so the softness would muffle the sound of his hooves. She'd been so far back, in fact, that sometimes the carriage had been out of sight, and she'd known it had stopped only because it had ceased to make noise.

She'd had a moment's fear it had turned off the road, and she'd missed it. The sounds of the men's voices carried through the night air too, however, complaining about the loose wheel with angry curses. At that point, she'd found an entrance to the field through an ancient wooden gate.

She hadn't known for certain her sisters would try to escape, but she'd wanted to be closer so she could help them better if they did. Thus, it had been planning on Lizzie's part, rather than luck, that had put her on the other side of the stone wall when Molly and Daisy had tried to climb the tree to get over it. If Molly hadn't swerved towards it on her own, Lizzie would have called to her to get her attention.

And then everything had gone horribly wrong again.

At first, Lizzie had been disappointed with her sisters for not trying harder to escape and at herself for not riding Herbert directly down the road so she could pull them both onto his back. And then her more customary anger had roiled her belly at the way the man with the bloody nose had grabbed Daisy and held her tightly with a grip that was obviously hurting her. Lizzie was used to that kind of abuse, but she didn't think anyone had ever hurt Daisy in her life.

Anger was a far better emotion for following one's captive sisters in the middle of the night than fear. Besides, just as when she'd watched the men load them into the carriage back at the convent, she couldn't be mad at her sisters for long. Daisy had bloodied that man's nose! Given the way they both normally did everything they were told, it was astonishing they'd had the wherewithal to rebel at all.

Thus, Lizzie was glad to see Daisy stop struggling by the time she was halfway back to the carriage. It would do no good for them to resist any longer. They'd tried to escape once. Their chances of doing so again were probably nonexistent. And thanks to Daisy's quick thinking, the men still didn't know about Lizzie.

Get help, her sister had said.

Lizzie could only ask, *from where?*

The fact that she and her sisters not only weren't princesses anymore but were supposed to be securely set up elsewhere meant nobody was going to believe a girl as ragged as Lizzie was really Princess Elizabeth, daughter of their former king. The idea was absurd on the face of it as well as delving ten feet deep.

While her sisters were being loaded into the carriage, Lizzie backtracked to the gate she'd come through initially. By the time the carriage started rolling, she was on the road again. Herbert the horse appeared as content with his new location as he had been in the field. But as he plodded along, Lizzie began to worry about the distance they might be intending to travel. The man had said their destination wasn't *far* but he'd sneered when he'd said it. What if she had days ahead of her? What was she going to do for food—or sleep, for that matter?

Her imagination carried her along another few miles, worries piling on worries. Then the carriage came to a crossroads and turned northwest to follow the right bank of a large river. Lizzie had never been here before, because she'd never been anywhere before. The journey with Earl Gilbert from Amesbury to St. Margaret's, like the journey tonight, had taken place in the dark, with the curtains on the carriage windows pulled closed. Before that event, Lizzie had rarely traveled more than a few miles from her convent, and that was always in the company of her grandmother.

But it was impossible to miss the massive castle that appeared ahead of them on their side of the river, visible from this distance because torches lit the battlements, and the trees for hundreds of yards around the castle had been cleared.

Four massive round towers rose two stories above the top of the encompassing curtain wall. A great square tower dominated the bailey, and on the north side of the castle, a many-storied keep squatted on a fifty-foot high motte. And while Lizzie didn't recognize the castle itself, she recognized immediately the banner that flew from the topmost towers.

Although she had never visited any of the places she'd learned about, her grandmother had made sure she'd received a proper education for a princess, in hopes she might one day take her rightful place as one. This meant memorizing the standards of every baron in England. She could hear her grandmother's voice describing this one as *argent,* a lion *gules* crowned *or,* within a border *sable bezanty.* In other words, the banner showed a red lion with a golden crown on its head, standing on its hind legs on a white background with a black border with gold dots.

The carriage that held Lizzie's sisters rolled through the front gate of the massive castle of Berkhamsted, seat of her father's cousin and close friend, Edmund of Almain, the Earl of Cornwall. A younger son and thus not eligible for the English crown, his father had been crowned King of the Romans, which was where the *Almain* came from, one of the names for the region of Europe he had ruled. It had been an elected position, however. As a son, Edmund had not inherited the title.

Also from her grandmother, Lizzie knew that Earl Edmund, or Almain as he liked his close companions to call him, was one of the survivors of that fateful evening in Lancaster where her parents and so many of the barons of England had died. She'd even met him, since he was also one of the few who'd ever visited them at Amesbury. In those days, before their grandmother's death, they'd called him Uncle Almain. To see the carriage carrying Daisy and Molly enter through the front gate of his castle had Lizzie nearly dizzy with relief.

And yet, rather than following immediately after them, she reined in beside the road. At first, she couldn't even articulate what stopped her. Uncle Almain *knew* her. He was probably the one person in the entire country to whom she could ride right up, say her real name, and be believed—especially since he'd just sent four men to collect her and her sisters in the middle of the night.

And maybe that was the problem. *He'd sent four men to collect them in the middle of the night.* While it was lovely to be remembered and cared for, all of her worries and concerns came roaring back. As their uncle, it would have been perfectly reasonable to want them with him. They were his nieces. He could have brought them home to Berkhamsted in broad daylight any time in the four years since their grandmother had died, and nobody would have objected.

The implications of that thought struck Lizzie like a bolt of lightning from the heavens.

Rather than doing any of that, Uncle Almain had allowed the world to think Daisy was married and living on the Continent, Molly was a nun, and Lizzie was being cared for by a custodian somewhere in the north of England. He'd known the truth and chose to keep up the lie all this time.

Unless he hadn't known? Could the ruse at that remote convent to which Earl Gilbert supposedly sent them have gone so far as to have involved actual imposters? Had a false Daisy genuinely married a nobleman and was there a real girl out there somewhere pretending to be Lizzie?

Regardless of the truth, *something* was very wrong here. Lizzie didn't know what, and she didn't know how she was supposed to find out. But she also knew that she had to.

The cold of the early morning air settled around her shoulders. Pulling the rough cloak tighter, she felt more alone in this moment than in her entire life. Most days, she'd managed to escape immediate supervision for a little while, hence her friendship with Herbert the horse. But those had been stolen moments rather than hours. Even as she'd longed for more time outside, now that she'd had a night of it, she'd had her fill.

Lizzie contemplated the castle's towers a while longer before sighing and turning Herbert's head in the opposite direction, all her hopes and dreams shattered on the ground around her.

It just went to show, just like her old abbess told her more than once, that she needed to be careful what she prayed for. God answered every prayer, but sometimes that answer was *no*—and sometimes the answer came in a wholly unexpected fashion that made a girl wish she'd never prayed at all.

8

Day Two

Molly

By the time Molly entered the receiving room, she had herself well in hand. It was a shock to discover her uncle was the one who'd sent the carriage, but also a relief. They *knew* him, a fact which she'd tried to tell Daisy as they'd walked across the bailey.

When they'd first seen the castle and the banners flying above it, her sister had appeared relieved as well, but then she'd turned pensive again. Ever since those men had appeared in the dormitory, Daisy had been far from her usual self. It was as if she was afflicted with a strange malaise that was turning her into someone Molly didn't know.

Molly ignored the moodiness and greeted her uncle with a gracious smile. "We've missed you!"

Uncle Almain laughed. "What beautiful young women you have become!" He kissed both of Molly's cheeks and then Daisy's.

Then he turned to gesture towards the only other man in the receiving room. "Neither Bogo nor I could wait another moment to greet you."

Even Molly had to hesitate over that, though she made sure it didn't show. Her uncle didn't appear to notice, and since he was already turning to introduce them, Molly felt she could assume he had no idea what she was thinking.

Although her uncle didn't say it, the full name of the man before her was Bogo de Clare. He was brother to Uncle Almain's wife (like Daisy, named Margaret, whom the sisters called *Aunt Maggie*), which furthermore made him brother to the ill-fated Gilbert de Clare, the man who had moved them to St. Margaret's in the first place.

Bogo rose languidly to his feet in order to bow over their hands. "My dear princesses, it is a true honor. What a blight on our nation that you have been hidden away so long in a convent."

Although nearly three decades older than either of the girls, Bogo was an extraordinarily handsome man: tall, blue-eyed, and dark-haired, unlike Gilbert, who'd been red-headed. Even without the coloring or the introduction, Molly would have recognized Bogo as a Clare purely by the way he tipped his head in greeting. These three—Gilbert, Aunt Maggie, and Bogo—above all else and no matter their occupation, the extent of their lands, or to whom they were married, were *Clares*. That meant something; almost as much as being the daughter of the King of England.

Molly's grandmother had had something to say about Bogo— as she'd had something to say about pretty much everyone. Although

Bogo had pretensions towards the Church, he had never been ordained and had otherwise used his role as a younger brother to the Earl of Gloucester to live a lavish and (again, according to Molly's grandmother) dissolute lifestyle. For whatever reason, and very unlike him in other respects, Gilbert had given Bogo anything he wanted.

Looking around the room, with its glorious tapestries and lavish furnishings, Molly had a frisson of memory of her childhood, much of it spent at Windsor Castle. Those had been happy years, for the most part, and the room gave her a good feeling, as if those days might be reproduced here. Daisy, on the other hand, though accepting of Bogo's compliments as he bowed over her hand, kept up the pinched look and appeared on the verge of speaking. Molly was quite anxious that she refrain from doing so.

Then Uncle Almain held out his hand to a woman lurking in the shadows. "This is Isabel, Bogo's niece. She can get you settled in your quarters. Bogo brought her here specifically to assist you."

Isabel appeared to be a few years older than either Molly or Daisy. Unlike her uncle, she was plain of face and wore a dark gray gown that didn't become her at all. She also gave Molly and Daisy something of a furtive look, shot a glance at Bogo that might have been adoring, and then curtseyed. "Welcome to Berkhamsted, my ladies."

"Thank you. Please lead the way." A lifetime in convents had taught Molly plenty about how to read undercurrents in a room, and she thought it best to remove Daisy from the situation as quickly as possible, before she said or did something they'd all regret.

But it was too late, and Molly knew it even before she reached for her sister's arm.

"It isn't that I'm not happy to see you, Uncle," Daisy said. "Please don't think we aren't grateful for your hospitality, but why did you send men to fetch us from St. Margaret's at such a late hour? Their manner was quite unpleasant."

Uncle Almain was solicitous. "My sincerest apologies, my dear. You are right that I should have come myself, but our plans developed so quickly that I left it to Bogo to instruct my men. They are usually very reliable. He said he had taken care of the matter." He sent something of a glare in Bogo's direction.

His disapproval rolled off Bogo like water off a duck's back. "The men will be censured for their treatment of you, I assure you," he said smoothly. "And really, we couldn't wait another moment to see you. But you must realize we also didn't want to call attention to ourselves—and to you. If I am not mistaken, nobody knew you were at St. Margaret's, and it was our thought that, until we are ready to present you, we should keep it that way—"

"You girls must be so tired." Uncle Almain cut him off. "Isabel. If you would."

"Of course." Isabel held out both hands to Daisy and Molly, gesturing them towards the far doorway. "No need to concern yourselves with the business of men."

"All will be made clear in the morning," Uncle Almain added. "It is too late for serious talk so long after midnight. We can be glad you are here now and safe."

Daisy still refused to obey. "What about Lizzie?"

"Lizz—" Uncle Almain looked puzzled for a moment.

To his credit, Bogo understood immediately. "It is very unfortunate your sister wasn't with you, but we will do everything in our power to find her." His expression hardened with an intensity that belied his earlier languor. He did want to find Lizzie—and soon.

By now, Uncle Almain had caught on as well. "Do you have any idea where she would have got to? Why wasn't she with you in your dormitory?"

"They kept us separated." Though Molly hadn't meant to, she'd made it sound as if the convent had been a prison. In a way it had been, but not in the sense she was implying, since they weren't actually locked in their rooms at night.

Uncle Almain's expression darkened. "There will be no more deprivation of any kind for any of you, ever again."

"Especially once Margaret is my wife." That was from Bogo, as it would be, casually spoken like most of what he'd said tonight.

Given the severe look Uncle Almain shot Bogo, he hadn't wanted to speak of this matter yet either. He needn't have bothered. Molly had known this was why they were here from the moment Bogo had raised himself so casually from his seat. To Molly's mind, it was about time someone appreciated Daisy's gifts, which were inappropriate, on the whole, for a convent. Molly's talents had also been wasted at St. Margaret's, but for different reasons.

From Daisy's calm expression, she had known the bargain too. In truth, this scheme was just so *banal*, Molly had to wonder at what point Bogo said to himself, *I'm going to seek out one of King Edward's daughters, marry her, and make a play for the throne*, though the last item hadn't yet been articulated. It was what he wanted. He couldn't have been more predictable.

Bogo's eyes were fixed on Daisy's. "Your niece, Almain, is an intelligent woman, as befitting her station, both as King Edward's daughter and my future wife. Even at this early hour of the morning, she deserves an explanation for why she is here. I imagine she was already halfway to thinking it."

Uncle Almain spoke through gritted teeth. "We would have discussed it in the morning."

Bogo dismissed Uncle Almain's anger with a wave of his hand. "It is morning."

"Barely." This was again from her uncle, though he'd mumbled under his breath. His reticence gave Molly some idea of the balance of power between them. Life in the convent had also taught Molly plenty about power too, who wielded it, who wanted it, and its cost.

Both men wanted the upper hand, and they were jostling for who should really have it. Her uncle carried a mantle of authority and he was older, but Bogo appeared a wild stallion. The only predictable part of him was his unpredictability.

Now he advanced on Daisy and took her hand again, this time in both of his. "I would be honored if you would consent to become my wife."

His charm was unmistakable. In those first moments of looking at him, Molly had been overcome by it. The feeling had been fleeting, thank goodness, especially now that Daisy was the only person in the room for him. Molly was almost embarrassed to be looking on.

"You honor me, my lord." Daisy pulled in a breath in a manner Molly recognized as an attempt to clear her thoughts. Her sister had never been as empty-headed as she pretended, and, in contrast to earlier, she was managing to keep her expression serene. "Are you also asking that we not speak of our true identities while we are here?"

"We think it best, for now," Uncle Almain said. "We have put out that you are my nieces, newly arrived because I am to aid in your search for appropriate marriages, one of which may be to Bogo, of course."

Even Molly had to react to that. "Are the people to understand we were entertaining inappropriate ones?"

Uncle Almain tipped his head. "As you say."

"Then perhaps you should call us Molly and Daisy, the names by which we were known at St. Margaret's," Molly said.

"That is very sensible." Her uncle smiled gently and added, "Your father always wanted to ally one of his daughters with the House of Clare. In the months before his death, he'd planned for

Joan to marry Gilbert, and I believe Daisy's union with Bogo would have pleased him greatly."

"I'm sure you are right, Uncle." Returning his smile as sweetly as she could, Molly tugged Daisy out of the room and held her hand as they climbed the stairs behind Isabel to an upper floor of the square tower.

Once they reached their room and were at last left alone to climb into their new big bed together, Molly rolled over to face Daisy, who had been staring up at the ceiling. Although Molly had been overjoyed in the first moments of realizing they were at Berkhamsted, with the conversation with their uncle and Bogo, the joy had faded, replaced by a cool head and cold assessment. She hoped her sister was capable of both. "You should take what he's offering."

"What?" Daisy turned onto her side too, so they could huddle close together, their faces inches apart. "You can't be serious."

Molly tsked. "You hate St. Margaret's, just as I do."

"I didn't know you hated the convent!" Daisy gaped at her to the point that Molly felt like tsking again.

"Of course I hate St. Margaret's. I was willing to tolerate it for a while, but we have never been appreciated there, and it has become clear to me we never will be. I would return to Amesbury, and Uncle Almain has the power to ensure that I can."

They were whispering, in part because it was so late, and in part because Isabel was in the next room. She was Bogo's choice for attendant, and Molly had guessed within moments of meeting her that she was also Bogo's spy. At St. Margaret's, they were encouraged to report on each other, and some girls took to the notion with more pleasure and gusto than others, at times Molly among them.

"I can't believe you are suggesting I accept Bogo's hand! You know what grandmother thought of him."

"What does it matter what grandmother thought? Are you waiting for a love match? When are you going to get a better offer? When are *we* going to get a better offer?"

"I don't like him. What's more, I don't trust him."

"Again, what does like or trust have to do with it? He's a nobleman, and he is offering you a way out of St. Margaret's. What's more, he is offering *us* a way out. I can't believe you would be so selfish as to question our good fortune."

Daisy had always been the timid one, without the courage of her convictions. She was perfect, in that sense, for Bogo. Why she was questioning everything all of a sudden was beyond Molly's comprehension.

"At the very least, you need to go along with it for now."

"Of course I will. I'm not entirely stupid."

Molly sighed. "I never said you were."

"But you think it."

"Because you insist on doing stupid things! Any questioning of the abbess and those men, as well as our attempt at escape, were for nothing."

"Not for nothing." Daisy had a stubborn set to her chin Molly also recognized. At times she felt like she knew her sister better than

Daisy knew herself. Though perhaps that was about to change. "There's still something wrong about all this."

"There's nothing wrong. We are in Berkhamsted, safe with our uncle."

"With me betrothed to a Clare." Daisy's tone was extraordinarily sour. "He isn't going to make the same mistake Earl Gilbert did either, waiting to marry me until *after* he's crowned, if that's the plan."

"It's the plan." Of that, Molly was certain. Nothing else made sense.

Daisy nodded. "Marriage is going to come first."

"Just think how much better everything would have been if Earl Gilbert had married you first, instead of being prideful about it and wanting to achieve the crown on his merits alone. You would have been his wife when he tried to take the throne. You would have been his wife when he died. The king might still have taken his lands, but he wouldn't have left you with nothing. On top of which, a widow has a say in her life where a maid does not." Molly had seen that in their grandmother.

"You're right about that." Daisy capitulated—at least in word. At the moment she was refusing to meet Molly's eyes.

Molly was willing to let it go for now because she knew she was right. She didn't lord it over her sister, either. That would have been petty. "Now all we need is Lizzie."

9

Day Two

Lizzie

When Lizzie woke the next morning, she remembered instantly where she was and why she was there. And was very relieved her dreams about being chased weren't real. Turning on her side, Lizzie watched the light travel across the floor of the abandoned croft she'd found, grateful the cloak she'd taken from the convent had kept her warm despite sleeping outside.

At what she hoped was a respectable hour of the day, Lizzie rose from her makeshift bed, feeling an unexpected moment of gratitude that she had spent her time at St. Margaret's being treated like a regular person instead of a princess. Because of it, she hadn't railed at not having a maid to help her get ready for bed nor even been particularly upset about not having a regular bed to sleep in. More times than she could count she'd slept curled up on the end of her sister's bed, or sometimes even under it on the hard wooden floor of the dormitory.

Finding the abandoned croft, which was out of the wind and supplied with fresh straw, had felt like a Godsend, like maybe her decision not to ride straight up to the castle and make herself known had been the right one. Since Lizzie had followed her sisters into the night, she had been alternately angry, fearful, and worried. What she hadn't been at all was unhappy.

Things could definitely have been worse. Even Herbert was content. He'd spent the night with her, the heat coming off his large body keeping the croft a little warmer. Now she led him outside. Because the straw was fresh and the corral attached to the croft was well-maintained, someone had to have been here recently, but they hadn't left a bucket by which to fill the trough. She couldn't in good conscience leave the horse without water, so she led him across the pasture to a little stream that flowed south to the bigger river that ran past the castle.

As the horse dropped his head to drink, she patted his neck and rested her head against his side. Though she'd taken him from the convent in great need in the night, by the light of day, it wasn't right to keep him. Given that they'd traveled a matter of a few miles from St. Margaret's, she hoped he might find his own way home. At the very least, someone in one of the villages through which they'd passed last night, through which Herbert would also have to pass again on his return journey, would recognize him.

She knew in her heart that she herself was never going back, but what exactly she was going *to* wasn't yet clear.

In preparation for her next move, Lizzie washed her face and hands in the same stream from which Herbert drank, braided her hair, and picked as much straw from her clothes as she could manage. After another pat and an actual hug, Lizzie left Herbert and set out on foot down the lane that would take her to the castle. It seemed the only available course of action, even though she had very little in the way of a plan for entering it, beyond pretending to be a servant and asking for work. Given her clothing's poor quality, she didn't think anyone would have trouble believing her story. A castle as large as Berkhamsted had to have a constant need for help.

Lizzie knew about servants, since she'd all but been one at St. Margaret's. As the youngest and most punished of the sisters, her experience with work of all kinds was considerable. She would even clean the latrines if it would get her inside the castle. In truth, because latrines were so necessary, located everywhere from the curtain wall to the top level of the keep, it might be the one job that could take her anywhere her sisters might be.

Again, oddly, her experience at St. Margaret's was suddenly something to be grateful for. It might even be that all these years of suffering could actually lead her to something good.

Unfortunately, the light of day hadn't answered any of the questions she'd asked herself in the night. At this point, Lizzie wasn't even considering proclaiming her true identity. Once she gained entry to the castle, if such a thing were possible, and snooped around for half a day (she was very good at snooping, if she did say so herself, almost as good as she was at eavesdropping), she would then decide whether or not to let everyone know who she was. If all was well and she had entirely misunderstood the circumstances of their departure from St. Margaret's, there would be no harm done. But if something was amiss, she would be very glad she was still at large in order to "get help" for her sisters as Daisy had begged.

Berkhamsted had looked enormous last night. On second inspection, with the eyes of a girl who'd spent the night in an abandoned croft, it was even larger than she remembered, and the walk along the road beside the curtain wall felt interminable. She was completely exposed to eyes from the battlements, and she reminded herself she was not a soldier, just a simple girl looking for work. To that end, she kept her eyes on the road and repeatedly told herself to put one foot in front of the other.

She had walked along the road blindly this way for some distance, looking at her feet and still a hundred yards from the main gate, when someone to her right said, "Girl! Give me a hand, will you?"

She stopped, blinking in surprise to see she had almost walked right past the burly man with a large belly who was talking to her. He stood on the edge of the road beside a wagon full of fresh hay. A wheel had come off. Apparently, if the examples of last night's carriage ride and this wagon were to be extended, wheels came off all the time.

Before her arrival, the man had been attempting to simultaneously lift the bed of his wagon and replace the wheel. He needed another pair of hands.

Lizzie had them, of course, and it simply wasn't possible to pass him by without helping. Besides, speaking to him might be good practice. He would be the first person she'd have to convince that she was not Elizabeth, daughter of King Edward, but a common girl on her way to the castle to seek employment. Even in the cool morning, she found herself sweating.

But she screwed up her courage and approached. "What can I do?"

The man's expression changed to one of hope—and then to one of concern. "You don't look like much." He wrinkled his chin. "But I'm desperate. If I lift up the wagon, do you think you can wedge the wheel back on the axle?"

"I can try."

Lizzie went immediately to the wheel, which he'd propped against the back end of the wagon, and hefted it. It was heavier than she'd expected, thanks to the thin metal plating hammered around the outside. Though she'd never had cause to fix a wagon before, with his guidance, she managed to fit the wheel as he directed and held it on while he secured its connection to the axle.

"That's good work. You're stronger than you look, little thing like you." Stepping back, he wiped his hands on his pants. "What's your name, girl?"

She almost said "Lizzie" but at the last moment changed her name to "Jonet", which she had always thought was pretty.

"One of Daniel's girls are you? How many does he have now … eight?"

Lizzie threw caution to the winds. "Nine." And then instantly felt bad about claiming to be someone else's daughter.

Worse, as soon as one of the other daughters was told she was in Berkhamsted, she was going to get caught, since they would tell everyone they had no idea who she was. It was too late to take it back, however, or it felt like it was. As her old abbess had told her, *even when she didn't think she had a choice, she still had one.* She just might not like the consequences of choosing it. Of all the things she'd done at the convent to draw her superiors' ire, lying wasn't generally one of them. She didn't see why singing in the corridors was a sin, but she definitely knew that lying was.

The man nodded. "I'm Bill. You look like you're headed to the castle. Has he sent you up here like your sisters to work?"

"Yes. I'm not sure they'll need me, but—"

"Oh, they need you, all right. Strong girl like you?" He made a motion with his arm. "Hop on, I'll give you a ride the rest of the way."

Lizzie said a quick prayer for forgiveness and climbed onto the seat of the cart to sit next to Bill. As she'd seen last night, the road followed the course of the river to their left and then turned towards the front gate of the castle, which was located on its south side. The portcullis was up and the gate open, providing free passage to anyone who wanted to enter. This morning, that included a great number of people, including servants, traders, and soldiers, most of whom were heading straight across the road to the bridge that would take them over the river to the town on the other side.

"How many in the garrison?"

"You have an eye for men, do you, girl?" Bill looked at her out of the corner of his own eye, misunderstanding the source of her inquiry. "Better put that thinking away right quick. Especially now."

"What do you mean?" She looked over at him. "Why specifically now?"

"What with the threat from France, King David has asked all the great lords to marshal every available man in case they're needed, so most of our men marched away two days ago, bound for Leeds."

"You mean because of what's going on in Aquitaine and Normandy?" Lizzie wasn't sure how much a peasant girl was supposed to know about these things, but by Bill's expression, he was pleased, indicating her reply had hit the mark.

"So you're a smart one as well as strong and pretty? That's exactly what I mean. You have the looks, I admit, but those here now aren't local men. They have been brought from Almain." He said this with a warning tone that implied the very fact that they were from Europe meant they weren't entirely human—or to be trusted.

"Are we going to have a war?"

"I shouldn't think so. It's just that King David is always one to be prepared. That French king should remember what happened at Hythe a few years back and know it was only a taste of what he would face this time. This time, we would be ready. I'm glad the king is keeping Englishmen at home to defend England, even if those other places across the Channel are part of the CSB now."

Bill was remarkably well-informed for a common man, and Lizzie was starting to think he wasn't as common as all that either, just like her, even if he was delivering hay to the castle.

By now they'd reached the gatehouse, and the soldier who guarded it put up a hand to call Bill to a halt. "What is your purpose?" He spoke with a heavy accent that if Lizzie hadn't talked to Bill she wouldn't have been able to place. Now that she knew where he'd come from, it was likely his first language was Theodiscus.

Bill's eyes narrowed, but he answered easily enough. "I'm delivering hay." He was right that this should have been obvious.

"Carry on." The soldier gestured them forward with a sweep of his arm.

Thus, her heart in her throat and clutching the edge of her seat, Lizzie rolled with her new friend into Berkhamsted Castle.

10

Day Two

Lizzie

O n its own, that first wooden gate in the exterior palisade wasn't particularly daunting. But then they crossed a moat, went through a second gatehouse built in stone that was somewhat more imposing, only to cross yet another moat to reach the massive barbican that guarded the entrance to the castle's bailey.

As a second guard waved the wagon through the main gatehouse without a second glance, Lizzie's mouth fell open. A square, many-storied tower took up a dominant position on the western side of the castle. Beyond was another barbican and the northwestern entrance. The keep sat high on a motte to the north of the bailey, looming over everything. It was accessed through its own fortified gate and protected by high stone walls on either side of a long stairway built up to the front door. At one time, it must have been the center of the lord's domain, but now, given the lack of activity on the stairs and with no guard visible at the top of the tower, it looked almost abandoned. Lizzie had never seen anything like Berkhamsted Castle in all her life.

Bill laughed to see it. "Earl Edmund has outdone himself here, hasn't he, child?" He'd returned to English, and she gave him a harder look, realizing only then that he'd understood the guardsmen's French and answered in the same language.

Rather than elation at the ease in which she'd infiltrated Berkhamsted Castle, Lizzie felt a tenseness in her stomach, like her arrival here had been too easy, given the efforts of the night and the fact that she'd lied to Bill. It was as if she was being rewarded, rather than punished, for her deception.

She couldn't stand the guilt. "Earlier I said I was Daniel's daughter. I'm not."

Bill raised his eyebrows. "Why would you lie about a thing like that?"

She looked down at her hands so she didn't have to see his face as she told him a real truth. "Because I wanted to be."

Bill was silent a moment, and then he nudged her shoulder with his. "No parents?"

"An uncle." She held her breath, wondering if the apology was enough, that she could be forgiven, and still knowing that she didn't deserve it.

Bill nodded. "You be careful, girl. Serving in a castle might be seen by some as an easy life, but they'll run you off your feet. You might look back at your uncle's farm and think it was a better living than this. If so, I'll take you home, no questions asked."

Here she was, a total stranger, and Bill had befriended her with hardly a blink of an eye. Lizzie wanted to shake her head in disbelief. Outsiders might think living in a convent would have acquainted her with all manner of charity, but that was entirely wrong. Had anyone ever been this kind to her, even once? If so, she couldn't remember it. At least not at St. Margaret's. And before her arrival there, people had to be kind to her because she was a princess.

Lizzie was within a hair's breadth of spilling the whole truth of who she was and why she was there, but she managed to swallow the words down and say instead, "Thank you. You've been very kind."

He scoffed, but before he could say more, his attention was drawn by a stableman who hailed him, saying, "Mayor Bill! I didn't know you would be bringing hay today."

"Just doing my share." Bill waved Lizzie off her seat. She had been staring at him, her suspicion that he was more than a mere farmer confirmed. "Including bringing some needed help. Her name's Jonet."

Lizzie had lied about that too, of course, and maybe Mayor Bill knew it because he winked at her. She felt compelled to whisper, "It's really Lizzie, but I liked Jonet better." And then, on impulse, she kissed his cheek.

He gave her a wide grin. "It will be our secret. You'll be wanting to start in the kitchen. It's just there." He indicated the large rectangular building near the square tower.

"Thank you again for the ride." Now on the ground, Lizzie bobbed a curtsey. It was a first of sorts. His station was so much lower than hers—or would have been if anyone knew she was a king's daughter—but somehow it felt right to treat him with respect.

"Save that for the earl." Mayor Bill waved the courtesy away. "Besides, you helped get my wagon rolling."

"I'm happy to be of service."

For that, she received another grin. "Give Cook Agnes my greetings."

Once Lizzie had seen how large the castle was and how many people it employed, she had been confirmed in her plan to behave as if she knew where she was going and what she was doing—and snoop about on her own. And while she'd already decided not to seek out Uncle Almain immediately, she did want to find her sisters. They needed to know she was here, not to mention alive and well. And while Lizzie's years in the convent meant she'd missed a great deal about how people behaved in the outer world, so her preconceptions about the running of a castle might be totally wrong, she didn't think servants were often stopped by soldiers, not when they were moving about with purpose. Now, however, with Mayor Bill still watching her with an avuncular smile, expecting her to go where he indicated, she had no choice but to do as he bid her.

Screwing up her courage and telling herself she'd made it this far, so she could keep on, she walked a bit stiff-leggedly towards the building Mayor Bill had indicated. Even without the smells coming from it, she would have known it was a kitchen from the way it was set apart from all other buildings and connected to the great square tower by a covered walkway to keep food from getting wet when it rained.

Uncle Almain may have hired foreign soldiers, but he must not have hired many, since she saw only one on her way to the kitchen. He glanced at her as she passed him, but, despite what Mayor Bill had said, she saw nothing lascivious in his look. Anyway, she hadn't needed Bill's warning to be careful. She well understood the dangers of men. That had been of particular interest to the nun in charge of novices at St. Margaret's, and she'd read them every story from the Bible that discussed the subject.

Her confidence growing, feeling that so far things had gone well and if she was careful and played her part, it might continue to do so, she pushed open the kitchen door. Truly, the removal of her sisters from the convent—and particularly the way it had been done— must have a good explanation, one she would discover within the next few hours. She would see that her uncle had their best interests at heart and, after that, it would be a simple matter to reveal Lizzie's true identity.

She and her sisters could all live happily together at Berkhamsted.

As princesses.

11

Day Two

Daisy

Daisy had not slept well. They'd been taught in the convent to free their minds from the cares of this world, but in the early hours of the morning she'd found it impossible to do so, and had lain awake long after Molly had fallen asleep. She kept envisioning herself celebrating her wedding mass with Bogo at her side.

As they'd come through the final gatehouse into Berkhamsted's bailey, Daisy had been unable to maintain her initial ebullience, not in the face of unsettling questions that could have only disconcerting answers. And that was before she'd realized Bogo was to be her betrothed. She hadn't told even Molly the real reason she'd acquiesced—to her uncle, to Bogo, and then to Molly. It was because of the look in Bogo's eyes there at the end. It had been impatient, and Daisy had felt, deep in her belly, that if she didn't behave as he wanted, he would abandon any pretense of her cooperation and take her to bed. Molly was right that likely he had learned from Earl Gilbert's mistakes.

Daisy shivered to think on it.

Before she'd died, Daisy's mother had related to her some of the reasons for long royal engagements, where children were betrothed even while still in their infancy. One was to give both families a stake in their future partner. Another was to ensure the suitability of that partner. And only as something of an afterthought was the hope that the two matched children would grow to appreciate, even love, one another before the marriage. Fear of abduction, and a subsequent forced marriage to a would-be suitor, was the main reason why heiresses—and princesses—were usually so well guarded.

But even had Daisy been enraptured by Bogo, the idea of tying herself to him for the rest of her life was too much to take in so quickly, not after so many years spent living as a nun.

Then again, as she could hear her grandmother saying, Bogo himself had been playing at being a priest for years without ever committing to it outright. Maybe he thought Daisy's commitment no deeper. And, of course, in that he would be right. She would be a hypocrite not to admit it. Even more, it would be wrong not to admit, if only to herself, that she was genuinely thrilled at the idea of becoming a princess again.

That was where her interest ended, however. Barring a few very notable exceptions, ironically Gilbert de Clare among them, divorce was forbidden by the Church and thus very rare. She was quite certain it would not be worth any amount of luxury to be tied to Bogo for the rest of her life. For starters, there were those character flaws her grandmother had pointed out. In addition, while Daisy would prefer any man she married to be handsome, Bogo was unreasonably beautiful. It was clear even from their brief encounter that he'd spent his life taking advantage of that fact. Priest clothes or no, he would have women falling at his feet every day.

Bogo's beauty wasn't his fault, any more than Lizzie's was hers. But Bogo lived and breathed what he looked like, while Lizzie appeared entirely oblivious to her appearance.

For Molly to insist that Daisy marry Bogo, even to accuse her of being selfish if she didn't, burned Daisy to the center of her being. She was usually happy to accommodate Molly's every wish, and certainly agreed that St. Margaret's was not the proper place for them to grow old—or to grow at all—but it wasn't Molly who would be saddled with an unsuitable husband for the rest of her life.

Once Daisy was upright and dressed, she dithered a long while at her sitting room window, from which she could see the fields and forests beyond the castle. Molly had risen earlier, gone off with Isabel to breakfast, and hadn't returned, a fact about which Daisy was not sorry. Daisy herself had made an excuse not to join them because she was still too tired from the events of the night and had a headache. No man ever argued with a woman's headache.

She was so deep in her thoughts, in fact, that at first she didn't hear the knock at the door. When it came with more force, she went herself to open it.

Isabel stood on the threshold. "My lady, my lord Bogo was hoping you were recovered enough to see him—"

The arrival of the man himself out of the stairwell cut off the rest of what Isabel had been about to say. Striding down the corridor, Bogo visibly brightened at the sight of Daisy framed in the doorway. "Ah, I see you are much improved."

Daisy could have put him off, but to do so would have merely deferred the inevitable. Besides, having answered the door, she was obviously well enough to stand upright, as Bogo could see for himself. He seemed to be one of the few men who *would* dismiss a woman's headache as the invention, in this case, that it was. Either that, or his need to speak to her was so urgent, he felt compelled to override what Daisy herself wanted. Given the events of the night, the latter supposition sounded most likely.

Resigned to her fate, at least for the moment, Daisy gestured that he should enter the sitting area and allowed him to bow over her hand again on the way by. "Good morning, my lord."

"I couldn't be more proud to have such a beautiful bride. And surely you must be hungry after the adventures of last night?"

"I am, thank you."

He looked at her with a severe expression. "Perhaps if you'd eaten earlier, your head would not have ached." And then from behind him, seemingly summoned by the thought, came a host of servers, huffing down the corridor towards Daisy's room with trays of food, which they proceeded to set out on the table next to the window.

Daisy's stomach actually growled at the sight and smell of the food, and she was able to look genuinely rueful. "I'm sure you're right. Next time I'll try to remember." She took the chair he offered and endeavored to appear pleased. He was right that she was hungry, and she *had* almost given herself a real headache by refusing to eat.

Then Bogo dismissed the servants, as well as Isabel.

Yet again, a cold feeling settled over Daisy. She and Bogo were betrothed, it seemed, which was the only way they could sit for even a moment alone together behind a closed door.

She said nothing about that either as he sat opposite her and dished food onto her plate rather than allowing her to make her own choices. Only when she had a full mouth did he say, "You must forgive the way last night went. I realize now I should not have spoken so forthrightly when you'd had such a trying evening. I was simply happy to see you and wanted to share with you the good news of our engagement."

Daisy managed not to choke, washing down the bite she'd taken with some of her uncle's very good wine. "Thank you, my lord. I did understand that, even at the time."

"Our union will be advantageous to everyone." Bogo's eyes were so lit up, Daisy felt momentarily chastened at the way she'd been doubting him and his motives.

She took another swig of wine, her eyes streaming a bit. "Excuse me." She coughed several times. While necessary to clear her throat, the last few were to give her time to craft what she needed to say next. "I can see how it might be hard to hold back your hopes for our future together."

"Hopes?"

The need to keep Bogo happy was like a maelstrom in her stomach, making it difficult to keep the conversation going—or keep eating. Daisy didn't have the courage of Joan, who had refused a marriage to William de Bohun after the death (by poison) of their elder sister, Eleanor. William's father had hoped that by marrying Joan, William could take the throne. Joan had entered the convent at Barking instead.

At the time, Daisy had wondered why the Bohuns hadn't turned their gaze on her. At a few months older than Lizzie was now, Daisy had been well within marriageable age, especially for a princess. Even if the throne of England had never come to pass, Daisy would have been the wife of the Earl of Hereford. She could have forgiven William for serving David as long as he treated her well. He was handsome, kind, and a favorite of the king. Surely she would also have had more freedom as his wife than in the convent.

But as had always been the case, no matter her age, she hadn't been given a choice in the matter. William had also refused to conform to his father's machinations, which had resulted in David taking the crown. Thus, when Earl Gilbert had come for them after their grandmother's death, he had seemed like a savior, for all that he was thirty years older than Daisy. She was older now and Bogo younger than Gilbert had been then, but somehow she didn't feel that made the situation any better.

When Joan had made her choice, Daisy had thought her mad. Nothing about Daisy's life in convents had made her change her mind. Even the death of Gilbert de Clare hadn't made her desire a life as a nun. But nor was she in favor of marriage to someone she didn't know.

"Perhaps you could explain to me again how this is meant to go, and how my sisters in particular fit into the plan? I'm particularly concerned about Lizzie, who is apparently lost, and Molly, who has a vocation as a nun."

"Does she? Am I to understand, then, that you yourself do not?" It was annoying that Bogo saw right through her carefully chosen turn of phrase.

"You are correct. I do not have a vocation, and I am not sorry to no longer be expected to take my vows. Molly, however, was given to the church at six years old. She should have the right to keep to her intended course." And then she threw in a good word for her sister, based on their conversation last night. "She would like to be returned to Amesbury."

"If that is truly her wish, then I would not stand in her way. I do not want any of you to be unhappy." Bogo had risen to his feet as he spoke, and now began to pace back and forth before the fireplace. Even nearing the end of his forties, close in age to her uncle, he was a vibrant man, fit and energetic. "I will tell you what is in my heart, Daisy, because it's clear you have much of your mother in you, and she would have demanded to know what was happening." He shot a wry smile in her direction. "You have been much more polite about it than she would have been."

"Thank you, my lord." Daisy set down her spoon. "Any comparison to my mother can only be a compliment."

He kept pacing. "Are you aware of what I've suffered these last years?"

"In what way, my lord?" Daisy could have detailed all the ways she and her sisters had suffered, far more than he, but she swallowed the words.

"In losing my brother. In losing my position at court." His face transformed to one of extreme intensity. "In having to submit to that insufferable Welsh bastard we must call king!"

Daisy felt herself settling further into her chair. He was going to tell her the truth. She hadn't been sure he would. "So this is about the crown."

He canted his head, returned to calm. "As you say."

"Your brother thought along much the same lines as you."

"We've learned a few things since Gilbert's attempt."

She wanted to ask what *things* exactly he was talking about, but she had other questions that were more pressing, and she had the sense that Bogo's patience with this story wouldn't be endless. "My presence here can't remain a secret, my lord. My uncle's servants already must know something about who we are. If we make any attempt to win the throne" (she thought the *we* was a nice touch) "the king will be wrathful. Why are you doing this now? Why do you think the outcome this time will be different from Gilbert's attempt?"

"The servants know you are relations of your uncle, but what of it?" His answer, when it came, was not directly to the point, though she had to admit her question had been many-faceted. "Almain is your closest living relative. It is his duty and honor to care for you." Then he made a dismissive gesture. "Besides, we won't fail. I am not my brother."

But, to Daisy's mind, that's exactly what Bogo appeared to be. If only she could make Molly see it too.

12

Day Two

Lizzie

To be neither caught nor recognized as an intruder was at the forefront of Lizzie's mind as she stepped through the doorway of the kitchen in search of the woman Mayor Bill had referred to as Cook Agnes. Lizzie had spent plenty of time in the kitchen at St. Margaret's, mostly on her hands and knees scrubbing the floor as punishment for one infraction or another. While the old abbess hadn't much liked her—particularly her *quick tongue,* as she invariably told her—Abbess Helen had seen it as her duty to drum all attempts at resistance out of her.

She hadn't been successful, as evidenced by the fact that Lizzie had run after her sisters without a backward glance. The problem, more in the matter of the new abbess than the old, was that Lizzie was as educated as anyone in the entire convent, even the sisters (other than Molly) who read scripture during meals. It might even be because Lizzie was so good at reading out loud that she had been asked to do it only once. Being left out that way was all the more frustrating to Lizzie, since it was the *one* thing, out of all the many things required of a nun, that she could do well.

Clearly obedience was at the very bottom of that list.

But she could obey if she had to. So, for Cook Agnes, she put on her most compliant manner and said, as sweetly as she could, in emulation of her sisters, "Mayor Bill brought me today and said I should see you about a position here. He thought an extra set of hands might be useful."

"Bill, eh? Is he here?"

"Yes, Cook. In the bailey. He brought hay."

"Well, he knows we are understaffed. Twenty workers went with the army when it marched away. I hired six girls yesterday, and I'd hire six more today if I could find them." She touched Lizzie under the chin to make her look up, examining her face. "How old are you?"

Lizzie did a quick canter around the possible responses, sent up a brief prayer for forgiveness in advance, and lied again, "Fifteen."

Agnes grunted. "Not yet ready for womanhood, eh?"

"It does not appear so, Cook."

She sniffed. "I would not have you mingling with these foreign soldiers. They mostly keep to themselves, but I don't trust them with my girls. Stay away from them, keep your head down, and you'll do all right. For now you'll fetch and carry and do whatever you're told. I'll inform Chamberlain you're here. I know he's missing help too. You'll be worked hard today. Can you bear that?"

"Yes, Cook Agnes."

"Hmm. I like your manner. What's your name?"

Lizzie decided she had to keep this particular lie going, even if she'd told Mayor Bill the truth. She didn't want anyone looking at her and thinking *Elizabeth*. "Jonet."

Lizzie's first job was to assist the man in charge of the cheeses with sorting and counting. He was very pleased to learn she could count. Then she helped the ewerer, who was responsible for providing water, both warm and cold, to the great hall and all the rooms, fetching and carrying pitchers and basins. Then it was off to fetch and carry firewood for the launderers, as one of the boys who usually helped with that task had marched away with the army.

All of that took place in the first hours of the morning. Mayor Bill had been absolutely right: working in the castle was *work*. The way she was kept constantly busy made her almost miss the breaks for the holy office at the convent that allowed her to sit for a short while.

It was only after she was passing through the kitchen, and Cook Agnes heard her stomach growl so loudly she almost spilled the cup she was pouring, that she allowed Lizzie to sit at the big table in the kitchen with a meal of bread and cheese of her own.

Cook Agnes stood looking down at her, her hands on her hips. "I talked to Bill. He says he picked you up on the road."

"Yes. He was very kind."

She grunted. "He said you helped him with his wheel, but at first you let him think you were one of Daniel the Cottar's girls."

Lizzie stared up at her, shocked that Mayor Bill had betrayed her. She had thought she could trust him. "I know, Cook. I'm sorry, Cook." She had just taken another bite of cheese, and the creamy goodness melted so sweetly in her mouth that she involuntarily moaned.

"Hmm." Cook Agnes made this particular noise often, and Lizzie wasn't sure what it was supposed to mean, except in this case it meant she was thinking. "You told the truth in the end, which counts for something around here." She grunted now, feeling Lizzie's upper arm. "And wherever you've been, you haven't been well fed."

A new wave of guilt came over Lizzie, because she was still lying about where she'd come from, not to mention her name and age. She put down the cheese. "I shouldn't have lied. I'm sorry, Cook. I'll go." She pushed away from the table, but got only halfway to her feet before Agnes's hand came down on her shoulder.

"No. Sit. We can use the help, and both Pantry and Water told me you did good work this morning."

After a morning of work, Lizzie knew who Cook Agnes was talking about. While she was to be called *Cook Agnes,* she referred to everyone else by what they oversaw. The kitchen was inhabited by not just *Water* and *Pantry* but by Pastry, Bread, Sauce, Vegetables, and so on. When Lizzie had first met her, she'd referred to the chamberlain as "Chamberlain" as if it were his actual name. Even the boy who stoked the fire was called *Wood.* It took some getting used to, but at least she had no trouble remembering anyone's names, as long as she knew their occupation. That so many people shared the same names—Thomas, Mary, Margaret, Elizabeth, William—was the reason she was Lizzie in the first place.

Cook Agnes went back to her cooking, and Lizzie to her cheese, until another girl sat down across from her. "Cook Agnes says you're to work with me next." She tipped her head. "You look like you could be my sister." Then she grinned and swiped one of Lizzie's chunks of cheese. "Mayor Bill has a soft heart."

Lizzie's mouth was full again, so she took a big swig of ale to wash it down before answering. "He does, and I am grateful for it. I'm sorry for lying at first. Though, to be fair, he asked if I was one of your sisters and I'd said *yes* before I could think."

"That's all right." The girl smiled. "There are a great number of us girls, and Cook Agnes says you were hungry. I'm Kate, number four." She reached out a hand to feel Lizzie's arm as Cook Agnes had done. "You are skinny for fifteen, and Cook thinks it's because you have been overworked and underfed."

"I don't mean to be a burden." It was becoming clear to Lizzie by now that not only did Mayor Bill like to talk and apparently would tell anyone anything, but the news of her arrival was all over the castle.

Here she was, casually eating in the kitchen, while everybody else was talking about her. Worse, the story of her arrival might soon reach her own uncle. It renewed the pit of worry in her belly and curdled the cheese she'd just eaten. Then again, Cook Agnes had just hired six other new girls. And Lizzie was going by the name *Jonet*. She thought she could assume as well that Uncle Almain would be very slow to entertain the idea that his niece could get herself hired on as staff.

"We have food. Not everyone is cut out for working as hard as is needed here, and I hear you've done all right. Better than I did, truth be told, when I first came."

"What do you do?"

"I work in the laundry." She held out both her hands, which were reddened and chapped. "They get so dry."

"Have you tried using lanolin?" Lizzie asked.

"Most nights. It doesn't last, but you're right that I should be better about remembering, so my skin doesn't crack and bleed. It's worse in the winter, and winter is coming." She gave a little laugh and made another motion with her head, indicating Lizzie should come with her. "You'll see."

Lizzie got to her feet to follow. "I've done laundry before."

As they set off across the courtyard, it came to Lizzie that she might ask questions of this girl, and it might even be worth a risk, now that she had a position, to inquire after her own sisters. It would be pretty silly to put so much effort into infiltrating the castle only to learn that Uncle Almain had already moved them somewhere else while Lizzie slept.

"Things seem busy today."

Kate flapped a hand in the direction of the gatehouse. "These foreign soldiers."

"I heard we have new guests too."

"Two young ladies!" Kate slowed her walk to speak more conspiratorially. "I don't know who they are exactly, nieces of Earl Edmund. He has put them in the quarters usually reserved for important visitors."

"When did they arrive?"

"Very early this morning."

Lizzie allowed herself to breathe again. "Why would they arrive at such an odd hour?"

"I wouldn't know." Kate shrugged, conceding that the actions of her betters weren't hers to question. "Maybe their carriage broke down. I think one of them is supposed to marry Lord Bogo." Now Kate's face was illumined from the inside. "He is so very handsome. And a Clare!"

That one of her sisters was to marry Bogo de Clare was news indeed. Given Earl Gilbert's plan to marry Daisy, it made a certain kind of sense that, with his death, Bogo might want to marry her instead.

Then, all of a sudden, Kate shivered.

"What's wrong?"

"Did I say something was wrong?"

"You shivered just now at the mention of Lord Bogo's family, the Clares."

Kate opened the door to the laundry facilities. This was a big castle, with a proportionate amount of washing. "The family has had such ill-luck, with the older sons betraying the king and paying the price for it." Her lips pursed. "I suppose you can't really call that *ill-*

luck, since they chose their path. But the curse on the family extends to Lady Margaret too. She's barren. Bogo also has no heirs. And Earl Gilbert had only daughters. While Thomas has been blessed with sons, ever since he tried to murder King David himself ..." Her voice trailed off.

"As you said, that isn't ill-luck so much as poor planning."

"That may be, but George says the family might be cursed." Gossip was more delicious to some people than the cheese Lizzie had just eaten. She could see it in Kate's face.

"Who's George?"

"One of the stablemen." From her tone, he was someone special to her.

While she had been talking, Kate had gone to a basket of linens. All of a sudden, Lizzie found her arms full of sheets, such that she had to peer at Kate around them. "If you think so, aren't you afraid to work here?"

"Of course not! It's just talk." Kate closed her lips over what she was going to say next, silenced by a glare sent her way by the chief laundress. "We should get to work on these."

Lizzie touched her elbow. "You can't leave it there! There's more to your story."

Giving in, Kate leaned closer to whisper in Lizzie's ear. "Bogo bears the mark of the devil. Missy saw it when he was bathing." She pointed to the back of her neck. "He's secretly Jewish."

Lizzie's expression must have conveyed her skepticism because Kate made a motion with her hand, dismissing the conversation. "Earl Edmund is safe because he's a Good Christian, like my family. His wife doesn't believe, though, and it sounds like those sisters in the tower don't either. I'm worried about them."

And then she was gone before Lizzie could ask more questions.

For the next hour, Lizzie worked as one of three girls whose job it was to stir the sheets in their cauldrons of water, which gave her plenty of time to consider what she'd just been told. Thanks to the prejudices of Abbess Helen, she was fully aware that *Good Christian* in this instance meant something entirely different from what was usually meant when spoken in general conversation by anyone but those in this castle. It was the reason Uncle Almain had pivoted with apparent ease from supporting Lizzie's father to supporting King David.

Because, to put it bluntly, he was a heretic.

Or rather, prior to King David's reign, he would have been called one. He'd founded an entire priory of *Good Christians*, Ashridge, to which he'd donated a phial of Christ's blood. Lizzie understood from what her grandmother had told her—as well as Abbess Helen at St. Margaret's—that initially everyone had thought the monks there were an offshoot of the Augustinians. In actuality, they were Cathars, a movement the Albigensian Crusade had spent years trying to stamp out. Cathars called themselves *bonhommes*, or *Good Christians*.

Among their beliefs was the assertion that the human body was in all ways sinful, and thus any marriage or relationship that produced children was also sinful. Some found a way to have sons anyway, and Kate certainly seemed to think having sons was a desirable outcome of marriage. Uncle Almain was married, but as Kate had rightfully pointed out, he and Aunt Maggie had no children at all.

Lizzie herself had never been particularly worried about her uncle's religious views. By the time she was made aware of his proclivities, he was in favor with the king, having survived Lancaster with his lands and reputation intact. How he'd become a Cathar, on the other hand, was a story in and of itself, and one Kate might have been delighted to have Lizzie tell. Uncle Almain's mother, Sancha, had been engaged—some say even married-by-proxy—to the Count of Toulouse, a staunch protector of the Cathars. Theirs had been a love match.

But when the Pope ordered a crusade against the sect, she'd been separated from him and forced to marry Uncle Almain's father, who was brother to the King of England. According to the story, whispered in the dormitory of the convent by one of the older girls, the pair had been cruelly separated by Sancha's sister, who happened to be none other than Lizzie's grandmother. Lizzie had already known from the dowager queen herself that she'd arranged the marriage. Lizzie's grandmother, however, had told the story with something of a different twist, in that she'd *saved* her sister from a ruinous marriage, never mind that Sancha had been madly in love with the count.

These days, nobody, not even the nuns at St. Margaret, spoke of anyone as a heretic. King David had supported Uncle Almain's right to practice his religion as he wished, as long as no harm came to anyone who did not share those beliefs. But the close proximity of Ashridge Priory was of concern to St. Margaret's abbess, as demonstrated by her frequent homilies describing Cathar beliefs in detail, as a way to ensure none of her flock ever strayed in that direction.

For that reason, Abbess Helen had expressed gratitude that Gilbert de Clare, and then Lord Tudur, rather than Uncle Almain, had become patrons of St. Margaret's, even though his lands were closer to the abbey. Lizzie had never realized how close until today.

The thought brought her up short, reminding her of her worries in the night and prompting a sharp word from the girl next to her about ceasing to stir the sheets in their cauldron. Lizzie got to work again, but inside, her stomach was churning as much as ever. All these years, she and her sisters had been living a matter of a few miles from her uncle, her father's closest friend in life. *Had he really not known they were there?*

These thoughts were strange and confusing, muddling her mind in ways it had never been muddled before. If nothing else, back at St. Margaret's, there'd been a purity to her resentments and hatreds that was suddenly missing. While she wanted to think the best of her uncle, it was becoming harder to do so with each hour that passed. The only thing she knew for certain was that she had well and truly entered what her catechism instructor would have called *the lion's den.* Lizzie could only hope to have as much faith in her survival as Daniel.

13

Day Two

Daisy

Daisy fought to contain an almost hysterical laughter welling up inside her. "When is this attempt at the throne meant to begin?"

"There will be no attempt. There will be only success." Bogo's voice grew momentarily cold.

Daisy shivered as his words gusted past her, despite the fire and the relative warmth of the morning, and realized, finally, her grave mistake. That he was telling her even these few details about his plot had to mean he had no fear she would tell anyone else. Either he trusted her loyalty completely, a dubious idea, or she wasn't leaving this castle until it was all over. He had no intention of giving her a choice about whether or not she would be participating—or whether or not to marry him. If Daisy were he, she wouldn't allow her even to leave this room.

Maybe it was because her situation had become so precarious that she decided to ask one more question, so the matter could be spread before her fully—like the breakfast she found herself unable to enjoy. "You seem to have planned for everything. But are you certain I'm necessary to the plan? I'm not entirely sure I want to marry anyone—" She broke off at his dark look.

"You do have other sisters."

It wasn't a cold wind she felt now so much as if she'd been dropped into a mountain lake. She was drowning, and she understood why Bogo had wanted all three sisters together. Any threat to Molly or Lizzie, as unsavory as their uncle might find it, would motivate Daisy to do as Bogo wanted. Or he would simply marry Molly or Lizzie instead of her.

It was yet another reason Daisy was glad Lizzie had escaped Bogo's clutches. One look at Lizzie and he might latch upon her as the ideal bride—beautiful, young, and most importantly, at only thirteen, biddable.

Which she might be, all previous evidence to the contrary.

Lizzie had been very young when their parents had died. They were hardly more than a fairy tale to her, one their grandmother had been very pleased to tell and embellish upon. Over time, Daisy had come to see that many of her stories were more than embellishments: they were outright lies. Lizzie couldn't know that. She'd experienced life as a princess the least, and she remembered her time at Amesbury as idyllic compared to St. Margaret's.

In truth, Lizzie wasn't wrong. It had been idyllic in comparison. But at thirteen, she was the perfect age to look up to an older man and think the answer to all her problems lay in marriage. Bogo could take her far away from a situation she detested. He could do that for Daisy too, obviously, and seemingly intended to, but in the end she might come to regret, or even resent, the bargain she'd made and wish she were back at St. Margaret's. Overall, it had been an unpleasant place to live for Daisy, but not the torture it had been for Lizzie.

Whatever the cost to Daisy herself, and far more so than she'd thought on the road to Berkhamsted when she'd protected Lizzie from the men her uncle had sent, she couldn't let Bogo anywhere near her sister.

With a straightening of her posture and a forcible reorientation of her thoughts, Daisy gave her betrothed the sweetest smile she could muster. "I was just trying to understand." She widened her eyes to look as empty-headed as possible. "I'm sure you know what is best for me, my lord, and I will follow your direction."

Her capitulation was sudden, but also more her usual guise, and it put a smile on Bogo's face. His manner became pompous and proprietary, sure of his course of action and her obedience to it. Daisy gave a silent hosanna of thanks for giving her that moment of insight. She knew what she had to do now, and who her true enemy was.

"Excellent, my dear. I will leave you to your meal." He gestured expansively. "Meanwhile, I will do everything in my power to make your stay here as comfortable as possible."

"Thank you, my lord." Daisy was struck with a sudden thought. "What of the story that I am married to some duke or lord of some far-away place?"

Bogo laughed. "He has died." He waved a hand dismissively. "You need not worry for a single moment about the matter."

Daisy tried to look pleased. "I am glad you have Isabel to attend to me, but I would have expected to be able to visit with Aunt Maggie. Where is she?"

"Visiting Thomas in France. They have four children, you know, and since Thomas can never return to England ..." His voice trailed off.

Then, without adding to the thought, he rose to his feet. Somehow, the mention of Thomas and Aunt Maggie had ended the conversation when other questions had not. The implication was that Aunt Maggie didn't approve of this plan of her brother's and had put herself well out of it by physically leaving England. Either that or Thomas was integral to Bogo's plot against the king, and she had been Almain and Bogo's messenger. Daisy didn't know her aunt well enough to guess which it might be.

As Bogo made for the door, Daisy relaxed into her chair, relieved to have survived as well as she had—which truly wasn't very well at all.

As for the immediacy of the problem that faced her, she could see now that no amount of sweet talk or persuasive argument was going to divert Bogo de Clare from his chosen course. Her only chance to extricate herself from his plans would be through rescue or escape, though the nature of this castle gave her little hope of either. To the rest of the world, she was already married and living in Europe. Or maybe, once a person was as completely forgotten by the world at large as Daisy and her sisters seemed to be, she was, for all intents and purposes, dead. Back in the carriage with Molly, Daisy had insisted they were not. But truth be told, during these last years at St. Margaret's, many times she had felt dead to herself.

And yet, her heart still beat. She breathed in the air of a new morning. And now that she was outside the convent, she was alive in a way she hadn't been since her grandmother's death. Surely as she was a princess in her soul, she hadn't been pulled from the grave that was St. Margaret's only to marry Bogo. Maybe she would make a great queen, but if that day ever came, it would be on her terms, not his.

Then the doorway through which Bogo had just departed was filled by the seamstress, ready to begin work on new dresses for Daisy.

Lizzie entered the room right behind her.

Daisy lifted her face to the ceiling, calling down another hosanna that Bogo had left when he had and that the corridor was dark compared to the brightness of her room. He hadn't seen Lizzie since their grandmother's funeral, and even had Lizzie been wearing a fine gown today, likely he wouldn't have recognized her, so vast was the difference in growth between nine and thirteen. Back then, Lizzie had been a foot shorter and nowhere close to womanhood. Now she was on the threshold, if not moving through the doorway.

More importantly, he hadn't looked back and seen the joy at the sight of her sister shining from Daisy's face.

14

Day Two

Molly

"There is more to *your* part of the plan, though, isn't there, Uncle?"

Molly and her uncle were alone, having enjoyed a meal together that had included Bogo and Isabel. After eating, those two had left on some errand for Bogo. It was a relief, at the very least, to have Isabel gone. Most of the time she ate with downcast eyes, but when she raised them, they tended to look at Bogo adoringly. Molly found the looks both irritating and concerning, given that Bogo was set to marry Daisy. And really, since a blind mouse couldn't be oblivious to Isabel's affections, that meant Bogo knew how Isabel felt and was using her for his own ends. He might even be bedding her. The thought made Molly's lip curl.

Meanwhile, Uncle Almain's eyes skated away. "What makes you say that?"

"Uncle." Molly knew in that moment she was right. Daisy had been the one to question last night, beyond the point Molly had thought reasonable, but the more time she spent with both her uncle and Bogo, the more she was beginning to wonder if Daisy had the right of it. It would be unusual, but not unprecedented. "Bogo is to marry Daisy on his way to becoming king. I see the benefit to him, but why are you supporting him? What do you get out of it?"

Her uncle gave her a long look while he poured both of them more wine. "I intend to get my life back."

"What does that mean?"

"Under your father, I was trusted. More than once, I was made regent during his absences. My advice was listened to and often implemented." Lifting his cup, he honored her with it. "Bogo is merely a means to an end."

"You think you can control him?"

"I don't need to control him. I can control Daisy."

Molly didn't actually snort into her cup and managed to swallow down any cynical retort. Before last night, Molly herself might have viewed Daisy as biddable. Now, she wasn't so sure. Her sister had revealed herself to be unexpectedly stubborn. And though she had capitulated to Molly's wishes in the privacy of their bedchamber, Molly hadn't been fooled. If Molly couldn't predict what her sister was going to do next, her uncle surely wouldn't be able to.

"Daisy will only be queen—" She broke off as the realization of what her uncle was really saying hit her. "You don't intend Bogo to rule for long."

Almain raised one shoulder in a careless shrug. "It's her birthright David usurped. Daisy is your father's true heir. She should be the next ruler of England."

Molly wet her lips at this easy talk of murder. "Bogo can't take the throne while the king sits on it."

"That is true."

Molly let the silence drag on through a few counts before asking, *oh so carefully* and perhaps more carefully than she had ever asked anything in her life, "You intend to assassinate the king?"

"He will die, yes."

"But he can't die. We know that. That's how Gilbert de Clare failed. And Thomas. We all know the story: he tried to murder King David with a crossbow, and in the very moment he could have died, the king escaped to Avalon. Even in our convent, we learned of it."

"Many people witnessed the event, yes."

Molly thought a low laugh would be allowed. "The news swept through England like a summer storm."

In truth, this miracle had sparked many a conversation among the nuns about the perils of going against what was clearly God's Will and David's divine right to rule. The King of France had Jesus's crown of thorns locked away in his holy vault in Sainte-Chapelle, but England was led by a living saint.

Or so the story went.

To add to the legend, while nobody would have blamed the king for hanging Thomas from the highest tower in London, he had chosen a different path. Refusing to orphan Thomas's four children,

David had instead released Thomas to his wife, with the promise that he would never again set foot in England or any territory associated with it. This was called *abjuring the realm.* Thomas had agreed, but doing so was becoming harder by the day, given that David was High King of Britain and the head of the CSB. It reminded her of questions her own father—and grandmother—had been known to ask, if not of Molly directly, then of those around her: "What is justice? And how does one know it when one sees it?"

Uncle Almain was not to be deterred. "That is true, but both tried to shoot him."

"And you think some other method will work better?" As her uncle continued to confide in her, some of Molly's confidence returned. She had been the prize pupil at St. Margaret's, after all.

"We have reason to believe he can be poisoned."

Molly sat back in her chair, a shiver running down her spine, since, of course, that was how her own parents had died—and her uncle himself had almost died. It took her a moment to get her thoughts in order. "Do you really think you can get close enough to him for that?"

"We already are." Uncle Almain smirked—and then as if he'd read her mind, added, "Justice, I say."

"You hate David that much?"

"Don't you? He killed your parents."

"I thought that was his food taster." Molly spoke as matter-of-factly as possible. "Also by poison."

"Well, yes, and it does seem that David had nothing to do with the specifics, but afterwards he encouraged the resettlement of Jews in Wales." Uncle Almain spoke so casually, at first Molly thought she hadn't understood what he'd said and had missed something in the conversation. Eyes narrowing in concentration, she leaned forward. "Why is that important? I thought you appreciated the king's acceptance of all religions. It has allowed you to practice your particular heresy in peace."

Between one breath and the next, her uncle was furious. "I do *not* practice heresy! My faith is the truth!"

Molly might not have spent much time out in the world, but she knew religion, and that knowledge would not let even her own uncle get away with such a falsehood. "The pope would beg to differ."

"He's in the pocket of the French king." Suddenly composed again, Uncle Almain made a dismissive motion. "I have no worries about what he thinks."

"All thanks to David." Molly felt confused again at her uncle's quick change of mood. She wasn't as good with reading people as Daisy, and it seemed it was more difficult for her than for her uncle to let the matter go. She knew she was pressing more than he wanted—more than her usual demeanor would suggest she could or should—but these were matters of faith, and Molly was an educated nun. "Do you think Daisy would have had the courage to do what David has done? Had she been the ruler instead of David, would she have allowed *you* to openly assert that *her* religious beliefs were counter to the teachings of Jesus?"

Molly herself had little use for Daisy's protestations about this marriage to Bogo. Last night she'd called her selfish for even considering turning it down. But Molly prided herself on her careful reasoning. If she pushed Daisy into a marriage that turned out to be a mistake, it was not a decision that could be walked back, and Molly would be to blame.

Uncle Almain scoffed. "That isn't the point, my dear. With your sister on the throne, with or without Bogo, the policies would not only continue, but be expanded. Except for England's Jews, of course. They will have to go."

Molly stared at him. Since the Cathars condemned Jews as servants of Satan, her uncle's antipathy shouldn't have been surprising. Nonetheless, she was taken aback at his vehemence.

Uncle Almain didn't notice. "I didn't agree with Gilbert about everything, nor that swine Montfort for that matter, but for all that we were often on opposite sides of any argument, they both had the right of it when it came to Jews. King Philippe was in the process of taking the proper steps before David thwarted him."

While her uncle's mention of *Gilbert* referred again to his brother-in-law, *Montfort* was a reference to Simon de Montfort, leader of the Second Baron's War. He and Earl Gilbert had been allies until Gilbert betrayed the barons and switched back to the royal side.

Before that happened, both men had led massacres of Jews throughout England. Ironically, Cathars had been slaughtered by the thousands by Simon de Montfort's grandfather, even as he apparently despised Jews too. Her own family had never held Jews in much favor, though everyone knew Jewish physicians were the best. Her father had been vigorous about ridding England of coin clippers. She remembered when he'd hanged hundreds of Jews for the crime before the first Welsh war—to pay for it, if David was to be believed. She could see why he thought so, since the money her father had acquired at these deaths was the same amount, almost to the penny, that he spent on the war.

Putting aside her own father's actions for now, and even Jewish denial of the truth of the Christ, these past few years of relative deprivation had given Molly new insight into the deprivation of others. The fact that her entire family was dead, but for her few remaining sisters, made her far less complacent about the idea of murdering anyone else's family for any reason—Jewish, royal, or standing in her uncle's way.

And really, all religion aside, with this elaboration of their plot, her uncle and Bogo were proving themselves to be less and less clever. *Murder the king? Really?* Molly could have come up with a dozen better ways to achieve their objective, if they'd asked. Which they hadn't. And at this point, she wasn't inclined to help them.

Her dramatic divergence in perspective from her uncle's made it all the more important that she not show him how distasteful she was finding the conversation—even as she pressed him about it a bit further. "Their existence impinges on you so much? I myself don't know any Jewish people."

"You have spent the last ten years in a convent. They're everywhere now." His hands clenched. "Sniveling about, demanding payment on debts when they're due. The interest alone is crippling me."

Understanding blossomed. "So it isn't truly a religious objection for you. You owe them money, and you want that debt wiped away. Expelling them from Britain would do that."

"They're *Jews*, my dear. I don't understand why you are belaboring this point."

Molly just managed to refrain from tsking through her teeth, in mimicry of Abbess Helen, truth be told. "You were always the one to loan my father money. What happened?"

"The new king has a different attitude."

"So don't borrow from them."

"The Italians won't loan to me anymore, as I've borrowed so much they don't believe I can pay them back. That leaves the Templars, who won't loan to me because of my religion."

Molly could have said that was appropriate, but it would have been rubbing salt on the wound, which seemed counterproductive if she wanted to keep her uncle talking. "So *that's* the reason for this sudden urgency? Why you made this move now when things have been going so well for you? They've called in your debts?"

His eyes narrowed. "I've said enough. None of this is your concern."

"It is if my sister is to be caught up in whatever game you're playing—to the point of being put forth as the next Queen of England!"

Uncle Almain's jaw bulged. "This isn't a game."

He was angry again. Molly had never seen a man angry before today. But then, she'd never before had a lengthy conversation with a man, much less pressed one to explain himself.

Molly found herself faced with the possibility of aiding and abetting a plot to overthrow the king. At one time, it might not have mattered to her that none of the men involved wanted to serve England. It was for their own ends, out of, quite frankly, greed. Somehow without realizing, she'd been infected by King David's vision as much as everyone else—to the point that she was offended they'd assumed she'd be on their side.

She studied her uncle for a moment, taking a sip of her wine to settle her thoughts. After another swallow, while her uncle took a deep breath and returned to his calmer manner, she decided to set the matter aside. He'd told her what she needed to know, and she didn't need to humiliate him further by asking the exact amount of his debt. "What happened with my sisters and me, Uncle? Why have we not seen you until now?"

"What do you mean?"

"You visited Amesbury before Grandmother died. And then we saw you at her funeral. Why didn't you take us into your household at that time? You could have protected us as well as Gilbert de Clare. Better even."

"Your grandmother wouldn't have it." He shrugged, his focus on the remains of his breakfast on the plate before him, still thinking about the Jews. "She objected to my religion."

Molly so very much wanted to snort, but she restrained herself. "What about after *Gilbert's* death?"

His mouth twitched. "What would have been the point?"

Another flower of understanding burst into bloom. "It was you who allowed for those stories to be put out about Daisy marrying a foreign lord and Lizzie in care somewhere in the north. Why?"

There was a moment of hesitation and then a sigh. "I suppose it does no harm at this late date to tell you Gilbert came to me as he was developing his plans, after he had spoken with your grandmother and she'd agreed that he could be the one to protect you. At that point, he asked for my assistance."

Even though she'd already realized what had to be the truth, Molly felt like he'd just slapped her face. He'd been wary of telling her, clearly, but had known it was required if any of what he said was to make sense. "So you gave it?"

He canted his head, studying her as he did so. "Not enough, it seems."

"But you gave him your blessing to marry Daisy when the time came?"

"Only after he'd achieved the throne. I made it a condition of my consent." He smiled gently, seeming to think somehow this made everything better. "Never fear, my dear, though you didn't know it, I have been keeping the three of you safe all this time." The smirk was back. "Gilbert was always the clever one. Bogo and I are greatly indebted to him."

Molly endeavored to keep her tone casual, not wanting her uncle to know how angry this conversation had made her. "Are you saying Earl Gilbert lied to us about why he moved us from Amesbury to St. Margaret's?"

"What did he tell you?"

"That we were in danger from the king's men, and our grandmother had chosen him to protect us."

"Does it matter whose idea it was originally? Once Gilbert's plans started to develop, leaving you at Amesbury was too risky."

"What did he fear?" Molly didn't tell him that it mattered very much to her whose idea it was. Never in her life had she had a conversation where she held so much back. It wasn't restraint so much as that, amidst the anger, *she* was afraid.

"That at any moment, King David could have remembered you existed and taken you into his household." He chuckled. "What he really should have done was have you all killed."

So far her uncle had put forth the possibility of five murders. Molly's horror meant she missed a portion of what he'd said next, and she came to herself to hear, "—precisely so a situation such as this couldn't arise. It is astounding how naïve the man remains, even after seven years as king. He doesn't have a devious bone in his body." Then he looked into her face, and perhaps he did read something there because he added, more gently, "Do not worry for your safety, my dear. Though it is Bogo now who will take the throne, his plan is far better than Gilbert's or Roger's. They each were far too arrogant and misread their moments. We've learned since then, and we won't be making the same mistakes they did."

"Did you say *Roger?* Are we talking about Roger Mortimer?" For the expanse of several heartbeats, Molly couldn't breathe.

"Of course." His unconcern was reminiscent of Bogo's the previous night.

"You backed him too?"

"Since Daisy was supposedly married, and you were with the Church, he couldn't have either of you, so I promised him Elizabeth. But, of course, nothing ever came of it."

Perhaps Molly shouldn't have been shocked at this news, given everything else her uncle had told her. It was just that nobody had known of his involvement in that rebellion. From what Molly understood, her uncle had marched an army to Skipton Castle to support *David* in the battle that followed.

She had to put it aside, like so much else. "The king has devolved much of his power to Parliament, Uncle. Whatever throne you imagine Bogo taking will not be the same position my father held."

He took an absent-minded bite of food and spoke around it. "Parliaments can be reined in."

As Molly gazed at him, it finally dawned on her that he thought simply by deposing David, the world would go back to the way it had been before he came. The idea seemed hopelessly naïve—far more so than he'd just accused David of being, even to a naïve almost-nun like Molly who'd spent one portion of her life as a privileged princess and the second in a convent. She'd been confused earlier by Uncle Almain's plan, but she thought she was beginning to see more clearly now. Limited as her experience in the world was, she knew enough of the events of the past to know that sometimes greed and chaos won.

"After Earl Gilbert's death, you could have taken over St. Margaret's. Why leave it to Lord Tudur?"

"If I had, someone might eventually have looked more closely as to why." Uncle Almain rubbed his hands together. "Moreover, it was an expense I didn't need."

Molly looked down at her plate. Sitting in this well-appointed room in her uncle's magnificent castle, she understood now that she had no more say in her life than the block of wood he'd just put on the fire. Like Earl Gilbert, he saw Daisy as a thing to be bought and sold, no different than a cow or an estate—or maybe even a country, for that matter. She and her sisters had been stashed away, like silver on a shelf in a pantry, to be brought out when the occasion was right. Until then, none of these men had cared one whit for their circumstances—and certainly not for their happiness.

She had been a fool to expect it.

She hated being made a fool.

15

Day Two

Daisy

Lizzie's expression held the same relief and happiness that had flooded Daisy, which made her hopeful that *every* decision she'd made since last night hadn't been entirely wrong.

"Stop staring, girl, and help me!" The seamstress, who said her name was Beatrice, snapped her fingers at Lizzie.

Lizzie jumped to attention. "Sorry. So sorry!"

"This one's a lady and not for you to be looking at." Beatrice spoke in English, which likely Beatrice thought Daisy didn't understand or else she might not have referred to her as *this one*. Then Beatrice switched to French. "Pardon the girl's rudeness. She's new here."

"I don't mind," Daisy said immediately. "She seems very sweet."

Beatrice shot Lizzie a dry look and reverted to English. "It seems you are forgiven."

"Would you like a bun?" Daisy moved to the table where her partially eaten breakfast was still laid out and picked out a soft honey cake for Lizzie to eat.

Lizzie kept her hands behind her back and looked down at the floor. She too spoke in English, continuing their practice from the convent. "Am I allowed to take one, Seamstress?"

Beside her, Beatrice snorted. "If a lady offers you a sweet, you may take it."

Lizzie didn't have to be told twice, and she leapt at the cake. Daisy remembered what it had been like to be thirteen and hungry all the time, though she'd been less starved than Lizzie. Even so, and despite her hunger, Lizzie couldn't put aside that she was a princess. She ate the cake quickly, but with dainty bites instead of wolfing it down in two.

The seamstress looked on with a somewhat disbelieving expression, whether at the fact that Daisy had given Lizzie the cake in the first place or at the way Lizzie ate it. Regardless, she made no comment. Lizzie was doing well to pretend not to understand French, but the fact that she *was* a princess—or at least a lady—was going to become evident in moments like this one. She spoke English well, as if born to it, but she hadn't been around people who spoke French since Amesbury. If she forgot, even for a moment, that she wasn't supposed to know it, she would be exposed as something other than what she claimed.

None of this did Daisy say to her sister, as much as the impulse to instruct had her biting her lip. Lizzie had made it this far on her own. It wasn't Daisy's place to tell her she was doing something wrong now.

Then the seamstress became all business, standing Daisy on a low stool so she could take her measurements. None of the sisters had worn made-to-suit clothing in years. They wore habits, which were designed to drive men away rather than entice them. At least her uncle had given a bit of thought, beyond the acquisition of Isabel, to what additional expenses and services having nieces in his household might require.

While Daisy was being fitted, she thought she could get away with speaking. "I'd like to ask about this girl with you. She seems quite capable."

"She's called Jonet, my lady, and, as I said, she just arrived." Beatrice glanced at Lizzie, who ducked her head at the scrutiny.

"Is she to work with you from now on?"

Beatrice had a mouth full of pins, but she managed to speak around them. "I don't know if that's been determined yet." She sniffed. "You are right that so far she has proved useful. A good worker, I might even say. Needs fattening up, though."

Daisy couldn't agree more and was just opening her mouth to suggest she could use a maid when, from behind the seamstress, Lizzie began shaking her head back and forth, mouthing, "No, no, no."

Daisy subsided, not happy about Lizzie overruling her, but again deciding to trust her sister's judgment. Lizzie would have seen more of the castle by now than Daisy, so if she had a plan, it was more than Daisy had in this moment. Daisy's instinct was to protect her sister, which was why she had thought to turn her into her maid. In retrospect, that might put her in Bogo's line of sight. Maybe it was better if she stayed as far away from Daisy's rooms as possible.

"Perhaps she would like another cake?"

"I'm sure she would, my lady, but Cook has her in hand. I wouldn't want to spoil the girl."

"Are you fitting my sister too? She has no more dresses than I."

"I am to go to her room next."

Daisy's breath caught in her throat. "Her … room?"

Beatrice glanced up at Daisy's face. "I was told her chamber is located one floor below yours."

"Yes." Daisy smiled gracefully, even though her insides had just curdled like week-old milk. "I forgot Uncle Almain said we wouldn't have to share."

Beatrice finally stepped back, inspecting her creation with a satisfied smile. "I believe this one will work well for you, my lady." She helped Daisy shed the dress and put back on an old one of her aunt's which was too large, akin in that regard to Lizzie's gray sack, which she must have acquired at the convent before she left.

Then, as Beatrice began to gather her supplies, Daisy motioned to Lizzie and said in slow and careful French, "Come with me a moment. If you are going to my sister's room next, you could take something to her from me."

Lizzie glanced at Beatrice, who nodded and repeated what Daisy had said in English before making a *go on* motion with her hand.

"My lady." Lizzie curtseyed before hastening into the bed chamber adjacent to the sitting room. Beatrice remained on her knees, packing her box of sewing supplies.

Daisy didn't dare close the door all the way, but she brought Lizzie well away from it. "I am so happy to see you, but I told you to get help!"

"I needed to speak to you first, to find out the situation before I did anything else. There wouldn't be any point in getting help if in the end you didn't need it." Lizzie kept her voice low too, and since Beatrice had started to hum a tune, Daisy hoped she couldn't hear. They had so little time!

"I'm to marry Bogo, who is making a bid for the throne."

Lizzie appeared to take this news in stride. "And from your tone, you don't want to."

"No!"

"I hear he is very handsome."

Daisy gave her a sardonic look. "Handsome is as handsome does."

"So said grandmother many times." Lizzie's hands were on her hips, between one moment and the next becoming even more the spitting image of their mother, though she wouldn't know it since she'd never really known her. "Escape would be so much easier if you could throw yourself out a window and travel to Avalon like Queen Marged."

Daisy had no notion where that idea had come from. While Lizzie wasn't wrong, the comment wasn't particularly helpful either. "I truly wish I could, believe me."

"It's probably smart not to try." Lizzie was referring to the occasional admirer of David who jumped from a tower or had a friend shoot him with an arrow in hopes of duplicating David's feats. A few had actually died in these attempts. In one of his speeches before he'd gone to France, David had begged the people to desist in their efforts. He didn't control his ability. God did. Or so he said. Maybe that was why these days the churches were fuller than ever, with people trying to prove they were pure at heart enough to qualify for a journey to Avalon.

Daisy did her best, but she had no interest in aiming that high. "Did you get a sense that anyone here knows who I really am?"

"Not that I've heard. Uncle Almain has put out that you are his niece, though the specifics of your relationship have been kept vague."

"Deliberately so." Daisy let out a breath. "That means we still have time to stop him."

Beatrice called from the other room. "My lady? May I be of assistance?"

"Just a moment!" They were out of time. Daisy stepped away from Lizzie and began searching a wooden box on the side table for something to give to Molly. The box belonged to her Aunt Maggie, brought in for a bit of finery until Daisy could accumulate her own. She picked out a green ribbon.

As she handed it over, Lizzie said, "We need to have a real talk. I think I have some ideas about how to get you out of here, but I don't know that I'll be able to come to your room again."

Daisy made an instant decision that felt right, given their years of convent life. "Meet me in the church after Compline."

Lizzie hesitated as she took the ribbon. "Are you sure you're going to be able to get to the church? It's all the way in the bailey."

Daisy frowned. "Why wouldn't I be able to get there?"

"There's a guard outside your door—"

But then Lizzie ducked her head, like a real servant might, as Beatrice nudged open the door to the room. "Is she being a bother again, my lady?"

"Not at all." Daisy smiled. "I'm sorry it took so long to find what I wanted."

Beatrice bobbed her head politely, but then directed a glare at Lizzie and switched to English. "What are you doing over there? You are taking advantage of her kindness!"

"I-I'm sorry—" Lizzie stammered.

Daisy hastened to intervene, back to French. "It is my fault, Beatrice. She has been no trouble. Truly. She waited patiently while I searched."

Beatrice looked slightly mollified, even as she held out her hand to Lizzie, indicating she should come with her. Lizzie hurried out the door, the green ribbon clutched in her hand and her eyes on the ground. Daisy followed them back to the sitting room. After another curtsey from Lizzie and something of a bow from Beatrice, the door closed behind them.

But before their footsteps receded fully, Daisy herself reached for the latch. She was suddenly concerned Molly might give Lizzie away. Daisy had been so distracted by the idea that her sister was now staying in a different room that she had given no thought to Molly's desire for Daisy to go along with Bogo's play for the throne. If Daisy went with Lizzie now, she could at least head off the worst of what Molly might do or say. However, pulling on the latch didn't open the door. She tugged again, harder. It still didn't open. Only after another tug did it dawn on her that the door was locked from the other side.

She stared at wooden planks, shocked to find she truly was a prisoner in this castle, never mind her well-appointed room instead of a cell in the tower.

Then, yet again gathering her wits, which had momentarily been scattered to learn of her imprisonment, she knocked on the door. "Excuse me! I need to use the latrine!"

There was a pause, followed by a scraping sound indicating a bolt was being drawn back. The door opened to reveal a man twice her age with graying hair and a thick beard.

"Hello," she said, thinking she'd start with politeness. "I'm Daisy. May I ask your name?"

"Roger de Marston." His French accent was the same as hers.

"Perhaps you could explain why the door was locked?"

"Your uncle's orders, my lady." Roger's cheeks flushed. "It is for your own protection."

Her eyes narrowed. "In what way?"

He cleared his throat, now even more embarrassed. "If your uncle hasn't said—"

"In. What. Way?" She emphasized each word, her eyes intent on his face.

Roger transferred his gaze to somewhere above and to the left of her head. "I was told you might desire to fraternize with members of the garrison. I am here to discourage you from doing so."

Daisy laughed. And laughed again. Holding her belly, she rested her head against the frame of the door.

If possible, this display had Roger looking even more uncomfortable. "My apologies, my lady—"

Daisy made a dismissive motion with one hand. "It is not your fault." She let out one last guffaw. "I assure you I have no interest in any member of the garrison."

"They are all foreign, anyway, my lady. I am one of the few Englishmen left at the castle." He patted his leg. "I twisted my knee the other day, preventing me from riding to Leeds with the rest of the garrison. I'll be joining them as soon as I can command a horse."

Lizzie hadn't mentioned anything about the garrison marching away, but then, their time had run short. She was glad to see Roger appeared interested in talking. It meant she could perhaps befriend him. For now, she said, "I would like to use the latrine."

She expected immediate acquiescence, but instead his expression turned sheepish. "You should have a bedpan in your room."

"I do, but ... I would prefer not to use it."

He flushed again and dipped his head, misunderstanding why that might be, as she intended. "Of course, my lady, I'm happy to escort you. It's this way." He gestured down the corridor.

Daisy preceded him, as if there was nothing out-of-the-ordinary about being escorted to the latrine. She had herself well in hand now. If she was going to play a part, she would play it well. She'd done so for years. "I am hoping to attend Compline tonight in the castle's church. I assume my uncle will allow me my prayers?"

So far, she had done nothing but embarrass Roger. She could feel this new wave come over him, even from a pace behind her.

"I will see to it, my lady."

This was the first step towards freedom. The rest was up to Lizzie.

16

Day Two

Molly

As when she'd shared with Daisy, Molly's new quarters consisted of a suite of rooms, with a bedroom and an outer sitting area. Molly had been staring out the window, one that overlooked the bailey, when a knock came at the door. Since Isabel was in the other room, doing whatever she did to keep herself busy, Molly let her answer it. She didn't want to talk to anyone right now anyway.

At first Molly was glad when she overheard Isabel sending whoever it was away, but then she appeared in the doorway to the bedroom. "That was the seamstress. I told her you were asleep, since it's clear you are not yourself. She will return tomorrow. The girl with her brought you a gift from your sister." Isabel held out a length of green ribbon.

Molly accepted the ribbon, winding it between her fingers as she gazed down at it. "How did she get it?"

"I assume it's from your aunt's collection."

Being a nun, Molly never wore ribbons in her hair, which must mean Daisy was using the ribbon as a means to send a message. For the life of her Molly didn't know what it was. "What did the girl who gave it to you say?"

"She spoke in English, of course, but I understand enough to know that she was telling me her name was Jonet. Then the seamstress explained the ribbon was from your sister." Isabel put her nose in the air. "I don't know what the chamberlain was thinking, hiring such a one. No serving girl should speak at all. You certainly would never need to know her name."

Molly looked up abruptly, and then away, not wanting Isabel to see her expression. Perhaps the seamstresses' assistant was some girl of no importance. Perhaps none of this meant anything at all. But Isabel was right to point out the unusualness of a servant giving her name. Though Lizzie had never been one for confidences, at least not with Molly, *Jonet* was the name she had given every doll she'd ever had when she'd been allowed dolls. If this was Lizzie, she would have said *Jonet* in hopes Molly would recognize it was coming from her. Lizzie could be that clever. And was, like Daisy, more clever than she showed herself to be much of the time.

Maybe Molly was reading far too much into such a simple act, but she found her spirits lifting for the first time since her conversation with her uncle. She clenched her teeth, determined to wrestle her emotions back under control. It would not do to betray what was in her mind, now more than ever. Molly commanded herself to *think!*

Daisy had sent the ribbon, which must mean Daisy also knew Lizzie was here. They'd been in each other's presence! So … if the fact that Daisy had sent the ribbon was a message, the ribbon itself might be one too.

A green ribbon. What did it mean?

And then Molly knew: this season's liturgical color was green. Daisy was telling her to meet her in the church.

She lifted her head. "Of course, Daisy and I will be attending Vespers together."

"Well—"

"I am a nun, Isabel, or have been one, as has Daisy." Molly used her best commanding voice.

"You never took your final—"

Molly overrode her. "We have not missed a holy office except when ill until today. I appreciate that we cannot be at every one any longer, not with Daisy's betrothal to Lord Bogo, but I must at least attend Vespers. Surely this request is not unexpected. We are not prisoners, are we?"

"Of course not!" Isabel actually looked offended. "My lord Bogo wanted to keep you in your rooms for your own protection."

Molly raised her eyebrows in an exaggerated fashion. "You are here to protect me?"

Isabel seemed to realize she'd said something wrong, but she didn't appear to know what exactly it was or how to answer. Instead, she flushed and bowed deeply. "I am here to serve. Your uncle has put a guard on Daisy's room for the same reason, to make sure none of the men of the garrison disturb your stay here."

Molly had to admire Isabel's quick thinking even as she brought more pressure to bear. "Nonetheless, we will be collecting her as the bell tolls for Vespers."

"Yes, my lady." Knowing she was defeated, Isabel backed out of the room.

Molly was left with a long afternoon in which to think. She passed the time at first with needlework and then with the religious books her aunt had left, including Goscelin's *Lives of Women Saints at Barking Abbey*. That was where her sister Joan resided, and Molly felt within her that the fact her aunt had the book was a link between them. Even more, that Molly was able to read it now was equally significant.

She closed her eyes to settle herself in prayer and then allowed the book to fall open naturally. Likely where it opened would be where her aunt often started, but even that would tell her something. Oddly, though at first the book opened to well-worn pages, the breeze from the window fluttered them, turning several more over until they settled on a page about St. Wulfhilda, who had been the Saxon abbess of Barking Abbey before being deposed by the queen, only to be reinstated twenty years later.

Molly read the pages carefully and then again. Were they telling her she was wrong about her uncle? That he had been wrongfully removed from his position of authority as he'd complained he had been and should now be reinstated? Was Molly's new resistance to his plan a mistake?

She frowned, puzzling over the matter, until she read again the passage that said the queen herself had been the one to reinstate Wulfhilda. There was no mention of murder, or evil dealings on Wulfhilda's part, only acceptance of her role and duty at the queen's command.

At the queen's *command.*

Molly surged to her feet to pace back and forth beside the bed. Was this really about the queen? Was she meant to go to her in Normandy? Given the impossibility of such a journey, Molly was left with Queen Marged of Wales, who was residing even now at Kings Langley.

Molly's breath caught in her throat, even as certainty filled her. As well as the chill of horror at what she now had to suggest to her sisters they do.

The more Molly paced around her room, the more sending Lizzie to Queen Marged became their best option. In fact, likely it was their only option. The test of this path would be if Lizzie truly was in Berkhamsted. If so, then she *had* seen Daisy, Daisy had sent her to Molly with the ribbon as a message, Lizzie had given her name to Isabel, prompting Molly to follow the chain of reasoning to reach this point.

All of a sudden Molly had a deep urge to see her older sister. Last Daisy knew, Molly had been in favor of her marriage to Bogo. Normally, Molly was not one for apologies, in large part because she was so rarely wrong. Daisy, however, would understand and forgive her.

And then they would put their heads together to figure out a way to persuade Lizzie to do what must be done.

17

Day Two

Lizzie

ook Agnes kept Lizzie as busy for the second half of the day as she had the first, giving her little time to think about what might be happening with her sisters. Most of Lizzie's chores were similar to her usual fare at the convent, except, somehow, they felt like less of a burden at Berkhamsted. She was also fed twice more between when she spoke with Daisy and when she was supposed to meet her in the chapel at Compline. Back at St. Margaret's, the nuns ate twice a day, and each person was given the same portion of food as every other, even the aged ones who spent their days in prayer.

At Berkhamsted, nobody gave the quantity of food Lizzie consumed a second look. Since Cook Agnes was keeping her *girls*, as she called them, out of the main hall, the food was laid out on platters on one of the work tables in the kitchen, with each person taking the amount they wanted and coming back for seconds or even thirds if they chose. For tonight, only men and the older female workers in the castle ate in the hall with the soldiers from Almain who made up the bulk of the garrison. There were twenty in all, not a huge number, but a heavy presence in the castle nonetheless. Cook Agnes kept muttering about *dirty* foreigners. It took Lizzie longer than perhaps was reasonable to realize she wasn't talking about how often they bathed.

Lizzie wasn't sorry to be kept safe. The less interaction she had with anyone close to her uncle, the better. Besides, eating with only women was normal for her. Mayor Bill had been the first man she'd spoken to in months.

By the time Lizzie and the other servants had eaten their evening meal, celebrated Vespers in the church, and returned to the kitchen to finish preparing it for the morning, Lizzie was falling asleep on her feet. Compline felt like a long way off and her bed in the dormitory with the other girls invitingly close. Like at the convent, everyone here worked long hours, which meant most slept from the moment the work was done. Because everyone else was doing it, and she really wanted to close her eyes, even for just a moment, she lay down on her pallet in the servants' little dormitory with the other girls.

It was a mistake, as one might have expected. The moment she lay down, she couldn't stay awake. She tried pinching herself, conjugating Latin, and reciting the Book of Psalms in order, but her few hours of sleep in the croft the previous night had been a *long* time ago, and she *had* worked hard that day.

Fortunately, as the tolling of the bell for Compline faded, one of the other girls got up from her pallet and kicked Lizzie inadvertently (at least Lizzie thought it was inadvertent) on her way to use the latrine. Lizzie, as the newest resident of the castle, had been given the bed closest to the door. While she had no interest in getting up, she forced herself to keep her eyes wide open while the girl was gone and, as soon as she returned and settled back on her pallet, rose and slipped out of the room. She didn't have to pass another girl to do it and was quite certain nobody would miss her.

Once the door closed behind her, Lizzie halted. Within weeks of arriving at St. Margaret's, being out of bed when everyone else was asleep became practically a way of life for her. Nuns, on the whole, worked just as hard as servants, and got less sleep too because it was interrupted for the cycle of holy offices. Unlike at the castle, the nuns attended all eight instead of just one in the morning and one in the evening. Lizzie had sleep-walked through most of them, whether day or night. They were certainly part of the reason she had no desire whatsoever to become a nun, given a choice in the matter (which, of course, she'd never had).

But here, she didn't have the castle to herself as would have been the case were she out of bed at night at the convent. The door to the kitchen was open, and she could hear men inside, talking. It was fortunate she didn't have to actually enter the kitchen to reach the church, which was located beyond the great square tower. Bracing herself once again for the total unknown, and telling herself she should be used to it by now, she set out across the bailey. She'd been inside the church with most of the residents of the castle a few hours earlier and seen Molly and Daisy up at the front with their heads together. For a moment, she'd been jealous to see them so close, not to mention placed at the front of the church. Like princesses.

The jealousy had been fleeting, especially since they were allowed to speak to nobody but each other. They came and went, Daisy on the arm of Bogo and Molly with the same woman who'd answered her door at her heels.

As far as Lizzie could tell, the service had been conducted in the exact same manner and with the exact same content as at St. Margaret's, barring the presence of men. So if the Cathars were practicing heresy, it wasn't obvious to Lizzie. She couldn't decide if that fact was disconcerting or not.

She was worried enough about being stopped not to walk directly towards the church. There might be only twenty members of the garrison, but they had made their presence known, pacing on the wall-walks and standing guard at the gates. She didn't want to encounter any of them directly, nor be stopped by one of the higher-ranked workers, Cook Agnes among them. She had kept Lizzie and the other girls in the kitchen after the holy office precisely so none of them would be doing what Lizzie was doing now.

The church stood alone on the western side of the bailey, separated from the other buildings, like the kitchen, though not for the same reason. Kitchens were kept apart so a fire in the ovens or fireplaces wouldn't burn down the whole castle if the flames got out of hand. As the church was holy ground within the castle itself, it had its own little churchyard surrounded by a three-foot-high wall to demarcate its domain—and to prevent the livestock, particularly pigs wandering the bailey, from digging up the bodies in the graveyard.

Lizzie had been worrying this whole time that Daisy wouldn't be able to get away again and trying not to think about what she would do or how long she would wait if her sister wasn't there. But as she approached the church gate, the same older, bearded man, who'd been guarding Daisy's door earlier in the day, stepped out of the church porch. He rocked back and forth on the balls of his feet, indicating the boredom of a watcher who didn't think his job was important.

Daisy had always been the peacemaker among the sisters. Lizzie had at times been jealous of her composure, even as she railed against it in equal measure. She had never understood how it was that Daisy never complained! Watching the man settle himself against a post that supported the roof of the porch, to all appearances resigned to wait as long as necessary, it occurred to Lizzie that by always being composed, polite, and obedient, her sister had been able to do what needed to be done when it counted. Because of it, Abbess Helen had never entertained the idea that Daisy was lying about Lizzie's whereabouts. And somehow, even on an afternoon's acquaintance, Daisy had convinced this guard to bring her to the church after dark.

The church itself was lit up from within, indicating that Lizzie wasn't too late to catch her sister before the end of Compline, so Lizzie allowed herself a moment or two to study the guard, to make sure he really did show no sign of entering the church. Then she sidled along the churchyard wall until she was at the back, near the vestry door. Daisy had done such a good job of befriending her guard that he also showed no concern she might slip out of the church that way.

Lizzie clambered over the wall and crossed the graveyard as quickly as she could, feeling the heavy silence all around her. When she reached it, the door opened easily on silent hinges.

Once inside the darkened vestry, she waited quietly as the priest sang the *kyrie eleison*, indicating he'd reached the end of the service. As the last notes faded away, Lizzie tiptoed forward. The church was built in the shape of a cross, and she found herself near the back within the precincts reserved for churchmen. From the shadows, she could see Daisy kneeling at the *prie-dieu* before the altar. A dozen other worshippers were scattered throughout the church.

While everyone's heads remained bowed for the final prayer, Lizzie flitted into the choir stalls and held herself still while the priest welcomed individual worshippers to come forward to speak to him if they wished. Slowly, the church emptied as, one by one, the parishioners departed. When the priest turned towards the vestry, preparing to leave, Lizzie moved at a crouch to the other side of the church, endeavoring always to keep herself positioned behind him. From his white hair and bald pate, he was an older man and possibly didn't hear or see well anyway.

Daisy, on the other hand, was fully in command of her faculties, and she had in no way missed Lizzie's movement around the church. When Lizzie retreated into an alcove, Daisy crossed herself, stood, and strolled serenely after her, ending up once again on her knees before the altar of St. Mary, whose shrine it was. Here, in a corner near a large sarcophagus with the supine image of a knight holding a sword, they were hidden from view.

By the time Daisy arrived, Lizzie had made herself as small as possible in a corner, out of the light. "Are you all right?" As far as she could remember, she'd never before asked that question of her sister. She wasn't used to thinking of Daisy as vulnerable. Or a person.

"For now." Daisy's lips barely moved, and though Lizzie heard her clearly enough, she didn't think her words would be audible beyond their alcove. "You were right. I'm under guard. Molly too. Roger will be wondering what has become of me. Yet again, I don't have much time."

"I saw him outside. And earlier that woman who answered Molly's door."

"Molly and I were able to talk during Vespers. She has come to see this is all so much worse than we thought!" Then, her voice barely above a whisper so at times Lizzie had trouble hearing her, Daisy related first Bogo's intentions and then told her of Molly's conversation with their uncle, including his plan to assassinate the king and put Daisy herself on the throne, presumably after the untimely demise of Bogo.

Daisy concluded with, "You've seen all these foreigners, I assume." Lizzie was barely able to nod, stunned as she was by everything her sister had imparted, "We are concerned about why Uncle Almain hired them."

That, Lizzie could answer: "To defend the castle while the garrison is—"

"Don't be naïve, Lizzie! They are a private army for Uncle Almain! He pays them to do his bidding. As mercenaries, they have no morals or scruples. They don't care about England. Their families are far away."

Lizzie subsided. She hadn't understood what a *mercenary* was until now.

Daisy put a finger under Lizzie's chin and raised her head so she had to meet her gaze. "Uncle Almain wants me to be queen so he can rule England through me. He thinks he can control Bogo—and maybe he can—but I do not want to be a pawn in his game of chess with King David. I don't want to be a pawn in *anyone's* game. Not anymore. Not ever again. I don't want *you* to suffer the same way either." She paused. "I've always thought maybe you wanted that for yourself?"

"Yes." Lizzie found herself breathless again, this time at her sister's adamancy. "You've never said anything like this to me before."

"I've never had the opportunity to express an opinion before."

"You did Earl Gilbert's bidding—"

"Earl Gilbert is dead for wanting exactly what Bogo wants. Roger Mortimer too. And Uncle Almain—" Daisy shook her head. "They're all mad, the lot of them. I want nothing to do with them. I think I finally understand now how Joan felt."

"So how do we stop it? I could sneak you and Molly out of the castle in a hay wagon if I could get you to the stables, but—" At the convent, they'd had fifty sisters, none of whom had liked Lizzie particularly, but Daisy had been quite popular. Here, they knew nobody except their uncle. Everybody else served him, and from the way they spoke about him, thought him a worthy lord and would never go against him.

Daisy made a rueful face. "Molly says you must go yourself to Kings Langley."

Lizzie's jaw fell open. "That's one of the king's palaces!"

"Obviously." Daisy was matter-of-fact. "It's the only logical thing to do, Lizzie. Our uncle is marshaling a challenge to the king. By extension, the king will be interested in helping us stop him. At the very least, he will want to know someone is trying to murder him!"

Every part of Lizzie rebelled against the idea. It was one thing to agree Daisy shouldn't be forced into a marriage she didn't want. It was quite another to speak to someone in the king's court about it.

She found herself shaking her head back and forth. "No, no, no."

"Do you have a better idea?"

Lizzie still shook her head. She would have run away right then, back to the abandoned croft maybe, or to Tim, wherever his farm might be, if doing so wouldn't mean leaving her sisters to their fate. As nauseating as speaking to one of the king's men might be, it had to be better than denying the hope in Daisy's face.

"Besides, it isn't as if you will actually have to see the king in person. It's only King Llywelyn, Queen Marged, and their children at Kings Langley."

Lizzie stared at her sister, more aghast than ever. "How does that help us?" Daisy had to know the real source of her grandmother's ire had always been Queen Marged, not David, who was a man and thus could be forgiven for behaving like one. "They are the least likely people in this entire country to believe me."

"Molly disagrees."

"Daisy—"

"You have to try, Lizzie. I cannot marry Bogo; I won't marry Bogo. I certainly don't want to see him on the throne, even for as long as it takes Uncle Almain to do away with him. The king and queen won't either."

Lizzie still wanted to push back. There had to be another way. She didn't like the idea of murder, obviously, but since King David had murdered her parents, it might be justice for him to meet his end in the same way. "*An eye for an eye.*"

"Lizzie." Daisy's censure carried all the weight of her seven years of superiority in age, as well as genuine moral outrage. "You don't mean it."

Lizzie looked down at her hands. Part of her meant it, certainly. And yet, while she could tell herself if David died, only Uncle Almain would have blood on his hands, under Daisy's penetrating gaze, she knew that wasn't enough. By *not* acting on what she knew, now that she knew it, if the king were murdered, she would be just as culpable as her uncle.

"But going to Queen Marged—"

"Is the only way."

While Lizzie didn't want to believe Daisy, she could nonetheless marvel at the transformation of her sister from a demure nun to a defiant princess. Because, really, that's how she was behaving. Truly, their grandmother would have been proud, other than the fact Daisy was turning down the throne her uncle was offering her.

"Fine. I will go to Kings Langley, but they aren't going to listen to me."

"You have to make them."

"How?" And when her sister didn't immediately reply, she nodded. "You see the problem? None of us are supposed to be here. You are supposed to be married to someone else and living in another country entirely!"

A gust of air swirled around the darkened nave as the door to the church opened, and Daisy's guard entered.

Instantly, Daisy was on her feet, stepping out of the shadows. "One more moment, if you will, sir?"

"Of course, my lady. I simply wanted to make sure all was well."

"I have much to be grateful for, Roger. Thank you for being so patient."

The church door closed again.

Daisy bent towards Lizzie. "King David is bringing about a new era, Lizzie. Women have the right to an education, to employment, and they can't be forced into a marriage not of their choosing. Well, I do not choose to marry Bogo."

Lizzie had no reply to that, as much as she wanted to shout *no* again at the top of her lungs. She herself wouldn't have been so quick to dismiss the idea of Daisy on the throne. But she couldn't deny her sister the right to her own life nor ask her to give up something Lizzie had every intention of claiming for herself.

Then Daisy reached for Lizzie's hand. "I have faith in you, Lizzie. So does Molly." Before Lizzie could snort her skepticism, Daisy overrode her again. "Truly, I think everything that has happened to us up until now has led us to this moment—led *you* to this moment. You can do this, Lizzie. Save us. Save England."

18

Day Two

Daisy

"**M**y dear, what are you doing out of your room so late?" The words dripped from Bogo's mouth. When he'd first appeared out of the stairwell, he'd been turning the other direction, but now he hastened towards her. When he reached Daisy, he dismissed her guard with a wave of his hand. "You are relieved for the night."

"Yes, my lord." Roger bowed, respectful as always, though the look he shot Daisy wasn't relieved at all, as she might have expected, given the long hours he'd spent on duty that day, but closer to *concerned.*

Over the course of the day, Roger's attitude had become friendlier, protective, even paternal, to the point that much of the afternoon she'd left the door to her room open so they could chat together. She'd stayed by her open window, working on a new needlepoint, and he'd lounged on a stool in the hallway. Her intent had been, quite frankly, to woo him.

In so doing, she had learned that Roger was a landed knight with a small estate some fifteen miles away, given to him by the old earl before his death. He had been married twenty years and had eight children. While he missed his wife, he was pleased to have been able to visit home more often in recent years since David had taken the throne and warfare, both within England and without, had become less common.

Not that there hadn't been a need for him to serve the king. He'd been at Windsor Castle when the king had held off the forces of William de Valence; at Hythe, although by the time they'd arrived there the victory had already been achieved against the French king; and at Skipton, in the company of her uncle, fighting again for David.

He'd also been among the men her uncle had brought to Westminster Castle for the crowning of Gilbert de Clare. He told the story of the king's arrival with an almost religious fervor, embellished by the additional first-hand account of his friend Walter, who'd been the one to admit the king to Westminster in time to stop the ceremony.

That said, Roger had no say in his duties at this castle. He certainly couldn't gainsay a lord as powerful as Bogo. Thus, despite what appeared to be true reservations about leaving her in Bogo's company, he departed.

Daisy waited until Roger's footsteps had faded before replying to Bogo. "My lord, I was in the church."

"Of course, you were, my dear. I should have thought of that. Castle life must be such a shock for you after so many years in a convent." Bogo's expression immediately transformed into one of contrition. "My apologies for my role in your removal from your former life."

It was as if Daisy had plummeted suddenly to earth from a great height. His words all but knocked the wind out of her, and she was rendered momentarily speechless. How on earth was she to reply to that? To say it was no matter? Apparently so, and she managed the appropriate platitudes, putting on a cheerful face and smiling sweetly at her supposed husband-to-be. "My father never intended me to be a nun. That was always Molly."

"I will apologize to her too. But surely she must see it would be inappropriate under the circumstances to leave her at St. Margaret's."

Again, his words left Daisy somewhat thunderstruck. Under *what* circumstances exactly? As Daisy had just said to Lizzie, women were allowed choices they'd never had before. But even in the old days, the Church had decreed that any woman who declared a vocation was to be allowed it, regardless of the man her parents, relations, or guardians wanted her to marry. She could always choose to veil herself, and no man, even the king, was to stop her. On her wedding day, when she stood before the priest, she could always say *no*.

Most girls knew, even so, that such a choice wasn't without consequences. Her own parents had genuinely wished for a love match, as they themselves had, for each of their daughters. But they were pragmatists too and would have forgone a true marriage to make an alliance that suited the crown. Daughters were a coin to be spent. Molly was truly in good company in her reasoning about the benefits of a union with Bogo, never mind that she had since been won over—though of course not out of concern for Daisy's heart. For now, it was enough of a miracle to have Molly on her side. In fact, her sister appeared as opposed in this moment to the scheme to take the throne as she had been in favor of it earlier.

Daisy could have made any number of responses when Molly had told her of her uncle's belief that she was the rightful ruler of England. The first was something she'd heard one of the novices say not long ago: *you've got to be kidding me!* She didn't know what goats had to do with disbelief, or if *kidding* could even be a word, but it appealed to her in the same way it had obviously appealed to the novice.

Another choice might have been invective. She'd learned some to-the-point curses over the years, strange as that might sound for a nun—though, of course, never spoken when she thought anyone else was listening.

Or, finally, she could have asked, *why me?* But she knew the answer to that question as a matter of course: she was King Edward's daughter. It might truly be, in this new world of David's, that a woman could sit on the throne of England, even when there were viable male candidates. But Uncle Almain was looking to Daisy only because of her bloodline, the value of which, even to Daisy, captive as she was at Berkhamsted Castle, was not obvious. Equally obscure was the part about *Daisy* being in any way qualified to rule a kingdom after spending most of her life in a convent. Daisy's father had been prepared from birth to rule. King David had spent his first fourteen years in Avalon and then the next six at his father's side, being groomed for leadership as a prince of Wales before he'd been crowned King of England by the English barons.

She wondered how much of Bogo's confidence, and her uncle's confidence in him, was because he was so incredible to look at. If he were at least somewhat less pretty, he would have been easier to doubt. She hadn't ever given much thought to the difference people's appearance made in how they were treated—and in particular how she treated them. Even now, it was hard to believe an angel's face could hide inadequacy and failure. Still, while others might be swooning, Daisy had the measure of him now.

He was planning to kill the king. Maybe his man already had.

So instead of pressing, which Bogo would not have liked, and which might have made him suspicious were he to entertain for even one moment that any girl might not be staring adoringly at his beautiful face, Daisy said, "May I ask about the welfare of my other two sisters?"

"Which two sisters do you mean?" Bogo's brow furrowed. "Molly is well. You just saw her in church."

"I was referring to Elizabeth and Joan."

His expression cleared. "Didn't your uncle say? He visited Joan himself last week. As has been the case for many years, she is ensconced in Barking Abbey with no intention of leaving or renouncing her vows."

Daisy felt a swell of pride. Joan was three years older, with a mind of her own. Unlike Daisy, she would also have the support of her abbess, who had been the one to take her in seven years ago after her aborted wedding to William de Bohun. Reading between the lines, it sounded as if her uncle may have attempted a similar removal of Joan and been roundly refused. Because Joan was older, even if only twenty-three, she would have made a perfectly adequate consort for Bogo as well.

"It seemed safe to let her stay there for the time being."

Let her stay there. He spoke as if he was doing Joan a favor. "I would like to see her. She will want to know where I am!"

"Of course. Of course. In due time." Bogo reached out a hand, almost as if he intended to take Daisy's, but turned the motion into a smoothing of his cloak at the last moment.

Maybe not surprisingly, given what she now knew about him, every third sentence out of Bogo's mouth put up Daisy's hackles. This time, she barely managed to restrain herself from asking, *What exactly does 'in due time' mean?* Though, of course, she already knew. The point of asking would be to force Bogo to say it: *until we have murdered King David and you and I are married.* The fact that Daisy and all her sisters but Eleanor had been alive when David had been crowned king seemed to have passed her uncle and Bogo by.

Regardless, neither would want to let Daisy out of his sight, especially to allow her to speak in private with an older and possibly wiser sister—especially one with her own mind, and especially not before Daisy was entirely contained as Bogo's wife. After that, there'd be no way out.

It was an ugly thought, and Daisy shivered.

Bogo saw it and immediately whipped off his cloak to wrap around her shoulders, mistaking her internal fear for a chill. "You shouldn't be out at this hour, nor standing in this drafty corridor." He started walking with her. "Promise me you won't leave your room so late again!"

"My lord, I must attend Compline."

Bogo sighed, perhaps momentarily regretting his proposed marriage to an almost-nun. "I would take delight in escorting you in future—and making sure you are warmly wrapped! I will speak to your guard for neglecting his duty."

"He did offer me his cloak, my lord. I refused. I wasn't chilled then. The problem must simply be standing in the corridor for too long." It was one thing for Daisy to suffer under Bogo's attention, but Roger had done nothing wrong, and she didn't want to see him censured for something that wasn't his fault.

"Again, my apologies." Bogo had left his hands on her shoulders after giving her his cloak, and he gave them a little squeeze.

Daisy smiled at him. "I assure you I am perfectly well, my lord. Thank you for escorting me back to my room." She was working hard to sound appropriately compliant. Thankfully, it was a demeanor with which she had enormous experience, and Bogo's expression took on a look of satisfaction, not unlike earlier in the day when she'd capitulated to his will.

Bogo had clearly forgotten—or intended not to answer—the rest of Daisy's question. She gave him a few more paces to respond, but then decided she had to prompt him. She didn't know when she'd get another chance. "And Elizabeth?"

Bogo's answer came immediately. "She was found, shortly after you left St. Margaret's, and remains safe in the care of the abbess. As with Joan, there we had no reason not to leave her there for now."

He was bold; she'd give him that. He knew what he wanted, and he was willing to do anything to get it. It was a quality her father had manifested throughout his life. Despite everything Bogo had said and done, Daisy couldn't help but find such bravura appealing.

But only to a point.

And certainly not to the point that she wanted to marry him and fulfill his dream of becoming King of England. He didn't appear to have the faintest notion of what it took to *be* a king. With his varied employment, he had no qualifications whatsoever for the job, any more than Daisy did.

The more Bogo talked, elaborating his initial lie into a compelling and wholly believable story, the more Daisy's stomach wound itself in knots. He was so *convincing*—and Daisy had spoken to Lizzie not a quarter of an hour ago! If Daisy hadn't known his words were a total lie, she could easily have believed him. It made her wonder if what he'd said about Joan was true either. He appeared to lie as easily as he breathed.

Apparently Daisy could lie too, as she'd just now done regarding Roger offering her his cloak (which he had not done). But in all her years, few as they were, Daisy had never encountered anyone with such an estranged relationship with the truth.

After a few more paces and a brief war with her emotions, during which time Daisy wrestled herself under control again, she managed to ask, "When can I see her?"

"We will have to see about the arrangements. Perhaps after we are married, you could take a trip to the convent, or she could be brought to you. The abbess seemed to think, however, that it wouldn't be good for Elizabeth to become overly excited. She is so well settled into convent life that the abbess thinks it would be unwise to upend her now."

Even had Daisy not just seen Lizzie in the church, she would have known this for the untruth it was. Bogo was speaking of Lizzie in a way adults often did when discussing the needs of young people in their charge—condescendingly and as if the younger person in question was a wild horse that could be tamed with severe limits and enough time.

Daisy was quite sure by now that no amount of time—and worse, severe limits—would ever have made Lizzie accept a life as a nun, no matter what the abbess inflicted on her to break her spirit or make her conform. Only thirteen she might be, but she'd had the courage and strength to leave the convent on her own, track down her sisters, infiltrate the castle, and speak to Daisy without anyone knowing who she was or what she was doing.

Daisy sensed Lizzie herself had no real notion of the power within her. For some time, Daisy had suspected it was there. Now she knew it. She had sent Lizzie to Kings Langley because they genuinely needed her to get help—the whole of England needed her to get help—but also because she truly believed her capable of finding it.

Earlier, Daisy's antipathy towards Bogo had so overwhelmed her she'd been a hair's breadth from telling him outright that she knew he was lying. But while to say so would have been very satisfying, she couldn't allow him even a hint of awareness that she didn't believe him or that this intimate walk down the corridor wasn't the highlight of her day. All of a sudden, the stakes, which had been high enough before, were very high indeed.

Before today, Daisy never dared rely on her little sister for anything. Now, she was relying on her for everything. Even when Lizzie had been particularly disobedient, every nun had known that when she had a plan, heaven help the person who went against her. If Bogo had known what was really going on at Berkhamsted, he would have been shaking in his boots.

19

Day Three

Lizzie

Part of Lizzie could have done without Daisy's pledge of faith. Or rather, most of her recoiled at the idea that anyone would rely on her for anything, and only a tiny sliver appreciated the trust. Lizzie had always been the troublemaker, the one dragging her feet, the last through the door, except for meals. She was the one who on occasion ruined the day for everyone else, simply because she could. More than one person (as in, the majority of the nuns in the convent) had spoken to her at one time or another about how they were a community, a family, and rowing the same boat. It was her job to get on board and row with them.

Lizzie had never seen why that should be. It wasn't her choice to be at the convent. Exactly nothing that had happened in her life had been her choice, and where there was no choice, there couldn't be responsibility either, no matter how much Molly or the abbess pretended otherwise. So, as she'd retorted more than once, she had no interest in traveling in their boat. She would rather stay on the bank, thank you very much.

Whenever she said those words, though true, she'd had to steel herself not to feel bad at the hurt look on the other woman's face. Lizzie didn't *like* hurting anyone's feelings (no matter what Abbess Helen said). She did like what happened after she sneered back. Early on in her sojourn at St. Margaret's, she'd learned that if she did a terrible job, repeatedly, at whatever task she was given, she wasn't asked to do it again. Or if she did end up doing it again, very little was expected of her in terms of finishing the job in a timely fashion. By making herself unpleasant, she ensured nobody wanted to be around her.

While that had left her with some of the worst jobs, it also meant, in addition to being left alone, that nobody expected anything from her. She had learned to perform with a remarkable perfection to everyone else's low expectations. And maybe to her own as well.

In summary, Lizzie had made it her life's work to become the opposite of everything her sisters tried to be.

That Daisy now assumed Lizzie was capable not only of something more but of *this* was truly terrifying. Lizzie herself didn't know if she was capable of it. Part of her was quite sure she wasn't—except for that tiny, aforementioned sliver that thrilled to Daisy's confidence and wanted the approval of those around her. Lizzie had tried to root out all such sentiments long since, but there it was again, poking itself up and demanding to take the lead.

Lizzie's only comfort, if she could even call it that, was the knowledge that she had a limited number of choices. Yes, she could stay on indefinitely at Berkhamsted Castle as a servant, but it was pointless to do so if it meant watching Daisy be forced to marry Bogo against her will. That was hardly the proper end for her sister, not after everything they'd been through. Besides, the more she thought about what Daisy wanted her to do, the more viable what she was asking seemed, especially taken step by step instead of as an intimidating whole. For starters, leaving Berkhamsted should be far simpler than entering. All she really had to do was walk out the door. She wasn't a prisoner like her sisters.

Thus, the first issue facing Lizzie was not whether she could physically leave, but *how* to leave. First Mayor Bill and then Cook Agnes and then even Kate had been welcoming to her, a total stranger, in a way that was wholly unexpected and left that tiny sliver of herself that wanted approval (the one growing larger by the moment) more than a little ashamed. She hadn't been liked by so many people in her life that she could easily discard any new acquaintance, no matter their station.

So while she could walk out the front gate of the castle, Lizzie could envision, even with her limited knowledge of the way servantry worked, that walking away without an excuse was going to mean she wouldn't be allowed back in. To return might be a crucial part of any rescue plan—on the off-chance anyone at Kings Langley believed anything Lizzie said.

Lizzie managed to fall asleep worrying at the problem and woke having decided, oddly for her, to tell Cook Agnes a bit of the truth. Arising at first light with the other girls, she made her way to the kitchen where breakfast preparations were in full swing. Cook Agnes would not like to be distracted in this moment, but it had to be done, and Lizzie went right up to her as she was peering into a cauldron of porridge. "Cook Agnes, I need to be excused today."

Cook Agnes frowned as she stirred. "Why would that be?"

This was already as hard as Lizzie feared it would be. "I need to leave the castle. I want to come back, and I hope you will have me back, but even if you won't, I will still go."

"Is it your time of the month?" Lizzie had expected a lecture. Every authority in her experience would have lectured her at this point, probably about responsibility and duty and sticking to a task once started.

Lizzie could have lied. It was on the tip of her tongue to do so, but she found herself shaking her head. "No, Cook. I'm sorry. It's something else."

Cook Agnes looked her full in the face. "Is it important?"

"Yes, Cook. Very."

She gave a sharp nod. "Then I suppose it's just as well I was waiting to see what needed doing to assign you anything for the day. When will you be back?"

"Soon, Cook. I hope. Very soon."

"Off you go, then, before anyone else sees you and wonders what you are up to and why I haven't boxed your ears." Her attention was already back on the porridge, gesturing with a big spoon to the young woman whose job it was to stir. "Get in there again. Don't let it burn on the bottom."

"Cook, what—" The woman, who was called Cally, another pet name, though for what given name Lizzie didn't know, had obviously overheard something of their conversation.

"Never you mind what Jonet's doing. Think about yourself."

"Yes, Cook."

Lizzie had been shifting her weight from one foot to the other, hesitating as she listened. Now, at a flick of Cook Agnes's fingers, she fled. She had no possessions other than what she stood up in, so her feet took her without a detour all the way to the gatehouse. Along the way, she worried at Cook Agnes's response, wondering why she had let her go so easily. It was true Lizzie had worked hard yesterday, and maybe that really was enough to earn trust. Maybe if Lizzie had worked hard that first day at St. Margaret's the entire course of her life there would have been different. But she hadn't. In truth, she was no judge of her own performance. It could even be that Cook Agnes didn't like her and was pleased to have been presented with a reason to get rid of her.

By the time Lizzie reached the first gatehouse, she'd shaken off the worry. It truly wasn't anything she could fix in this moment. What was done was done, as her old abbess used to say. Lizzie had what she wanted, and it appeared Cook Agnes was not so upset with her request to leave that she'd told her never to come back. Lizzie had taken a risk by going to her instead of disappearing without talking to anyone, as was her first instinct. Thus, by almost any measure, this was a victory.

That didn't mean, however, that Lizzie didn't still have a tightness in her chest as she walked past the guards as if she were on an errand instead of leaving for good. She had been treated (in her estimation) alternately well and poorly since her parents' deaths. As the dowager queen, her grandmother had ruled Amesbury like it was her own estate, and the abbess had done her bidding. The three sisters had lived in their own quarters, adjacent to their grandmother's, with all the luxuries (food among them) befitting their station. Other than living exclusively among women, it hadn't been that different for any of them than their lives at Windsor Castle.

All that had changed when they'd come to St. Margaret's. Lizzie had assumed, with her admittedly limited experience, that the only way she would ever be treated well was to once again become a princess.

Against all expectation, a single day at Berkhamsted had taught her it was possible to be liked and respected as a common person—and maybe even just for being herself.

20

Day Three

Elen

Gwenllian wadded up a piece of paper and threw it at Elen's head.

"Hey." Elen patted her hair, tucking one of the long red strands behind her ear. "What was that for?"

"You are going to be fourteen years old tomorrow, a grown woman. What are we going to do about it?"

"Your mom is planning a party, you know that."

"I know *that*. What are *you and I* going to do about it?"

Elen eyed her cousin/best friend who was, even more, a sister. Elen's mother, Elisa, and Gwenllian's stepmother, Meg, were actual sisters. Gwenllian's biological mother had died when she was born, in June of 1282, making Gwenllian nine months younger than Elen, thirteen to Elen's one-day-short-of-fourteen. From almost the moment Elen had come to Earth Two a year and a half ago, she and Gwenllian had been inseparable. They shared a room, lessons, clothes, thoughts, dreams, and pretty much everything else. As with any set of sisters, sometimes they didn't get along, but those times were relatively few and far between. They had each other, no matter what life threw at them.

They occasionally even managed to convince various visitors to the court that they were twins, though they figured they were believed only in the sense that nobody would admit a princess was lying to them. Though younger, Gwenllian was taller, blonde, and what Elen had heard described as *willowy. Like a willow tree?* Elen wasn't entirely sure that was a compliment, though the speaker hadn't otherwise implied an insult. Elen herself was barely over five feet tall with a few more curves than Gwenllian, perfectly straight red hair, and the same color blue eyes as her cousin.

"As long as it isn't what we did for *your* birthday."

Gwenllian pretended to pout. "It was fun."

"We went hiking through the mountains in the pouring rain, mist, and fog, never mind that it was June. We got lost. Aunt Meg was three minutes from calling out a search party for us." Elen wrinkled her nose. "I thought you wanted to go shopping at the market?"

"You don't even like shopping. Besides, we always knew which way was down." It was a non sequitur, but Elen knew what Gwenllian meant.

She eyed her cousin. She herself had been adventurous enough from the very start to be all in on coming to Earth Two, regardless of the drawbacks, of which there were many. She was as much in favor of indoor plumbing and heating as the next person, but their absence wasn't enough to stop her. She certainly wasn't going to abandon Christopher, her brother, who'd spent a year on his own in Earth Two before they arrived. Gwenllian, on the other hand, yearned to return to Avalon. It had been her decision to jump out of the window of Westminster Castle with David's son Arthur and travel there during Gilbert de Clare's insurrection. In so doing, she'd saved Arthur and changed the course of everyone's life. For the better, as far as Elen was concerned.

The universe (or God or Merlin, Elen's opinion on the issue varied with the day) had arranged things so Christopher had been right there at the Bryn Mawr train station to pick them up. He hadn't known who they were initially, but he had a soft heart and had gone to check on them when he didn't have to as they stood alone near the tracks.

The rest was history—or rather, Earth Two's history—with Christopher returning with them in his car and killing Gilbert de Clare with the front end as they came in.

Weirdly, Elen and Gwenllian hadn't even *met* in Avalon. Elen had been *right there* in the same town, but she had spent the day at a babysitter's house. At the time, Elen had been eleven years old, left to play children's games while Christopher saved their cousins. It had taken nearly another year and a couple other strange turns of events to arrange Elen's own arrival in Earth Two with her family.

Gwenllian turned onto her stomach on the bed, her chin in her hands. "If shopping is out and hiking is out, what then—"

"Hello, girls, what are you up to?" Elen's Aunt Meg poked her head into the room.

"We were just discussing plans for my birthday." Elen rolled her eyes in a way she thought her aunt would appreciate.

Aunt Meg immediately pointed a finger at Gwenllian rather than at Elen. "No hiking!"

Gwenllian scoffed. "We know, Mom."

"Good." Aunt Meg took a step into the room and switched to English. Up until that moment, they'd been speaking in Welsh, which Elen could attest was no easier for English speakers to learn than it had been twenty-five years earlier when her aunt had first come to Wales. Speaking from experience, few managed it beyond some key phrases. "I want to introduce you to someone." She waved a hand into the corridor. "Come on in, Jonet."

The girl approached with one of the wariest expressions Elen had ever seen—and she'd seen wary a lot. The Americans in Earth Two tended to be far too informal and disdainful of tradition for the residents of Earth Two. Especially for princesses. Elen wasn't really a princess, but because her family lived with Gwenllian's family, and her cousin was the King of England, saying Elen was not a princess was really just splitting hairs. Though David had been wary about anointing members of his own family with honors, just before the France trip, he had told Elen's parents he was giving them the Earldom of Gloucester. There was a lot to unpack there, Aunt Meg had said later, but nobody was sorry he was doing it.

Elen put on her most welcoming face. "Hi Jonet. Welcome to Kings Langley."

Aunt Meg stood with a hand on Jonet's shoulder. "She has just joined the staff here. She was thirteen ... when?" She looked inquiringly at Jonet.

"In August, my lady," Jonet supplied the answer through stiff lips. She was standing poker straight too, like she couldn't wait to get out of there and back to wherever she'd come from.

Aunt Meg nodded. "I thought you two might make her feel welcome. You are all about the same age."

Gwenllian knew the drill as well as Elen. She'd already swung her legs to sit on the edge of the bed. "It's so nice you've come to Kings Langley, Jonet. I turned thirteen in June. What day in August is your birthday?"

Even more than Elen, Gwenllian was fluent in Welsh, English, and French—and read Latin. Her English, however, came out with an American accent, like Elen's, since she'd learned it from Aunt Meg, who'd raised her from when she was two.

Because of that, Elen thought at first Jonet hadn't understood her, but then she blinked and said, "The seve—" She swallowed. "The seventeenth."

"Nice," Gwenllian said. "Elen turns fourteen tomorrow."

Jonet appeared to have swallowed her tongue at this casual conversation with two high born girls. Everything about her demeanor indicated a fight or flight response was in the offing. But for now, she remained frozen where she was.

Aunt Meg came to the rescue, with a rueful look at both Elen and Gwenllian. She really should have known that any friendship, if possible at all, was going to take time. For now, Jonet was uncomfortable and tongue-tied in their presence. Aunt Meg's arm went around the girl's shoulders and squeezed. "I'm sure Chamberlain Donald has a few more things to show you before you retire for the night. Welcome again to Kings Langley."

"Thank you, my lady." Jonet curtsied and practically ran from the room.

As soon as she'd gone, Elen pulled a face. "That was awkward."

Aunt Meg sighed. "We'll keep trying. True equality is going to take time. She seems very bright, just in the bit I've spoken with her. We'll see how this goes, but I'm hopeful for her. Girls that young can be retaught if they are treated as if they have worth."

"It's still weird we have servants at all," Elen said. "I should be able to get myself dressed. It's hard to get past that to become friends."

"Elen's right, Mom," Gwenllian put in. "I wish you wouldn't bring by every stray who comes in. It makes everybody uncomfortable."

"She was hungry and cold and walked all the way here in the pouring rain from somewhere up by Berkhamsted, according to the guard at the top of the tower who watched her come in." Aunt Meg's tone had a bit of an edge to it. "Besides, do you really think I'm going to let her stay a servant? She's thirteen!"

Gwenllian subsided at that. Elen herself had initially been surprised Aunt Meg was making Jonet a servant at all, so important was her initiative to educate children—and particularly girls—which full-time employment prevented. But families needed money too, and most hated taking charity. Besides, as Elen's own mom had said, *there wasn't anything wrong with a part-time job.* It was when children worked sixteen hours a day, every day, leaving them no room either for education or for *being* children that it became a problem.

Elen and Gwenllian were being educated, of course. And the exciting, real difference between being in Avalon versus Earth Two was that at fourteen Elen could start training at the university in Llangollen to be a teacher. Oxford and Cambridge were still primarily focused on producing church scholars (*fine as far as it went*, according to Aunt Meg), but to have a democratic society, the realm needed an educated populace, and Aunt Meg saw training more teachers as one way to achieve it. Many were even itinerant. And unlike Cambridge or Oxford, both of which nominally admitted women but were really continuing to drag their feet on the matter, Llangollen University admitted women as equals.

David was pushing for change, to the point of threatening to revoke the special tax status of both Oxford and Cambridge if they didn't comply. He was busy right now with other things, but had promised, by next year, that girls and women would be admitted fully to both. There wasn't even an *or* to add to that. He didn't throw his weight around all that often—not like he could as king—but when he did, people knew he meant it. As he'd said, *what was the purpose of being King of England if he didn't* use *it every once in a while.*

Once Aunt Meg left, Elen returned to the matter of what to do for her birthday. "Maybe I'll just sleep in."

"You are such a party pooper." Gwenllian flopped onto her back and gazed up at the ceiling. The shadows from the candle flames danced across it. Elen liked watching candle flames, so at first she thought they'd distracted her cousin, but then Gwenllian spoke again, indicating she'd simply been gathering her thoughts. Gwenllian often gave the impression of being flighty or unserious, but she noticed everything and could think deeply when she wanted to. "There was something off about Jonet, don't you think?"

"She was terrified of being with us, that was for sure. Her feet were stuck to the floor. I've never seen anyone actually run away from me before."

"I don't think she was running away from us. It was Mom she feared the most. When Mom's arm came around her shoulders, did you see the look on Jonet's face?"

Elen frowned. "I guess I didn't notice that particularly."

"It wasn't fear she was feeling, I don't think." Gwenllian was frowning now too. "If I didn't know better, I would have said it was *disgust.*"

21

Day Three

Lizzie

Lizzie had walked out the front gate of Berkhamsted Castle without much of a plan—scratch that, *any* plan—beyond getting to Kings Langley and entering the castle.

Somehow.

She figured she had seven miles to come up with something. She had entered Berkhamsted easily enough because of meeting Mayor Bill on the road. She would allow for that possibility again, or she would think of some other means of getting inside. Worst case, she would apply yet again for employment.

It took her several hours to reach the village, the last half of the journey in the pouring rain, for which she was woefully unprepared, even with her sturdy cloak. Initially, she hadn't intended to go straight to the palace but thought to investigate the village and surroundings a bit first. But as she trudged down the main street to the green, the villagers' houses were closed up tightly because of the rain and not a soul was about. It rained all the time in England, but maybe this rain was a little much even for hardy peasants. Not a single person poked his nose outside his door as she passed by. Either they were remarkably incurious or incredibly unwelcoming. Or maybe, they had so many people walking through Kings Langley every day that they didn't care enough about strangers even to gawk at them. Whatever the reason, there was no Mayor Bill to save her this time.

The palace of Kings Langley wasn't smaller than Berkhamsted so much as a very different place. It wasn't designed to defend against assault, beyond the bare minimum of a curtain wall that encompassed the whole of it. It had a large gatehouse, but no real keep, not like Uncle Almain's fortress, and otherwise was somewhat sprawling, with many multi-storied buildings, including a hall, stables, bath house, kitchen, and living quarters, most of which she found out about later.

Screwing up her courage, Lizzie walked directly to the front gate. The straightforward method had worked for getting out of Berkhamsted. Maybe it would work for getting into Kings Langley. Lizzie came to a halt, still in the rain, but standing on the paving stones in front of the gate. Her dress was muddy to her knees, which meant her legs would be too, underneath. She was thoroughly wet from head to toe, her cloak long since having given up keeping her dry. Then, as she gazed somewhat blearily at the guard on duty, rain blew particularly hard into her right side, and she staggered at the force of it, barely able to keep on her feet.

The guard on duty must have been out in the rain recently too, given his wet hair and beard, but he appeared wholly unsympathetic. "What are you doing here, lass? This isn't an inn."

Taken aback, Lizzie righted herself and pulled her useless cloak even more tightly around herself. By now, its only real benefit was to keep the rain from actually hitting her skin. Otherwise, it was hardly more than a wet rag.

"You have no work for me here, then?" All of a sudden, a lump formed in Lizzie's throat, and she had to force the words around it.

"Not today. Go home."

"I don't have a home."

He snorted. "You came from somewhere!"

"My parents are dead. I don't have anywhere else to go." The stark truth came blurting out before Lizzie could stop it. In that moment, everything had become simply too much to bear. The struggles of the last few days crashed down around her. She couldn't be turned away. She truly did have nowhere else to go. Despite her best intentions, tears began to leak out of her eyes, though likely the guard couldn't tell because they mixed with the raindrops already on her cheeks. "Please." Her voice broke.

"Harry, you know better. I thought we talked about this. Bring the poor child inside." A woman swathed in a thick black cloak stepped out of the doorway of the left tower. "The last thing you want is for the queen to learn you left a girl standing in the rain."

"But Dilys—"

Even Lizzie knew that was a Welsh name. She couldn't remember ever meeting a Welsh person before. By her grandmother's description, they all had warts and double chins and spoke a language no reasonable person could ever be expected to understand, much less read. But this woman's English was perfect. She was also approaching middle age, with blue-gray eyes and dark hair streaked with white that was just visible from within the hood of her cloak.

"Harry."

"My apologies." His words were, on the surface, polite, but otherwise his manner was very grudging. Nonetheless, Harry motioned Lizzie forward.

Before Lizzie had taken even a step, the woman herself closed the gap between them, unhooked Lizzie's own cloak at the throat and, in a fluid motion, as if it were the most natural thing in the world, swung her own cloak around Lizzie. "Let's get you someplace warm. What's your name, *cariad*?"

"Jonet." Stunned, Lizzie could only acquiesce. She was inside Kings Langley, which was what she'd wanted, so she couldn't argue with Dilys's actions. But she also could hardly comprehend the woman's accepting manner, especially after Harry's opposition.

"How old are you?"

"Th-th-thirteen." Lizzie was so befuddled she forgot to lie.

"You poor dear." Dilys led Lizzie across the courtyard to a building she couldn't identify until she stepped inside, when a wave of warm, moist air hit her. In an instant, Lizzie forgot about her grueling walk in the rain. Berkhamsted also had facilities for laundry and bathing, as did all castles, but this was the most luxurious bathing room Lizzie had ever seen. This was also, what with a blazing fire heating cauldrons of water, the warmest Lizzie had been in days, if not months. *Years?*

"What is this place?"

Dilys laughter tinkled. "It's a bathroom, and one fit for a queen, according to my lady."

"Your lady?"

"Queen Marged. Another queen, Eleanor, wife to King Edward, may he rest in peace, had the sense to have it built in the months before she gave birth to her last daughter, Elizabeth." Dilys tipped her head. "The girl would be about your age by now."

Despite the heat, Lizzie's feet were frozen to the floor. She had been thinking about her parents a great deal since the men had come to St. Margaret's. In coming to this place that had once belonged to her father and mother, she'd been bracing herself for … well, she didn't know what.

To hear their names spoken, with gratitude, along with her own name, and to know her own mother had ordered the bathroom built, on this spot where she now stood, rendered Lizzie incapable of coherent thought in an afternoon that had already been full of surprises.

And then she further humiliated herself by bursting into tears.

"Oh my sweet. You must be so cold." Dilys began to bustle about, soon aided by the arrival of two maids to assist in the efforts.

In a few moments, they had Lizzie out of her sopping wet clothes and into a warm bath—her first warm bath since she'd left Amesbury, truth be told. Though, even there, as the youngest of the sisters, she'd always bathed last, when the water was no longer truly hot. The nuns at St. Margaret's believed in bathing too, but the temperature of the water was at best tepid and more often the same temperature it had been when it came out of the well. This was especially true for the youngest and least appreciated of their number. That, Lizzie knew, was her own fault. At the time, she hadn't been uncomfortable enough to change her behavior.

Lizzie allowed herself to be scrubbed from top to bottom, her hair washed, and then her body thoroughly dried. It was only after she'd gone through all that and they were layering warm, dry clothes on her that it occurred to her they didn't know anything about her but her false name.

She knew who she was, of course, *but they didn't*. She was only a girl to them, a random stranger who'd appeared at the gate. Their kind treatment was so confusing and unlikely as to be nonsensical. Given that she'd just been ruminating about how well she'd been treated at Berkhamsted, someone who didn't know better might think the owners of these two castles were on the same side.

This time, she actually thought about her question before she spoke, though when she did, her words were no less abrupt: "Why are you doing this?"

"Doing what?" This was a new voice, and Lizzie whipped around to see who had spoken.

A woman stood in the doorway, older than Dilys, with dark hair also streaked with gray and loosely coiled at the back of her neck. She wore a burgundy dress that would have left Daisy drooling, and one which even Lizzie, who didn't care for fashion, had to admire as perfectly fit to her and of the highest quality.

"Being nice to me. Taking me in. Giving me a bath and dry clothes." Belatedly, Lizzie curtseyed. It was obvious the newcomer was someone of status. "My lady."

The woman nodded as if it were no more than what she expected, though with no pretension or a nose in the air. "I'm Meg." Then she tsked through her teeth. "None of you will call me that, of course, so you may call me *ma'am*."

Lizzie mouthed the word to herself before speaking, "Yes, ma'am."

Again, the woman nodded, and Lizzie realized only then that she was speaking to Queen Marged of Wales herself.

From deep within Lizzie, an uncontrollable feeling of revulsion welled up that was so strong it made her head spin, and if she hadn't had her teeth clenched together she might have vomited on the floor. Here was David's *mother*, the person primarily responsible for every bad thing that had happened to Lizzie since she was three years old. If she'd had a knife in her hand, she might have stabbed her in the chest and damn the consequences. Almost worse, but certainly because of her loathing, it was completely impossible in this moment to tell her what Lizzie had come to say: that her son was in danger, that Bogo de Clare was colluding with Lizzie's own uncle to murder him—and may already have done so.

And if she wasn't going to go so far as to tell her that, or her own true identity, how could Lizzie even begin to explain about the need to rescue Daisy and Molly? Lizzie bent her head, knowing she could not let even a hint of her hatred show. While she wrestled her expression back under control, she shielded her face with the fall of her hair and pretended to be overawed.

Thankfully unaware of what was going on inside Lizzie, the queen approached, though not to talk to her. She and Dilys had a conversation in what must have been Welsh, given the strange sounds coming out of their mouths. After what appeared to be an accord, the queen touched Lizzie's shoulder with her right hand, softly, with a few fingers, nothing more. "No one is ever turned away from this castle or any castle from which my husband or son rules. Any and all are welcome to eat in the hall when meals are served. Someone will be speaking to Guardsman Harry on the matter, to remind him of his charge."

Lizzie forced herself not to wrap her arms around her body. She *had* to control the way she was shaking inside. Still with her face turned away, she said, "I wouldn't want him to lose his position on my account. He didn't know me—"

Dilys laughed lightly. "Do not worry that he will be dismissed, starved, or dropped into an oubliette."

At Dilys's words, the queen suddenly grinned, and even through the red haze that had covered Lizzie's vision, she could see it lit up the room. "We don't have one of those anyway. He will simply be encouraged to be more open in the future to bedraggled girls who arrive in need of succor." Her next words were for Dilys, a last exchange in Welsh. Then the queen departed.

After that, the afternoon was taken up with what Dilys called, *sorting her out*, which included an explanation of how things were done at the castle. Lord Tudur, whose name Lizzie had been pronouncing wrong all this time, had gone to London with King Llywelyn to consult with Earl Carew. They'd also taken the six-year-old royal twins, Padrig and Elisa, a fact which seemed to please Dilys greatly, though she hastened to assure Lizzie that the children were very polite and occasionally thoughtful, but *busy* in a way Dilys found exhausting.

For her part, Lizzie managed to relate to Dilys a passably coherent tale of the death of her parents and then her grandmother, with whom Lizzie had been living until she'd died too. With nobody else to whom she could turn, she'd come here.

"I'm so sorry, my dear." Dilys gave Lizzie's shoulders a squeeze. "When did you say your grandmother died?"

"A few weeks ago."

"Then you're grieving too. I'm glad you had sense enough not to try to live on your own." Dilys paused. "But why come all the way to Kings Langley? Why not simply apply for work at the castle at Berkhamsted? They are much larger than we are."

"I've heard strange things about Earl Edmund's religion." Personally, Lizzie thought this was an inspired response, but Dilys just waggled her head a bit, not necessarily agreeing, but not arguing either. Regardless, Lizzie's answer seemed to satisfy her. At no time did Lizzie mention the convent, her sisters, or anything else that was true about her life.

And then Queen Marged returned to take her to meet the princesses.

22

Day Three

Gwenllian

"Mom?" Gwenllian pushed open the door to the room to find her mother sitting up in bed with papers spread in front of her, obviously working. She stopped. "Sorry, I'll come back later."

"You will do no such thing." Mom set aside what she was reading. "I always have time for you. What's up?"

"It's that new girl, Jonet." Gwenllian hitched herself onto the edge of the bed, and then, when her mother swept more papers out of the way, came all the way to her side and got under the covers. Gwenllian was thirteen years old now, so most of the time she didn't come into her parents' room to snuggle. But sometimes it was nice not to have to be so grown up.

"What about her?"

"She speaks French."

"How do you know?"

"I was in the kitchen. When I'm there, they speak French."

"Old habits. That was required back in the day because many, if not most, of the people in Edward's court spoke no English."

"Yeah, but Jonet was there too, and I could tell she was following along perfectly well. As I was leaving, I stopped by where she was folding aprons and asked how she was doing—in French. She answered back that she was well," Gwenllian paused, "in really perfect French."

Mom made a *hmm* sound. "That is in keeping with what Dilys told me earlier this evening. Jonet dropped a log for the fire on her toe and swore quite fluently." She tsked. "It seems she didn't think anyone was listening."

"She's no village girl from Berkhamsted."

"It would seem not."

"So who is she?"

"I have no idea."

Gwenllian had been considering the matter for the last quarter of an hour as she'd walked from the kitchen to her mother's room. "Do you think she's a spy?"

"That was Dilys's first thought too. If so, she is not a very expert one, is she?"

"Not very, not to give the game away so easily and be tripped up by answering in a language she isn't supposed to know." Gwenllian's expression turned wary. "Unless it's all a clever ruse."

"She came to us wet and hungry. That wasn't feigned."

"It rained so much today, she could have walked a quarter mile in it instead of seven and would have been equally wet. Everyone knows the king's castles are open to the hungry and in need. We could be being taken advantage of." Her tutor would have commented on the terrible way she'd constructed that sentence, but Gwenllian was feeling quite earnest now—and worried—and didn't care.

"Dilys didn't think the tears were feigned."

"Don't dismiss me, Mom."

"Never." Mom pulled Gwenllian closer. "I would never."

"Everyone's gone, and I'm worried about them all the time. And now Jonet's arrival is just too weird, given everything else that's happened. Just last month, King Philippe tried to take over Aquitaine! Everyone had to escape from Paris with their lives. The world isn't anything like a safe place."

Mom kissed Gwenllian's temple. "I'm sorry. I truly don't mean to diminish your fears. They are real, deservedly so, but your brother and father can take care of themselves. You have to let them."

"Can they, though?" Gwenllian forced the next words out of her mouth, ones she'd felt building up inside her for years and been afraid to say. "Dad went to Cilmeri, Mom, even though you told him not to. Because of it, in Avalon I spent the rest of my life in an English convent, never learning Welsh or even knowing who I really was. He doesn't always do the right thing."

Gwenllian's head was on her mother's shoulder, so she felt her take in a deep breath and let it out before answering. "This is something you really need to discuss with him. I don't want to speak for him, but I do know your father had his reasons."

"If so, they weren't good ones."

"They were compelling at the time. Sometimes we make choices we wish we really could time travel to the past to do over." Now Mom turned so she could look into Gwenllian's face. "You are not that girl, and your father is no longer that man. Hindsight says it was absurd to ever think he could trust the Mortimer brothers, but he didn't have that perspective. He was coming off some big victories and desperate for an edge that would really win him the war. And they went so far as to put their pledge to him in writing."

"You warned him."

"Here I did, but not in Avalon."

"Where he died. And Wales fell."

"It wasn't because he didn't love you, honey."

"He didn't even think of me." The knowledge was a fist of pain in her chest.

"I—" Mom closed her eyes for a second and took in another breath. "I'm not trying to put you off. Maybe you're right. Maybe he was so angry by that point that he didn't care about anyone or anything but his vision for Wales and that made him blind to the risks."

Gwenllian looked down at her hands as they rested on the blanket.

Mom swept a lock of hair back from Gwenllian's forehead. "You may have your chance to talk to your father sooner rather than later."

"He's coming home?"

"Not yet. He's got another day or two in London. The twins have apparently not yet destroyed the entire city." Mom smiled wryly. Gwenllian hadn't been separated from her brother and sister very often, and she missed the sound of their running feet in the corridor.

The communication network established throughout England was imperfect but improving. They had three ham radios that could communicate long distances. David had one in Normandy, one was in Angoulême with Callum, and one was at Westminster, which was how her father could talk to David all the way in France—and really why he'd gone to Westminster in the first place. Her mother and father would have communicated that day through radio telegraphy via morse code.

Then her mother went on, her joy and relief palpable as she spoke. "David probably has something to say about this too. He really is on his way home!"

From an earlier conversation, she knew David had been planning to return to England to address the members of the CSB. They just hadn't expected him so soon. He might even be in England already, sailing up the Thames to London. Lili initially, and then David more formally, had invited Normandy to join the union of nations that was the CSB, but David didn't actually have the power anymore to make that happen. It seemed people needed to be persuaded. And the matter voted upon.

Even the movements of the King of France were less concerning at the moment. While Philippe was angered by Normandy's quest for independence, he had cleaned house of his advisers loyal to Noga-ret, leaving him with lesser men and those loyal to David himself, among them Archbishop Romeyn, John Jr, and Matthew Norris, the master of the Paris Temple. Philippe had also lost his best military commander (captured, not dead) in the failed attack on Angoulême.

Still remaining was the accounting of what had been King Philippe's ideas and what had been Nogaret's. Certainly, the French king had to take a significant portion of the blame for the devastation of his court, if only because it was he who'd allowed Nogaret free rein in the first place. Besides which, Philippe *had* freely agreed to expel the Jewish community from Paris and still thought David unreason-able in his objections to the action. Peace with France was a long way off, but war with France currently appeared to be too.

Gwenllian hugged her knees to her chest. "You've been wor-ried too!"

"Yes, I have been worried."

Gwenllian gave a little grunt. "You act like you're not."

Mom gave her a wary look. "If I shared with you just how worried I was about the welfare of your father and David—not to mention the twins, Anna, and you, it would scare you. Perhaps it was wrong of me not to let you see it more because it made you more afraid—and afraid to talk to me. I'm sorry." Her mother's eyes held real pain. She'd never talked to Gwenllian like this before. "I do truly believe, between your brother and your father, that most anything is in good hands. Can you believe that too, a little bit?"

Gwenllian nodded, deciding for now she could, still shaken by what she'd seen in her mom's eyes. After a hard swallow, she asked, "Any update on Peter?"

"He may walk forever with a limp, but he will recover."

"And the babies?"

"All the babies are fine."

"So how are we going to find out what's going on with Jonet? Are we wrong to think she isn't what she seems?"

"I'm pretty sure she isn't what she seems." Mom made a *maybe* motion with her head. "But that she means us ill isn't at all clear. My heart tells me something else is going on with her. There was a moment when I met her, when she first realized who I was, that an expression crossed her face I didn't like. Anger, maybe?" She shook her head. "Don't mind me. I'm probably imagining things."

Gwenllian was not at all sure about that and said so. "Honestly, I thought I saw something like that too when you put your arm around her in our room. Maybe we should have Rhys investigate?"

Rhys was a member of her father's personal guard and the best tracker in Wales, according to pretty much everyone.

Mom laughed. "Rhys is a Welshman, so perhaps a bit less subtle than I think we need to be in this moment. Whatever is happening, I don't want to spook Jonet."

"So what do you want us to do? Elen and me, I mean."

"Befriend her."

Gwenllian made a face. "Somehow, I thought you were going to say that."

"Yeah, well, that isn't to say I don't want you also to be a bit cautious of her. We'll take her with us tomorrow, whether she wants to come or not, and we will see what we will see. I don't want her roaming about Kings Langley on her own until we know more about who she is."

"Where are we going?" Normally she would be expected to be in school, but lessons were the last thing Gwenllian thought they ought to be doing on anyone's birthday, much less Elen's. That was why, for Gwenllian's birthday in June, she'd persuaded Elen to play hooky with her.

"You'll see in the morning. No mountains involved." Mom shot her an actual smile. "At least, not the geographic kind."

23

Day Four

Elen

"Up, Elen!" Gwenllian shoved her shoulder. "It's time to get up."

Elen woke from a deep sleep to find her cousin standing over her, her hands on her hips. The shutter that blocked the window at night was open, and the sun was shining brightly into the room. Elen rubbed the sleep from her eyes and pushed up off the pillow. "What time is it?"

"Happy birthday!" Gwenllian was alight with happiness.

Elen's expression twisted a bit. "I was dreaming!"

"You were going to sleep all day, and we couldn't stand it any longer. We're going on a little trip, with a picnic for lunch, so you need to get up!"

Given the rain of yesterday, a picnic had seemed unlikely last night. But a trip sounded more interesting for her birthday than the regular party they had talked about and that Elen had thought her aunt was planning. "Where are we going?"

By the look on her face, Gwenllian was warring with herself as to whether she ought to keep it a surprise, but finally as Elen wrinkled her nose at her, she capitulated. "To St. Albans. There's a Roman ruin Mom wants to see, and, of course, the abbey. She wants to speak to the abbot."

Elen knew what that was about. Jewish people had been arriving in England in some numbers for a while, and Aunt Meg had taken it upon herself to ensure nobody was preaching against them. St. Albans had influence because it was the oldest Christian site in England. Alban had been a native Briton (so, in other words, Welsh), beheaded by the Romans for his faith, before the Romans themselves converted to Christianity. This was the kind of thing a girl was required to know when she lived with Aunt Meg.

Elen frowned. "We're riding?" She knew how to ride, but she wasn't as proficient as everyone else she lived with who'd grown up with horses.

Gwenllian was practically jumping up and down with excitement. "Of course we're riding! It will take but a moment to get there by horse. It's only five miles. I'm tired of being cooped up here all the time, so get going before Mom changes her mind!"

Elen rolled out of bed, entertained as usual by Gwenllian's enthusiasm. A perfect birthday for Elen herself would have included sleeping the first half of the day and reading a book for the rest, but she could appreciate that it wasn't sufficient for everyone else. In

Wales, fourteen was a momentous birthday, and even if they were currently living in England to support David's endeavors in France, they were still Welsh.

Gwenllian bustled about the room, gathering her things. Elen joined her, knowing what was necessary. They planned to be gone for just the day, but one never knew what might happen when one left a castle. More than once during their journeys a horse had gone lame on the road, a fierce storm had blown up, or someone had fallen ill, and they'd had to find shelter somewhere other than their intended destination. Admittedly, St. Albans contained both a monastery and a convent, so plenty of guesthouse space if they needed it, and, at only five miles from Kings Langley, they could walk back if they had to.

Elen also got herself into clothing suitable for riding, of the type Lili had made famous. All the women of the court possessed one of these split dresses with leggings worn underneath. Elen's was deep green, her favorite color, with a cloak to match. There was something to be said for bespoke tailoring, not a luxury she had encountered before coming to Earth Two. Into her backpack last went her e-reader and solar charger, just in case. It wouldn't do to be caught away from home without plenty of reading material.

The girls emerged from their quarters to find Aunt Meg waiting for them, along with two stablemen; three kitchen workers in charge of food; a half-dozen armed guards; and Jonet. If Elen hadn't known about Gwenllian's conversation with her mother the previous evening, she might have thought the inclusion of Jonet was odd. Nobody was acting like it was strange, however, probably because Aunt Meg could do whatever she pleased.

Elen made her way to her aunt to get a birthday hug and then greeted Jonet in English. There was no need to indicate they knew she spoke fluent French until she was ready to tell them how she knew it. "It's so nice you are coming with us."

"Happy birthday, my lady." Jonet replied in the same language and dropped a curtsey.

"You can ride?"

"Yes, my lady."

"Please call me Elen."

"Yes, my lady."

Elen rolled her eyes. It was always this way until someone really got to know her. Aunt Meg had been fighting an uphill battle for years to get anyone to call her *Meg*, or even *Queen Meg*. As far as Elen could tell, she'd made exactly zero headway, especially in England. It made no sense, really, since David got to be known by his first name: David—or Dafydd in Wales. But she supposed nobody called him that to his face. In person he was exclusively *my lord* or *sire*.

They mounted their horses and headed out. She knew from her family's stories that there was a time they never would have ridden anywhere without a genuine army. But England was at peace, never mind what was going on in France. David could keep his *teulu*, though he'd spent plenty of time roaming about without them too.

The road from Kings Langley to St. Albans was not as well-maintained as the high road, or king's road as it was called, from London. Because Aunt Meg could never resist a good historical fact, Elen knew the road was so good because the Romans (maybe even the same ones who'd beheaded Alban) had built it a thousand years before.

Not so much the road to St. Albans. A carriage might be shaken to pieces, especially with the puddles and mud that were still all over the place from yesterday's rains. Being on horseback meant they didn't have to keep to the narrow lane, and it wasn't long before Gwenllian gave a *whoop* and set off into the field beside the road. Aunt Meg laughed and followed, with everyone else grinning madly and racing to keep up, even the servants, who'd probably been chosen in the first place because they could ride.

That was pretty much the way the whole journey went, all the way to St. Albans. The Roman ruins were more overgrown than Elen had expected, but her aunt walked among them for quite a long time, and it was where they had their picnic lunch.

Up until that point, Elen herself hadn't made anything in the way of progress with Jonet, even though the girl had stayed close to her for most of the journey, keeping to the back of the group of riders because Elen was the slowest. Whenever Elen tried to start a conversation, she answered every question with as short a response as possible and a *my lady*.

"I was noticing how well you ride, Jonet. Where did you learn?" Typically, Aunt Meg was determined to break through Jonet's reticence. She made a gesture of welcome. "Come. Sit."

Jonet had little choice but to obey. Whoever she was, with her perfect French, she knew better than to gainsay the Queen of Wales.

"Thank you, my lady." Unlike Elen, Jonet didn't sit cross-legged on the blanket they'd brought, but knelt, pulling tight the fabric of her dress to smooth it over her legs.

In the process, Jonet hadn't answered the question. As the silence lengthened, Aunt Meg kept her eyes fixed on the girl, who looked more and more uncomfortable with every moment that passed, truly like a deer caught in the headlights.

Elen could almost see her internal convolutions until she finally came up with an answer. "The farm next to ours had a horse meant for riding. The boy who lived there and I were friends, and he taught me."

The coolness of the delivery meant Elen couldn't tell if what she told them was a true-but-difficult memory or an outright lie.

"Bareback?" Gwenllian asked.

Jonet nodded. "I learned to use a saddle too, but mostly we rode with just a bridle."

Suddenly inspired, Elen put in, "I wanted to thank you for staying close to me today. You ride far better than I do, and sometimes everyone else gets really far ahead."

"She doesn't jump, in other words." Gwenllian popped a bite of cold potato salad in her mouth.

Jonet looked from Gwenllian to Elen. "I thought Lady Elen did well—"

"You are too kind, really." Elen laughed. "The rest of that sentence should be *for someone who never sat on a horse before two years ago*. Actually, I haven't been here even that long. The sad part is there were farms near where we lived. I could have learned to ride. I would never have thought learning to ride was harder than learning Welsh."

"If it's any comfort, I didn't know how to ride before I came to Wales either," Aunt Meg said, "and I was quite a bit older than you and lived pretty much in the same place."

Jonet had been looking from one to the other, though now she included Aunt Meg in her query. "Um. So—"

Elen could guess the question before Jonet asked it. "I grew up in Avalon too. Yes, it's real. No, it isn't anything like the legends say."

"David is though." Gwenllian sprawled back onto the blanket and lay looking up at the sky. "You can believe pretty much everything you hear about him. *The perfect brother.*" Her tone was very sour, and for a second even Elen thought she was serious. Then she lifted her head and winked at Jonet.

Aunt Meg was on the other side of her and didn't see it. "None of that." She poked her daughter. "We've talked about this. You need to let David be David. You are someone different, and that's a good thing."

Gwenllian rolled onto her side, her head propped in her hand. "I'm teasing. You should know that."

"You are remarkable too." Aunt Meg's gaze took in each person sitting around her. "All of you."

She'd included Jonet, who, at the comment, looked down at her hands. She had remained just barely perched on the edge of the blanket, but now she bent forward to start collecting the remains of their lunch. "Excuse me, ma'am, I'll just take these now."

Elen watched her go, and then said in Welsh to the others. "Was that bit about the horse a lie? I couldn't tell. She *can* ride, but she rides better than she could have learned from the boy on the farm next door, saddle or no saddle."

"Some of it sounded true." Aunt Meg herself now rose to her feet—a little stiffly in regards to her knees—and stretched her back. Her eyes weren't on Elen, but on Jonet, who was packing the leftover food items into a satchel with the help of one of the other workers. "Maybe there was a boy and a farm, but just not where she learned to ride. As for the rest ..." Her voice trailed off, and she shook her head. "I still don't know."

After the picnic, they went to the monastery, where the abbot, who'd been warned by a messenger the previous night that they were coming, had whipped up a special birthday feast in Elen's honor. He'd invited the abbess of the nearby convent too, which Gwenllian instantly saw as suspicious and thought was to encourage the girls towards a vocation in the Church. Most royal families had at least one nun in the family, and so far David's did not.

Elen certainly was not going to be the first, she knew that much. Nor Gwenllian. The idea was laughable. But other than that slight hiccup, she enjoyed the evening. They'd even made a cake for her! She hadn't felt the need to pull out a book and retreat into it even once.

Jonet had revealed a little more of herself in the process as well. Initially, in fact, she'd refused to come inside. "I'll stay with the horses."

Under other circumstances, Aunt Meg might have accepted her choice, but not today, not when they knew so little about her. Leaving her alone in a strange place was not in the cards.

"We have stablemen for that." Aunt Meg had held out her hand to Jonet. "Come. Again, you are welcome."

Jonet had obeyed. As before, nobody could deny Aunt Meg what she wanted when she put her mind to it. That didn't mean the girl didn't drag her feet along the way. They ended up eating all together at two long tables. Although Elen sat with Gwenllian and Aunt Meg, she kept an eye on Jonet sitting at the far end. For once, she wasn't eating like it was her last meal in this life.

There was a great deal more they still had to learn about each other, and when they ended up side-by-side again on the way home, Elen risked another question: "I'm glad you ate with us in the hall. You really were welcome."

Jonet shot her a look Elen found unreadable. "Thank you, my lady."

"It really is *Elen*."

Again, Jonet gave her a look, this time implying she wasn't going to call Elen by her given name in a million years.

They'd come a couple of miles from St. Albans by then and had that same distance still to go. It was growing darker by the minute, so their escort rode with torches taken from the abbey and were also trying to move a little faster than they'd ridden in the opposite direction that morning.

"It *was* a pretty nice day, wasn't it?" Gwenllian threw the words over her shoulder. Elen, as usual, was riding at the far back, struggling a bit to keep up, truth be told, which was why it was kind of Jonet to stay with her. "Even I will agree it was way better than getting lost."

"Admittedly, that's a pretty low bar," Aunt Meg said from further ahead, in a perfectly delivered wry tone.

Elen was just opening her mouth to say that, really, this had been one of the best birthdays of her life—

—when the world exploded with fighting men.

24

Day Four

Lizzie

Lizzie had been hanging back with Elen, congratulating herself on the way she'd evaded any question that got too close to the truth about who she was, and even managed to answer the query about how she'd learned to ride without telling a complete lie. She *had* learned to ride bareback, and had ridden that way all of two days ago. For a time too, she'd had a friend in Tim, the farm boy.

From the start, Lizzie had been struggling with how to talk to them at all—and not just in regards to herself or Elen's birthday. Half of her had wanted to murder every single one of them, and the other half had been berating herself continually for not confessing the truth about who she was and why she had come to Kings Langley. Her sisters needed their help. *What was she waiting for?*

But every time she tried to force words past her lips, words that might include *I need your help,* they stuck in her throat. It was pride, really, that had kept her hanging back and avoiding the queen's eyes. On the way to St. Alban's, at first she'd stayed beside Elen because it kept her far away from the queen, and then because Elen seemed the gentlest and least threatening of them all.

Elen had been very open about having little experience with horses, and Lizzie's practiced eye agreed with the assessment. She constantly forgot to keep her elbows tucked in, and much of the time the only reason the horse was going in the right direction was because it was a gentle soul itself and was following after the other horses. Really, despite Lizzie's vast and deep reservations about coming to Kings Langley, and whether or not Daisy was right that they could trust these people, Lizzie felt the need to keep an eye on Elen. She, at the very least, could not be blamed for anything Queen Marged and her children had done.

For that reason, and really only that one, she was beside Elen when the attack came. Lizzie had actually been considering thanking Elen for including her in her birthday party.

In the time it took for her to open her mouth, men appeared all around them, some leaping from the trees and hedges on either side of the field and others seemingly arising out of the grass, as if by magic. They shouted at each other in a language Lizzie didn't understand but one she'd heard just yesterday. It was Theodiscus, which meant these were the same men who'd been guarding her uncle's castle; the same men who even now stood between her own sisters and freedom.

For a few dozen heartbeats, it was screams and fear and chaos all around them. Although the queen's guards gave a good account of themselves, they were only six to the attacker's dozen—and unprepared to boot.

In the end, it was no contest.

Elen might not have been a particularly good rider, but someone had trained her how to handle a rearing horse and how to clear her feet from the stirrups before it dumped her off. She was on the ground before Lizzie fell off her own horse practically into Elen's arms. Evading their horses' hooves, they rolled together down a slope. The horses then gathered themselves and bolted, right over the top of them.

Lizzie ended up with her face pressed into the grass, Elen's arm wrapped around her shoulders. The earth had a sweet smell that reminded her of Tim. She managed a deep breath, finally, and said, "Let me—"

"Stay down." It was a command, one that brooked no argument, and not a tone Lizzie had yet heard from Elen. "They aren't here for you. Play dead. The moment their backs are turned, you run, you hear me? Run!" Then Elen flung her own gorgeous green cloak over the top of Lizzie, pushed off the ground and ran back up the hill, calling, "Gwenllian!"

Lizzie dared lift her head enough to see Elen some twenty yards away, standing above her at the top of the slope, silhouetted against the late evening sky. Instead of risking them both by staying under the cloak too, Elen had chosen to protect Lizzie, unknowingly saving her from men who very much would have cared about who she was had they known she was there.

Elen may not have been much of a rider, and until now she had been as kind as the day was long, but underneath she had a spine of Damascus steel.

It was unaccountable, like so many things that had happened to Lizzie over the last few days.

She couldn't see beyond Elen, but she could hear just fine as Gwenllian screamed, "Ellie!"

Lizzie couldn't bear to watch, but she couldn't bear not to either, so she kept her head up slightly and thus saw the moment when a man appeared on horseback, scooped Elen up by the waist, and carried her out of sight. His manner was rough—rougher than the treatment meted out to Lizzie's sisters by the men who'd come for them at St. Margaret's.

Lizzie covered her head again, trembling under the cloak and uncertain what to do or how to do it. Elen had told her to run, but every time she thought about moving, her breathing quickened and her head spun. It felt remarkably like those moments she'd stayed hidden behind the curtain in the dormitory. Her sister had told her what she needed to do but she'd been afraid to do it.

And now this.

Lizzie had spent the day thinking these people were her enemy. The nicer they were to her, the more she'd hated them. For that reason, she'd said nothing to them about who she was and what she wanted.

They were to have been the saviors of her sisters.

Now it was too late.

She wanted to cover her ears, to pretend this wasn't happening. She knew if she looked up, she'd witness the death of the woman she'd hated for as long as she could remember. The moment of final victory had come, but she couldn't be grateful or pleased or anything but so sick inside she kept swallowing down bile.

She'd been a coward all day and knew herself to be a coward still.

"Don't hurt her!" It was Queen Marged's voice. "What do you want with us?"

The man replied in heavily accented French, which only confirmed Lizzie's suspicion of his identity. "You are Queen Marged, and these are the girls, Gwenllian and Elen. Don't bother to deny it."

He pronounced Gwenllian's name the English way, without the strange /sh/ sound in the middle that Dilys had spent a quarter of an hour teaching Lizzie the day before. Lizzie still didn't have it right, but she was better at it than this man, who hadn't even tried.

Then again, it was a small matter when compared to attacking the party of the Queen of Wales.

"Yes. You are correct." The queen didn't threaten him or ask questions. And rather than defiance, Lizzie heard a calm certainty in her voice.

"Then you are the ones we seek."

Lizzie heard the man say something more in Theodiscus to his own men, and Queen Marged speaking in Welsh to Gwenllian and Elen. Lizzie herself didn't dare look up again. She felt (more than heard) them depart, presumably on horseback, though even that she couldn't be sure of. All she knew was, after a few more steadying breaths on Lizzie's part, they were gone.

25

Day Four

Lizzie

izzie lay still for just a few heartbeats longer, her face in the grass, telling herself *Get up! Get up! Get up!*

Running up the slight slope to the main part of the field felt like climbing that mountain Elen and Gwenllian kept laughing about. What she found at the top was incredibly far from amusing, however. The attackers had left the bodies of the queen's companions lying in the grass. Hastily Lizzie went from one to the next, urgency a physical force filling every muscle and sinew. With some joy, she discovered at least half were still alive, many unconscious but breathing. One man had been felled by a sword through his gut, and she feared if she did nothing for him, he would die right then and there. She pressed on the wound, tears streaming down her face.

He pushed at her hand. "Never mind us. You can't save us." When she didn't give way, he found the strength to grasp her wrist. "Find the queen. Get help."

That was yet another person relying on her to *get help*, a quest on which she'd so far failed utterly. And yet, he was only telling her what she already knew. The moments of nauseating stillness before she'd risen had given her time to consider the way history was repeating itself. Men had come for Lizzie and her sisters in the middle of the night. It made a certain kind of absurd sense that Bogo and her uncle might think abducting more women—the Queen of Wales among them—would give them even more leverage in their quest for the throne.

That this logic was bound to fail under the weight of its own inadequacies didn't seem enough to stop them. With her sister's help, and with great reluctance, Lizzie had come to see that the throne wasn't simply a prize to be taken. David could be dead, but marrying Daisy still wasn't going to put Bogo on it. Both her uncle and Bogo were mad to think they were going to gain what they wanted in the end.

These thoughts set her mind back into its proper channel. As she bent over the dying man, she reminded herself that the conspirators behind the ambush might not actually *be* Bogo and Uncle Almain. She was quite certain foreigners had attacked their little party, but her uncle was hardly the only person who could hire mercenaries. It would do no good at all to run back to Kings Langley to tell Dilys of the abduction and not be able to report exactly where they'd got to. She might as well not report it at all.

It was full dark by now, and stars lit the sky. By them she could see the shapes of several horses in the pasture on the other side of the road. It was the same trackway they'd avoided that morning, in favor of riding across the fields, which were dryer and free of giant puddles. Feeling again as if she was reliving that night at St. Margaret's, Lizzie abandoned her vigil over the man and the other wounded and clambered over the wall to recapture one of the horses. This was the one Gwenllian had been riding, and it was definitely more feisty than Herbert, though not more than Lizzie could handle, especially since it came with saddle and bridle.

Once mounted, Lizzie urged the horse back into the field in which the attack had taken place, though she averted her eyes from the fallen as she passed through, knowing she was already very far behind and maybe shouldn't have checked on them at all.

Because the attackers hadn't ridden down the slope to where Lizzie herself had lain hidden, nor even looked in that direction, she knew better than to bother searching south or east. That left north and west, whether by road or field. The mercenaries had managed to surprise everyone so easily because they'd launched themselves from a small wood adjacent to the field. By now, it was too dark to see anything in there if they had retraced their steps. Instead, Lizzie found a path that skirted the wood before heading northwest.

She couldn't move fast since she was looking for hoofprints, to make sure her assumption they were headed to Berkhamsted wasn't the wrong one. Her uncle, if it truly was he who'd sent these men, held many estates. She could see the sense in holding these new captives somewhere else. Because she was going slowly, she picked up a glint in the path before her. Even as she feared further delay, she slid off the horse and bent to the ground.

A silver brooch lay embedded in the dirt, one that not a half-hour before had been holding Elen's cloak closed at the throat. Since that selfsame cloak was now an extra layer around Lizzie, it made sense that Elen had still been holding the brooch in her hand when she'd been captured. Lizzie had to think she'd dropped it in the hope that one of the helpers Lizzie brought back to the field might find it.

Now that Lizzie knew she was on the right track, she rode faster, almost to the point of giving the horse its head. Tending to the wounded and recapturing a horse had delayed her, but the riders ahead of her were burdened by their hostages. Lizzie caught up to them before Berkhamsted, and for the second time watched prisoners disappear through the outer gateway.

Her uncle had truly outdone himself this time. Even she could see there was no retreat for him now. Lizzie hoped she would be welcomed back into Berkhamsted, were she to follow, but help wasn't to be found there, and she had all the information she needed. Hated Queen of Wales or not, there were now three more women in Berkhamsted for her to rescue.

Determined now, and finally certain of what she must do, she turned the horse's head in the direction of Kings Langley.

26

Day Four

Gwenllian

"What castle is this?" Crossing the bridges over the castle's moats had required that the horses move closer together and, for the first time since their capture, put Gwenllian close enough to her mother to speak to her. They'd been separated for the journey, each held on a different horse. Thankfully, they had been allowed to sit upright, and it was a matter of a few miles from the field where they'd been ambushed to wherever this was.

"Berkhamsted."

Gwenllian stared at her mother. "Why?"

They were speaking in Welsh, which she was just plain going to assume their captors didn't know.

"Because Edmund of Almain wants something from your brother he shouldn't—and can't—have, no matter what he does to us."

Gwenllian digested that bit of news for a breath or two. Her mother was so calm that it calmed her too. "Who are these men? I don't understand a word they say."

"They are speaking Theodiscus. We'd call that German if we were in Avalon."

Gwenllian wanted to snort and would have if her throat hadn't closed around her derision. By then, they had passed through the last gatehouse into a large, entirely deserted, bailey. Gwenllian had lived in castles her whole life and knew, even after dark, that people were always about. But not here.

They were separated again and, for a moment, Gwenllian was terrified they were going to be held separately as well. But then they crossed the bailey to the far side, where they stopped in front of another gatehouse protecting a motte and keep.

The man who'd been leading her horse dismounted and came to where she remained perched, her hands tied in front of her. For most of the ride, she'd wound her fingers into the horse's mane to stay on. A glance behind her to Elen showed her cousin to have a white face and pinched lips. Somewhere along the way she'd also lost her cloak.

"Down." The man made a motion with his hand.

Though she really wanted to kick her heels into the horse's sides and race back out of the castle, they'd come through three gatehouses to get to this inner bailey. She needed to save her defiance for when it might make a real difference.

So she swung her leg over the top of the horse's head, in a move she'd practiced a thousand times, because it looked so cool when done right, and dropped to the ground. At that point, a man came up behind her, grabbing her more roughly than needful, and pushed her forward towards this final gatehouse. The keep it guarded was to be their prison. She almost vomited on her captor's boots.

It would have been satisfying, but she managed to swallow down her revulsion. By now, the three of them were bunched close together, with Mom in the middle. Elen clung to Mom's other side, her arm looped through hers. Somehow, Elen hadn't been tied like Gwenllian. But since she wasn't going anywhere anyway, it didn't exactly give her an advantage.

Out of the side of her mouth, Mom said, "Just do as they say."

Elen clung even tighter. "Are they going to kill us?"

"No." And then Mom elaborated. "If Almain wanted us dead, we would be dead already."

Mom's response seemed to satisfy Elen, but Gwenllian found her mind churning. Her grandfather, Gruffydd, had been kept in the Tower of London, imprisoned by her great-uncle, King Henry of England, and had died when the rope down which he was attempting to escape broke. Hanging on to her mother as they jumped or descended from a high window could ensure that wasn't going to happen to them. What was going to happen looked bad enough.

Gwenllian measured the keep with her eyes. Combining it and the motte, it was a long way to fall, if rescuing themselves was required instead of waiting for it to come to them.

"Possible?" she asked her mother.

"Eminently," Mom said. "Higher than most. Almain doesn't appear to believe in Avalon."

"Or we're not going to get a window."

"Don't even think it."

Gwenllian didn't speak again, deciding to wait to share her thoughts until they knew where they were going to be kept. As Mom had implied, if Almain were smart, he'd put them in a basement with no windows. Instead, the soldiers urged them up the motte to the main doorway of the keep, and then up the long curving stairway to the top floor, exactly where high-born prisoners would be expected to reside.

The room, when they reached it, even had a largish window, which would make sense, since the keep once would have been the main home of the lord who owned the castle. This room might even have been his. As it was, the moment the guard released her from her bonds, Gwenllian made a beeline for the window and looked out.

Berkhamsted's defenses consisted of a double moat and rampart system. While it was to their benefit that the motte and keep lay *outside* the main curtain wall that encircled the lower bailey, to escape they'd still have to navigate multiple barriers. These included the moat directly below them, the castle's outer stone wall, another moat, and finally a wooden palisade.

Directly across the moat from the keep, a small, narrow door had been left in the outer wall: the postern gate. Nobody guarded it specifically, just a single man whose charge it was to walk the entire length of the wall-walk on that side of the castle. Gwenllian found hope there, if only a little.

She had been so preoccupied with the setup, in fact, that she hadn't had time to be afraid, but now her fear returned as the door closed behind the departing guard.

"What—Almain's not going to come in here to monologue?" Elen's first impulse was to make a joke.

Gwenllian loved her for it and responded to the unspoken message that fear would do her no good right now. "It could be worse."

"It could always be worse." Mom and Elen spoke at the same time, repeating a common mantra in their family, and then laughed.

It felt good to laugh.

By now, Mom had begun her first circuit of the room, starting with its large bed, which they were going to have to share. Of late, Gwenllian preferred nobody to be touching her while she slept—and apparently nobody wanted to touch her either since she was known for pushing her bedmate (usually Elen) to the edge of the bed. Then her mother ducked down to look under the bed and, smiling, pulled out a trundle bed. "For you, Gwenllian."

The only other furniture was a small table against one wall with a pitcher of water and a basin. Underneath was a bedpan.

"Why didn't they tie you up, Elen?" Gwenllian asked as she peered into the pitcher, wondering how fresh the water was and if she might taste it.

"If I couldn't move my hands, I couldn't keep my seat on the horse." Elen wrinkled her nose. "I confess to playing up my ineptness to ensure it."

"You risked being tied more than we were," Mom said.

"Not if they wanted to make decent time, which they did. Besides, they don't care about us at all. You could see it in their eyes. This was a job to them. Nothing more."

"Did you gain anything from your bit of freedom?" Mom's eyes went to Elen's face.

"I dropped the brooch for my cloak." Then she explained about saving Jonet.

Gwenllian found herself staring at her cousin, wondering if she too could have been so smart and brave, given the opportunity.

"Come here." Mom spread her arms wide, and the girls came into them, their arms tight around each other's waists, holding on until each one relaxed.

"Why did he do this now, Mom?" Gwenllian asked. "David is as powerful as he's ever been."

"I was wondering that too. The men who took us aren't from his normal garrison, and did you see how empty the bailey was and how few guards are patrolling the walls? Almain has sent some of his own men and workers away, to where I have no idea. It looks to me as if he has been planning this insurrection for some time. Unfortunately, we—I—walked right into his trap by making our little journey today. That we are here is *my* fault. I assumed the English countryside was safe and failed to take proper precautions."

"That isn't true, Mom. You can't blame yourself." Restless, Gwenllian returned to the window. "The fault lies with the men who abducted us and the man who ordered it."

"I put us in the position to be abducted." Her voice was soft but firm. "But I agree that blaming myself gets us nowhere in this moment."

Gwenllian kept her head turned away, finding it hard to swallow around the lump that had formed in her throat. The last time she'd been imprisoned like this had been with Lili and the boys at Westminster Castle. She had sat in a window much like this one, Arthur on her lap, and dropped out of it into Avalon, where Christopher had found them. She had survived that. She couldn't fall apart now. She had to be strong for Elen and for her mother, who would need her. For what exactly, they didn't yet know.

So she cleared her throat. "Well, unless *Almain* shows up here and, as Elen said, lays out his evil plan in detail for us, we can only guess why we're here."

"Can you guess more, Aunt Meg?" Elen said.

"You know me, sweetheart. I can always come up with an answer. It's just a question of whether or not it's the right one. But we have to assume we are a lever in an attempt to take the throne."

"That's always what these things are about, isn't it?" Elen said.

"It's an interesting choice, isn't it?" Mom spoke without inflection, and Gwenllian almost laughed again, which no doubt had been her mother's intent. She knew better now, though, after their talk last night, what might lie behind the jest.

"Given this, do you still think Dad's okay?" She might be mad at him, but that didn't make her less worried. "What's to stop Almain from ambushing *Dad* on his way back to Kings Langley?" Truthfully, after tonight, it was harder to blame him for what happened thirteen years ago.

"I do, Gwenllian. Really. We both know he has survived far worse than what Almain can throw at him. He will not have made the same mistake I just did in setting out with too small a guard. Besides, Almain doesn't need Dad when he has us. In fact, I think your father remaining free is exactly what Almain wants. If he isn't free, he can't act."

Elen plopped herself on the bed. "Does that mean surrendering the crown?"

"Like that's going to happen." Of this, Gwenllian was sure.

"Or is that easy," Mom said. "Your father doesn't have that power."

"David does." Gwenllian still wasn't ready to settle. "Why don't we just go, Mom? Stop all this before it starts."

"We could." Mom made a rueful face and looked out with Gwenllian at what remained a long drop to the ground. Nothing had changed since she'd looked down the first time. "I kind of feel like we should wait to see what this is really about."

Elen spoke from behind them. "Why didn't you time travel when they ambushed us, Aunt Meg?"

"It must be that my life wasn't in danger. And anyways, I wasn't going to leave you two behind, and I couldn't take you with me because we weren't connected to each other."

Gwenllian gave a little snort. "You think that matters to—" she flung out a hand, suddenly inarticulate, "whatever controls this?"

"It has up until now."

27

Day Four

Molly

Uncle Almain's lips were pinched and his color was high. After a lifetime of living in the company of women who weren't allowed to express their emotions—or, what's more, even speak of them—Molly could tell just by looking at him that he was utterly and completely furious.

Bogo's manner, as usual, conveyed nothing more or less than utter calm, sure to the very center of his being that he was the cleverest person in any room he entered. "It was the right choice."

"We. Are. Not. Ready." Uncle Almain's words were punctuated, but he left off the pointing finger in case anyone else in the hall was watching. In truth, they all were watching. They were always watching. Really, once Bogo revealed he'd done something contrary to what Uncle Almain wanted, he should have cleared the room of everyone, so Uncle Almain could speak more plainly. But that was probably why Bogo had made sure they weren't in private.

"Contain yourself, Uncle." Bogo glanced towards where Daisy and Molly were sitting a few paces away on the other side of the hearth. They were in the main hall, but ensconced in comfortable chairs reserved for the nobility. It was in that moment Molly also realized how, for all his dismissive manner, Bogo's shoulders were stiff and his jaw tight. He wasn't feeling as easy about her uncle's anger as he pretended. A moment earlier, he'd folded his arms across his chest in a classic posture of resistance and defiance. Now he carefully unfolded his arms and laid a forearm on each arm of the chair, smiling casually as he did so.

That the sisters were here at all was because Bogo had insisted he and Daisy take a last drink in each other's company before retiring, apparently not wanting to waste an opportunity to further their acquaintance.

Bogo leaned forward and dropped his voice to a whisper. Given her knowledge of the topic, even if she couldn't hear him, Molly would have been able to read his lips: "I have had word that David is returning to England. We have been promised he will be dead before he arrives. If we are to be ready, it was now or never."

Rather than respond directly to Bogo's news, Uncle Almain signaled to his lute player to begin a tune, a clear attempt to cover up the disagreement and tension, since it wasn't just Daisy and Molly he was trying to convince that all was well. As it was, servants, eyes downcast, hastily refilled trays of food and jugs of ale, pretending they hadn't noticed that their lord and his co-conspirator were at odds. Others gathered at the various tables in the hall averted their eyes, while at the same time dragging out their consumption of late evening drinks so they had an excuse to remain.

"I think caution is no longer our friend, sister." Daisy had leaned in to whisper in Molly's ear, but now rose to her feet in an abrupt movement.

Molly looked up at her, the same aghast feeling she'd experienced at the convent filling her throat. Ever since Molly had learned of her uncle's plans, she'd worked hard to pretend she had no objections to his endeavors. When last they'd talked, Daisy had agreed to do the same.

But Daisy, as appeared to be her wont lately, ignored Molly's horror and carried her cup of wine to the cushioned bench next to Bogo where she sat and placed a gentle hand on her betrothed's arm. "What terrible thing has my affianced done now to draw your ire, Uncle?" She spoke lightly, with amusement in her voice.

Molly had seen other women behave in this simpleton fashion, depending upon who was in the room, usually in the company of men who, like Bogo, were sure of their own authority and intelligence. Even Abbess Helen had feigned an excessive degree of acquiescence when the delegation from Canterbury had come to visit. Molly had a flashing thought that maybe she was actually cleverer than she let on. Having seen the type of woman the Archbishop wanted to lead the convent, she'd molded herself into that person in his presence so he would appoint her.

Despite her vapid expression (or maybe because of it?), Uncle Almain narrowed his eyes at Daisy and said, "This matter is not your concern."

"I find that highly unlikely." Molly shocked herself by not only moving to the bench beside Daisy, but by speaking, as some hitherto unknown reckless part of her took over, apparently deciding she wasn't Abbess Helen and had no interest in being her anymore.

"Women should be seen and not heard, my dear." That was from Bogo, as it would be.

Molly was quick with her retort. "If you thought that, you should have considered marrying someone other than the daughter of Queen Eleanor of England."

Bogo gazed at Molly through a count of three, and then he threw back his head and laughed. The sound rolled out of him, to the point that everyone around him found themselves smiling too, including the two sisters, though, of course, their smiles served a greater purpose.

The laughter also eased the tension in the hall. The people present went back to their own conversations, and fewer heads turned towards the fire. Everyone but Daisy and Molly liked Bogo and enjoyed his company, which made it easier for them to convince him they were on his side. He had no experience *not* being liked or, at the very least, being able to charm himself into the good graces of those who didn't immediately give way before him.

Relaxing now, Bogo stretched his arm languidly in a proprietary manner across the back rail of the bench on which Daisy was sitting, willing to humor his audience. "I have a spy at Kings Langley, as well as in Normandy. When Queen Marged of Wales, her daughter Gwenllian, and her niece Elen, set out this morning for St. Albans, he let me know about it." As he began to speak, it was clear he believed his own plan extremely clever and resented her uncle's ridicule of it. "On their return journey, I sent men to fetch them here. They are now ensconced in the top room of the keep."

Molly couldn't entirely keep her shock and surprise from her face and body, but when she spoke, her voice didn't tremble. She thought she might even successfully be conveying an amusement she certainly didn't feel. "Is that so? Why would you do that?"

"Leverage." It was Uncle Almain who answered.

"Short of abducting the king's son, what better leverage could we have? Gwenllian is even—" Bogo waved a hand in dismissal. "Never mind."

Molly had come to see that Bogo's mind was a mishmash of well-constructed plans and hare-brained schemes, ones which he seemed to be, at one and the same time, implementing with a wild incoherence and a certain kind of sense. He'd abducted Daisy, the eldest available daughter of King Edward, as a marriage prospect in order to legitimize his claim to the English throne. What he had almost revealed just now was that Gwenllian could be another weapon in that particular arsenal if Daisy and her sisters failed him. Gwenllian happened to be the great-granddaughter of King John, through his youngest daughter, Eleanor.

"Why do you need this kind of leverage, exactly?" Even as Molly kept up her smile, she gripped Daisy's hand tightly.

In truth, she thought it was a toss-up whether Bogo would answer, and from the look on Uncle Almain's face, he was a hair's breadth from telling him not to. Rather than reply directly to Molly, Bogo sought to reassure him. "Nobody saw them, Almain. I cleared the bailey and the keep for their arrival and bundled them up the stairs before anyone could guess their identity. In addition, I used the mercenaries, who have no provenance. For all intents and purposes, the women have disappeared into thin air, just like these girls here."

"The people—"

"Don't know who they are. You worry too much."

"You don't worry enough. Someone will start asking questions."

"And lose their position here, their livelihood, their families? No." Bogo shook his head. "They will keep their heads down and say nothing, especially once you explain they are more nieces, along with their mother, being protected from yet another predatory suitor. Your people trust you. They will accept it because they need to."

"And if they don't?"

"We will think of something else."

"To fully convince the people of the ruse, I think I should visit them." Daisy spoke again, as relaxed as Molly had ever seen her. It was almost as if, with the worst that could happen exposed before her, she had no fear.

The look of horror that crossed Bogo's face was almost comical. "Why would you want to do that?"

Daisy's face was a mask of innocence. "The two girls are the same age as our sister, Elizabeth. They must be frightened out of their minds. I want to assure them you mean them no harm."

At that, Uncle Almain visibly swallowed, and when Bogo didn't immediately reply, Molly put every last scrap of feminine horror she could muster into her voice to ask, "Are you saying you *do* mean them harm?"

Bogo was quick to appease her. "Of course not." He shot Uncle Almain a look that was unreadable from where Molly was sitting. "We would never harm them. You have no need to be concerned for their well-being. Their every comfort is being seen to. Still, they need to understand they will not be leaving Berkhamsted until—" He broke off.

"Until what?" Daisy asked, not letting it go.

Molly thought to soften her question. "You were speaking of leverage, my lord."

"The leverage becomes important once David is no longer an issue."

Molly internally winced, but Daisy was able to ask, "I am completely lost. There's the matter of King David's—" her throat constricted, but she carried on, "abdication, but I thought—"

Bogo smiled gently. "Oh, my dear, I'm so sorry. Did you think I intended to go to war? To *fight* for the throne?" He started to laugh. "Nothing could be further from the truth."

"Then what?" Daisy's eyes were wide.

"Once he is gone, I intend to force the barons to live up to *his* principles, those to which they've sworn allegiance all this time. David claims the people chose him as their king, but we know it was really a handful of barons who saw him as the lesser of any number of evils. Without David, the barons will be back in the same position they were in 1288. Your uncle, then, becomes a neutral arbiter in the dispute because he has no desire to be king himself. He will be the voice of reason; he will demand they live up to the principles David so avidly promoted. The barons will have no choice but to call an election and put it to the vote, just as has been done in Scotland and Ireland."

"You think you'll win." Molly asked a question that wasn't a question.

"Of course I'll win." Bogo was languid again. "Leverage, remember?"

Molly nodded. "If King Llywelyn puts himself forth as a candidate, or objects in any way to what you are suggesting, you will threaten him with harm to his queen."

Bogo shrugged. "Daisy and I will be married in a very public ceremony, overseen by your uncle, who will be one of the leading voices for democracy in Britain. At that point, the people will be ready to vote, and furthermore, will be overjoyed to vote for me."

He was utterly mad. But still, Molly could see why he thought this could work. "You would really be content to hinge your rule on a vote every five years?"

Bogo laughed out loud once more, quick and barking, less this time with amusement than a certainty that resonated from deep within him. "Of course not, my dear. Once I'm in power, we will restore the English throne to its rightful place in the world."

28

Day Four

Lizzie

Lizzie knew only that it was late as she approached Kings Langley, coming straight down the road from Berkhamsted as she'd done the first time. Again, she was walking because her horse had pulled up lame a mile earlier. Thankfully, it wasn't raining.

Up until her horse had gone lame, she'd been making good time, urging the horse faster and faster and probably infecting it with her own anxiety. In retrospect, the mad rush down the road had been a mistake. Even the high road from London, well maintained as it was, wasn't entirely smooth, especially in the dark. At least the walking had forced her to calm, to consider what was going to happen, and what she was going to say when she arrived at Kings Langley.

And really, was there a proper way to inform the royal court that the mother, sister, and cousin of the King of England had been abducted by Lizzie's own uncle?

With every moment that passed, she was further overcome with shame and guilt at her own cowardice. If she'd told the truth, even standing in Kings Langley's courtyard that morning, they could have been on alert. Likely, the queen would never have left the palace at all. But Lizzie had lied, and now two other girls, never mind the queen herself, were in as much—or maybe more—danger than Lizzie's sisters. This was entirely Lizzie's fault, and she couldn't pretend anymore that her actions didn't matter.

She was a good fifty yards from the main gate when a shout came from the battlement, which was bristling with spearmen and archers. It meant the king's court already knew at least something of what she had to tell them. Still, she kept walking. Whether they listened or threw her into the oubliette the queen claimed they didn't have, made little difference. Lizzie was coming.

Then the wicket gate flew open, and Dilys tumbled out. "Jonet! Thanks be to God!"

Lizzie allowed herself to be embraced, even hugging Dilys back. She honestly couldn't remember the last time anyone had hugged her. Thinking back, Queen Marged's family had been unusually affectionate, touching each other all the time. She'd thought at several points over the course of the day that Queen Marged had been about to hug *her,* settling instead for light touches.

Dilys's grip was so tight Lizzie could barely breathe. Under the circumstances, it seemed like a small matter. "You know about—" All the way down the road, Lizzie had rehearsed what she needed to say, but now, like the traitors they were, tears pricked at her eyes.

This whole time, she'd been focused on keeping herself together, staying strong because she had to, and Dilys's show of affection had almost completely undone her, just like the last time she'd approached this gatehouse. *What* was *it about Kings Langley that made her perpetually want to cry?*

"A farmer fetching his sheep came upon our people, dead and wounded, and sent his boy running all the way here to tell us. By the time our people arrived, the alarm had been sounded in St. Albans too."

"How-how many—"

"Some live." Dilys's voice was gentle as she herded Lizzie back through the wicket gate. "Queen Marged—" Her voice broke.

In one sentence, Lizzie knew she could put Dilys's initial fears to rest and give her new ones. "They're not—" Again, the words stuck in her throat, but she forced herself to talk past the lump. She kept seeing the men rise out of the grass and then descend, swords and axes swinging. In her mind's eye, Elen's horse reared again and again. "They're not dead. Or, at least, last I saw, they were alive. They were abducted."

"Were you hurt too?"

Lizzie shook her head. "Lady Elen hid me with her own cloak."

Dilys pulled in a breath. "We feared the worst, though perhaps our *worst* is not yours."

Lizzie didn't understand exactly what that meant, but there was no more time for questions because Dilys was marching Lizzie across the outer courtyard, the horse having already been taken by a stable boy. The courtyard was also full of men preparing, from what she could see in her limited experience, for war. It was Lizzie's job to direct them towards her uncle.

She forced out more words. "I followed them. I know where they are. Is there a way to send a message to—"

"The king is here. He arrived not a half-hour ago, having no idea of what had transpired. He sits in council as we speak. I will take you to him."

"You mean—" All of a sudden, Lizzie could barely breathe. King David was *here*? That meant Bogo hadn't murdered him yet. It wasn't too late. She clenched her hands into fists, warring with herself. Bogo could not be allowed to win, but how easy would it be to say nothing about the traitor in the king's midst? She had so much to tell them, and every single part of it was painful.

Dilys marched on undeterred, not noticing Lizzie's hesitation or maybe ignoring it. "Relate what you know as fully as you can. You will not be censured, no matter what news you bring."

They had reached the hall, which was full of men too. If they were eating, it was an afterthought. She recognized none of them. Judging by the gear laid out on the tables, these were the king's guard. She heard mostly Welsh. Dilys led her around the dais to an archway, which took them to a corridor and then to a closed door. As they reached it, Lizzie found her feet sticking to the floor, and she resisted Dilys's tug forward.

Here too were guards, and Dilys looked at one of them. "Fetch some mulled wine if you will. It seems we'll need more of it."

With no help for it, Lizzie allowed herself to be led through the doorway into a receiving room containing many fewer men, more like half a dozen, gathered around a table. She could tell they were the king's men not only by their gear and clothing, but also by the set of their shoulders. They were prepared for action.

They turned as one when Dilys said, "My king."

Lizzie was expecting to see a young man, since David was short of thirty years old, but the man who looked up was much older, with dark hair shot with gray and an all-but-white beard and mustache. He was tall and unbent, however, and his gaze was penetrating.

"Sire, Jonet, here, was with the queen and the princesses when—" Dilys swallowed, "—the event occurred. They are alive, she says."

In an instant, Lizzie had the full attention of every person in the room. This king, of course, was Llywelyn, pronounced with the same difficult /sh/ sound as Gwenllian's name. Lizzie didn't know whether to be disappointed or relieved. It did give her a reprieve from the immediacy of telling anyone about Bogo's plan to poison his son. With David still in France, there was nothing they could do about it from here.

But then King Llywelyn looked at her, and she felt like he was seeing all the way into her heart. "We are relieved to see you, *Jonet*."

The way he said her name was odd, and for some reason, it caused him to purse his lips, as if he disapproved of it or maybe of her. Leaving the table, he approached closer. She felt him looming over her, right before he went down on one knee, requiring him to look up into her face instead of her into his. He grasped each of her arms to hold her steady, and his smile was gentle. "Tell me what happened, as much as you can remember."

Once again, Lizzie found her throat tight. She stuttered at him, even as he continued to smile at her. Here was *King Llywelyn*, whom her grandmother had hated as long as she'd hated his wife, longer maybe, because he was the one who had refused to bow to England for all those years, leading rebellion after rebellion against first her husband and then her son. Ultimately, after Lizzie's father's death, Llywelyn had further humiliated the English by demanding—and getting—his own kingdom.

"Jonet." He said her name one more time. "Where is my wife?"

She'd had trouble marshaling her thoughts to answer the more general question, but this one had a straightforward answer. "In Berkhamsted Castle."

Llywelyn reared back, returning to his feet. Lizzie's news had the men behind him talking amongst themselves, but the king kept his eyes on Lizzie's face. "Earl Edmund of Almain?"

"Yes." She swallowed hard, because she knew without actually having to say it that the next name was going to cause even more consternation. "And Bogo de Clare."

"Bo—" But instead of cursing or turning white or doing anything that might have indicated anger or fear, Llywelyn barked a laugh. "Really."

The king swept his gaze over his advisers, finding one face among the dozen before him. "Rhys."

Rhys replied in Welsh. Whatever it was, it was incomprehensible. Then he disappeared out the door.

Once he'd gone, Llywelyn motioned with one hand. "Jonet, Dilys. Come forward." Chairs were pulled out or brought to the table, and everyone sat around it. This was a war council, and Lizzie was at the center of it. She obliged by relating everything that had happened from the moment they'd ridden out of Kings Langley that morning. It still wasn't the whole truth, but she told herself it was enough for now.

The king listened with an intensity shared by everyone else at the table. When she finished, he sighed. "Thank you. Your bravery matches that of any man here. If you had not followed those mercenaries before riding to us, we would not have known anything beyond what we saw in that field until Almain or Bogo revealed himself. We are behind, but because of you, we have been given time that, up until now, we hadn't known we needed." He paused. "Why did you do all that? Why not simply save yourself? From what I understand, you arrived at Kings Langley only yesterday."

Lizzie met his eyes, which were a pool of blue, like the sky on a summer day. In fact, they were not far off in color from her own. If only he knew how difficult she found it to help him, a man she'd hated her whole life. He couldn't know what she was feeling, and though she still couldn't tell them who she really was, she could speak a bit of the truth. Really, she was understanding only now what hadn't been clear to her before. "I couldn't leave them there."

"Are you saying—" Dilys started to speak, but Llywelyn put out a hand to stay her question. From what Lizzie understood from her grandmother's memories, it would be unusual for a woman to speak in council, though Dilys had asked several other questions during Lizzie's story. In this moment, Lizzie didn't get the sense the king cut her off because she was a woman, but because he didn't want that question asked, whatever the question would have been.

"Dilys," the king said instead, "we have much to prepare. Would you mind seeing our young friend to her bed? If we have more questions, the morning will be soon enough."

"Of course, my lord."

Dilys was on her feet in an instant, gesturing that Lizzie should come with her.

"Sleep, *Jonet*," the king added, as she departed, "we will speak in the morning."

The door shut behind them. Dilys had Lizzie by the elbow, and they were halfway across the great hall before Lizzie came to an abrupt halt. Why had King Llywelyn said her name so strangely?

"Jonet, come."

"I can't." Lizzie didn't budge, even as Dilys gave her arm a tug.

Dilys looked at her, puzzled. "What is wrong?"

Lizzie twirled to walk back the way they'd come. "I have not been completely honest."

Dilys hustled after her. "Jonet—" She caught her arm again, trying to pull her to a stop. "You cannot simply reenter the king's presence, not until you are once again summoned!"

Lizzie shook her off. "The amazing thing is that *I* can."

29

Day Five

Llywelyn

Once the women had gone, Tudur was the first to put up a hand. "I feel I must bring up what might be an uncomfortable subject, my lord. We have to consider another alternative to what the girl has stated. It may be your wife is not *in* Berkhamsted, but in Avalon."

Tudur had been perturbed when Dafydd had not included him in the project in France, what they'd taken to calling *The French Connection*, for reasons that weren't entirely clear to Llywelyn but which provided his wife with significant amusement.

Llywelyn thought he knew as well as anyone could what went on in his son's head, how he had spent the last seven years as King of England working every day to be less revered and less powerful rather than more. His efforts had mostly been in vain, each year adding to his power instead of subtracting from it. Few complained, in truth, and those who did were men who wanted his power for themselves. Like Almain and this Bogo.

Tudur could have been such a man. According to Meg, he was one of the few in Avalon who'd survived Edward's purge after Cilmeri. Llywelyn had long since forgiven Tudur for that betrayal, in large part because it had been less a betrayal of Llywelyn himself than of Dafydd, Llywelyn's wayward brother, who could not be trusted to lead the country. Because of that history, rather than scorn Tudur, Llywelyn had sought to nurture him, to the point that he, along with Nicholas de Carew, was the trusted adviser left behind in England upon Dafydd's departure to France, *just in case*. Carew's loyalty was unquestionable, and before Llywelyn's very eyes, all thoughts of rivalry and resentment in Tudur's mind were being swept away at Dafydd's prescience. Llywelyn could not be prouder of the man his son had become—and still Dafydd continued to outdo himself.

"It seems clear she did not travel there when the men attacked. It is certainly possible she might choose to go in the interim, but she would never go without the girls." Llywelyn knew this for the truth it was. In the past, every time he and Meg had separated, as they often had to over the years, he would look into her eyes and tell her, "Go, if it means keeping yourself safe. Don't worry about me." And then he'd kiss her like it might be the last time. He was quite sure, after today, that he would never let her out of his sight again.

"Sometimes she can't help it," Tudur said. "We can't assume too much."

"Are we sure about this girl's information?" This was from Goronwy, Llywelyn's oldest friend in life. "As you said, she arrived in Kings Langley only yesterday."

Since it was past midnight, that would be two days ago now, but Llywelyn didn't correct his friend. He knew what he meant. And anyway, the point stood. "She did. Something is definitely amiss with her story and her timeline, I grant you that. And you are correct that her stay in this household has been very short."

Bevyn took up Goronwy's objections. "That's because Almain sent her to deceive us. Didn't you hear? She was a maid at Berkhamsted until she came here." Then he hesitated, suddenly less abrupt. "You know all this—and still you believe her story. Why?"

"Because—" Suddenly, Llywelyn was feeling very grave. This was the moment to confess the truth about the girl's identity. He honestly didn't know if he should because he could still be wrong about who she was. That niggling doubt was what had prevented him from saying anything earlier.

Then the door to the room was flung wide, once again revealing King Edward's youngest daughter. She hesitated on the threshold, as well she might, whether or not she was born a princess.

Behind her, Dilys reached out a hand. "Jonet! Come back here—" She broke off at the sight of Llywelyn watching and curtseyed deeply. "My apologies, my lord. I couldn't stop her."

Llywelyn gestured with one hand. "Let her come in."

The girl had traveled far in order to disguise herself as a servant in his household, all for a reason—one likely very pressing. The fact that she was the sole able-bodied survivor of the ambush wasn't only because of Elen's spirit.

And she was looking quite remarkable now, even hesitating as she was in the doorway.

Her eyes flicked around at his advisers, all of whom he trusted but she clearly did not. He found it astounding that she might actually trust *him.*

"I didn't tell you everything. I need to do so now."

"Come to the fire, Jonet." Llywelyn strode to the sideboard to pour mulled wine into a cup for her. Thrusting it into her hands, he said, "Drink."

She obeyed, taking several large gulps, and then several more gulps of air afterwards. She was going to faint in a moment if he didn't calm her down.

"You must be about the same age as my daughter, Gwenllian."

"Yes." Another deep breath.

By now he had found her a chair. Though some of his men, particularly Goronwy or Tudur, would have come closer, he waved them off. In this moment, he wanted her to look only at him. Whatever she had to say was *for* him.

He still hadn't called her by her proper name, Elizabeth. He was waiting for her to confess to it, which would bring about an uproar amongst the men behind him. Some among his council might distrust what she had to say if they knew the identity of her father. Perhaps they would be right to. They'd all survived for as long as they had by not trusting Normans. Perhaps Llywelyn was mad to give this daughter of England the benefit of the doubt and think she wasn't involved in the abduction of his own daughter, niece, and wife.

And yet, he had come to know thirteen-year-old girls fairly well, given that his household contained two of them (though admittedly Elen had just turned fourteen). Even if Elizabeth had come to him as a last resort, something of which he had little doubt, she had also come out of genuine fear. He had heard it in her voice when she'd entered the room. That Almain was one of her last living relatives made it all the more astounding she had chosen to come to Kings Langley instead of simply siding with him.

Meg had mentioned her (as Jonet) when they'd spoken the evening before, but he hadn't given her another thought until she'd arrived in the room an hour ago. All he'd needed was one look at her face to know who she was, however. Her sister, Eleanor, now dead from poison in the leadup to Dafydd's crowning, had looked very much like Queen Eleanor, the girls' mother, as a young woman. Elizabeth, in turn, was the spitting image. It showed how old Llywelyn was, and the travails that had afflicted England since Edward's death, that Llywelyn himself was the only person in the room who had met Edward's queen in the early years of their marriage. Even Goronwy hadn't been so privileged.

Dafydd hadn't dismissed the original staff at Kings Langley, so it might be that some had known Eleanor before her death in 1285, but even that was ten years ago now. She'd been in her forties when she'd died, still beautiful in her own way, but also worn by the births of sixteen children. Meg, who was the same age now that Eleanor had been then, could still easily pass for a woman a decade younger.

As he crouched in front of Elizabeth, Llywelyn sent up a prayer of thanks that he had returned to Kings Langley tonight. He hadn't intended to travel at all, and it had been a spur-of-the-moment decision that morning, after he'd finished up the last of the important discussions with Carew about the running of the country. He knew Meg would do right by Elen, but the girl was now the exact same age Dafydd had been when he'd come to Wales, and Llywelyn had thought to give the moment all the honor it deserved.

He was also grateful that Nicholas de Carew's wife had begged to keep the twins for a few more days as entertainment for her own young children. He didn't have to worry Padrig or Elisa with fear for their mother, and perhaps she would be returned to them before they even knew she was gone.

"Bogo's plan is to marry Margaret, King Edward's daughter. Through her, he will then claim the throne." Elizabeth took in a breath. "Both Margaret and Mary are also being held against their will at Berkhamsted."

Though several advisers exclaimed at this news, Llywelyn took it in stride. He was still waiting for the confession that they were *her* sisters. "You saw them?"

"Yes! Though that was—that was a few days ago."

Llywelyn kept his expression interested but neutral, as if he didn't believe her. "I was told you were at Berkhamsted before you came here."

"I know that sounds strange, but yes, until two days ago I was a servant there."

Llywelyn was looking into her face, but she wouldn't meet his eyes. They were getting closer to what she must feel was a dangerous truth. *The* dangerous truth.

"How do you know that's who they are? Is it common knowledge at the castle?"

"Earl Edmund has put out that they are his nieces, two of many. So far nobody has connected them with King Edward's daughters."

"Neither of whom are supposed to be at Berkhamsted." It wasn't a question.

"Exactly." The girl ducked her head.

"So how do *you* know that's who they are?" The silence behind Llywelyn was absolute. Even the slowest of his advisers, and none of them were slow or they wouldn't be his advisers, would be starting to see that something here was very much amiss.

Llywelyn could see the moment *Jonet* screwed up her courage to tell the truth, a truth that had driven her to return to the room in the first place. "Because I am their sister."

The uproar behind him was, he had to admit, quite satisfying. Also satisfying was his ability now to put a hand on Elizabeth's knee and say gently, "Welcome to Kings Langley, Princess Elizabeth."

30

Day Five

Lizzie

"Th-th-thank you." Lizzie couldn't seem to stop herself from stuttering. She was very cold too, despite the fire and the blanket Dilys had brought for her.

The king saw it and refilled her cup with the mulled wine. "Drink. It's time for you to start again, this time at the real beginning." He retreated a pace to another chair placed near the fire and sat in it.

"But sire—" Lord Tudur voiced a protest that Llywelyn cut off with a wave of his hand.

Llywelyn's men had remained hovering around the table. Now, he motioned for them to come closer. "We'll hear this now, and then we will decide where to go from here." His gaze bent again on Lizzie. "I won't tell you not to worry, because likely that's impossible, but please believe we will do everything in our power to rescue your sisters, not just Marged and my girls. All of them."

The others gathered around, Dilys among them. She pulled a seat close to Lizzie's left side and put a hand on her shoulder. "Take your time."

Everyone waited, silent, until finally Lizzie couldn't stay quiet any longer, and she looked up to meet the king's eyes. All her life she'd heard about him, how he'd taken on the mantle of leadership fifty years earlier at an age hardly older than Lizzie was now. *She wished her father could have lived as long.* That thought was followed immediately by a plaintive *why did Llywelyn get to live while her father died?*

She ruthlessly thrust the thoughts aside. That was childish thinking. She knew that now. She didn't want to be a child anymore.

So she began, hesitantly at first, but then with growing confidence, relating how Bogo's men had come to St. Margaret's and everything that had happened after that. When she arrived at the part where her uncle had explained to Molly his plan, including that he had someone ready to murder David with poison, the words initially stuck in her throat, but she forced them out anyway.

The king leaned forward. "You're certain of this? Do you know the identity of the spy?"

"No." She shook her head. "I'm sorry. He didn't say anything about who he or she was, at least not to Molly. I never spoke to him at all. I made sure I never went anywhere near Uncle Almain either."

"That was very sensible." Dilys patted her arm, though as she did so, Lizzie saw her gaze go to Llywelyn. She wanted to take Lizzie away again. The king wasn't having it.

"My lord, I think there has to be a spy here in Kings Langley too, otherwise how would they have known to ambush us on that route?" Lizzie said.

"You may be right, Elizabeth. We clearly have some work to do here." Llywelyn's jaw was like granite. "But first a few questions for you, the most important being: why were you not where we've thought all this time? How did you *get* to St. Margaret's?"

She wrinkled her chin, realizing she'd started at what she'd thought was the beginning, but yet again, it hadn't been the *real* beginning. "Before he died, Earl Gilbert de Clare moved us from Amesbury."

"He what?" That was from one of Llywelyn's advisers, one she thought was called Bevyn.

Llywelyn himself gave one of those barking laughs, as if he was surprised and at the same time entirely unsurprised. In the last quarter of an hour as she'd been speaking, she'd entirely forgotten how much she hated him. He was hard to hate sitting in front of her, treating her like his own daughter.

Meanwhile, his advisers responded similarly to when she'd told them who she was. Lord Tudur actually swore, fluently, in French and then in Welsh—or at least that was what she thought had happened, given the censorious look Llywelyn sent in his direction. By all accounts, even her grandmother's, the King of Wales was a devout servant of the Church.

Into this momentary disarray strode the castle's chamberlain, a man named Donald, whom she'd met earlier and who was a holdover from her father's time. Were she the king, he would be the first she would question about a spy in Kings Langley—him and that guard, Harry. Given Bogo's confidence that King David would be dead before he reached England's shores, the poisoner had to be traveling with him.

Behind the steward came a Norman lord, who was obviously an important man since his presence had everyone but Llywelyn on his feet. And then, even the king rose to a stand, somewhat lazily, once the nobleman was all the way into the room. "Bohun. It is good to see you."

"And you, my lord. I feared you would not be here." The man was Humphrey de Bohun, one of the most powerful men in England.

"I returned this evening. That reminds me—" King Llywelyn gestured to one of his men, another Welshman, and said words that Lizzie, as usual, didn't understand. All she caught was *Clare*. The man nodded and left.

"What has happened?" Bohun looked at each of the men in turn before his gaze fell on Lizzie. She tried not to shrink in her chair. "Why have you just sent off Cadwallon?"

"Nothing to do with you, at least not yet, I assure you," Llywelyn returned his attention to the great lord, "though certainly something worth hearing. First, let's consider your news, since we would not be seeing you at this hour if it weren't important."

"It is very important. It concerns the king."

Since this looked like a conversation that should not be had in her presence, Lizzie made a motion to rise to her feet, but Llywelyn stopped her. "I would have you stay, if you will."

Lizzie settled back into her chair, astonished at Llywelyn's request, but at the same time not arguing.

The king looked around the room. "The rest of you should sleep while you can. We will reconvene at dawn, by which point we should have heard from Rhys."

Given that Berkhamsted was all of seven miles from Kings Langley, Lizzie hoped to have heard from him far sooner than that. But by putting this plan into the king's hands, it was now entirely out of hers.

While he waited for the room to empty, Humphrey poured himself his own cup of wine from the carafe on the side table and gestured with it to Lizzie. "Who is this? Not Gwenllian. Not Elen." He looked at her closely. "Is she—"

Llywelyn cut him off. "She can wait. What is it, old friend? Why are you here at this hour?"

"Old friend." Bohun was still hesitant. "We *have* known each other a long time."

"We have indeed." Llywelyn touched his cup to Bohun's. "We have been enemies."

"Not anymore." The way Bohun spoke gave some kind of special meaning to the words, though Lizzie didn't understand what that meaning might be. She knew some of the history behind this tension between them, the way they'd been alternately allies and enemies for decades. These days, they were, at least on the surface, united behind Llywelyn's son.

Llywelyn laughed and shook his head. He laughed a great deal for a man under as much strain as he had to be. Come to think on it, the entire family laughed a great deal. "Consider all of the ways the world has changed since you came to Brecon to warn Meg, when she was pregnant with Dafydd, of Gilbert de Clare's betrayal." He gestured with his own cup to Lizzie. "And here he rears his ugly head again. I well know how much I owe you."

"And I you." Bohun nodded, though his eyes crossed a bit in confusion, and Lizzie herself wasn't certain if the king's last comment had been for Bohun or for her.

"So what is it?" Llywelyn asked.

Earl Bohun glanced once more at Lizzie, questions still in his eyes, and capitulated. "Edward's son, Edward, whom we believed dead nigh on these seven years, is alive."

31

Day Five

Lizzie

A magnificent joy filled Lizzie's entire being—in the single instant before King Llywelyn *laughed.*

Again.

Both Bohun and Lizzie stared at him. Bohun spoke first. "You think that's *funny*? He is only eleven now, but that is dangerously old enough to collect supporters around himself. He will have been raised to make a play for the throne."

Llywelyn guffawed one more time before getting himself under control, sobering completely a moment after that. "It's funny because of who is sitting next to you, Humphrey. May I introduce King Edward's youngest daughter, Elizabeth, who herself has just appeared at Kings Langley with news that Bogo de Clare, with the help of Edmund of Almain, is even now making his own play for the throne. His plan includes assassinating Dafydd first, via poison, from the hand of a traitor in his company. In addition, Bogo has abducted not only two more of Edward's daughters, Mary and Margaret, but my wife, daughter, and niece."

Bohun's mouth opened and closed like a landed fish. The king's explanation was about as succinct a one for Lizzie's presence at Kings Langley as she could imagine giving, and made her realize how closely he had listened to her.

Because of it, reason returned to Lizzie too. "Where is my brother now?"

"In Castile." Bohun was still looking tense.

"How did he get there?"

"Through the actions of one Philip de Willoughby, who buried a different boy in your brother's place and then fled England with Edward. Or so I am led to believe."

Llywelyn was back to looking amused. "Willoughby was the Chancellor of the Exchequer under King Edward." He looked at Lizzie. "I see the sense in this, if it's true. Your mother was born in Castile and, like you, was the youngest surviving daughter of the king. Your brother, Alfonso, was named for your mother's brother, whose grandson now sits on the throne, only ten years old himself."

Lizzie understood that Llywelyn had said all that in case she hadn't known her own history. "How are we to know the boy who died was a stranger and the boy who lived my brother? Perhaps Edward really did die like we believed and, in the aftermath, Willoughby saw a way to eventually return to power. He could have taken any four-year-old boy with him to Castile after David's crowning."

"That is true." Bohun was now looking musing. "There were rumors Willoughby himself had an illegitimate child. I wonder ..."

Llywelyn leaned forward. "Don't wonder. Find out. We need to know the truth, whatever it is."

It was Bohun's turn to bark a laugh. "Always the truth with our king."

"Always." Llywelyn's eyes were on him. "Thank you, my friend. You are welcome at my council at dawn, if you care to stay."

"I will. Thank you."

"I hope you know you are *always* welcome." Llywelyn gave special emphasis to *always*. "Though your news is important, and I am grateful you came, our most pressing issue is what is happening at Berkhamsted."

Lizzie had a sudden thought. "My lords, do you see these two pieces of news as related?"

Bohun spread his hands wide. "Almain is your father's cousin, since his father and your grandfather married sisters, but those brides were from Provence. He himself has no connection to Castile, which was where your mother was born." He heaved another sigh. "You don't seem much concerned about any of this, Llywelyn. Your wife and daughter are captive, your son is under threat, and yet you sit here sipping wine with the daughter of the man who ordered your assassination. Twice."

Lizzie blinked, having not heard that story before, but Llywelyn replied before she could ask about it.

"I'm quite sure it's three times." He waved a hand, to all appearances dismissing Bohun's cares and these attempts on his life as of no matter. "I am doing everything I can do, and I don't see how worrying will help."

"You could—" Bohun broke off, shaking his head, and she thought she heard him muttering something in French along the lines of *I will never understand the Welsh.*

"My chamberlain will show you to a room, Bohun. Get some sleep, if you can. We will meet in a matter of hours."

Bohun pushed to his feet. "I will do that." Then he bowed to Lizzie. "My lady."

As he departed, Llywelyn looked at Lizzie. "You too, my dear. I suspect Dilys has been hovering in the corridor all this time, waiting for me to release you."

But Lizzie herself wasn't ready to leave. "Why didn't you send me away before you spoke to Lord Bohun?"

The question had burst from her. It had been happening too often of late, though she supposed she'd never had anyone to ask questions of before.

Llywelyn didn't even blink. "You are a king's daughter and proof, if Lord Bohun needed it, that what I told him about Almain is true. He too knew your mother when she was young. I think he recognized you the moment he walked in."

"You don't think I will run to Uncle Almain and tell him your plans?"

"For the moment, we don't have any, so there's little risk there." He laughed. "But even more, you were the one who told us where his men took my wife and daughter. Without you, we would not have known that. I am quite sure we were not meant to know it. You may not trust us, and for good reason perhaps, but you don't trust him either, and you need us to rescue your sisters."

That, too, was a succinct assessment of Lizzie's predicament. She rose to her feet, realizing she was dismissed, though so gently she wasn't entirely sure she'd understood correctly. "What are you going to do?"

He laughed once more, this time very much under his breath. "I'm going to sit here and—despite what I said to Lord Bohun—allow myself to worry."

32

Day Five

Lizzie

Lizzie hadn't wanted to sleep. She hadn't thought she could, but suddenly dawn was on its way. It had rained hard earlier, which had made Lizzie want to pull the covers back up over her head and never move again.

Dilys opened the shutters, and fresh air flowed into the room. It smelled like wet grass. Outside, men were talking. Many men. "I know you didn't get enough sleep, but it's time to get up. The king wants to see you."

Lizzie sat up with a start. "Is there news?"

"That is what the king would like to discuss with you."

Lizzie was given a clean dress, and she stroked a hand down one arm, luxuriating in the fine fabric. She hadn't worn a dress this soft and warm since she'd left Amesbury. And maybe not even then.

Dilys saw the motion. "It looks lovely on you. Gwenllian picked it out herself. The riding habit you wore yesterday was also once hers."

Lizzie looked up. "That was before—

"Before we knew you were a princess. Yes." Dilys tipped her head. "I can see that surprises you. This is a new world you live in. It took some adjusting for my husband and me. In time, this will all become easier, my lady."

The honorific pulled Lizzie up short, and she said out loud what perhaps she shouldn't have. "It's been a long time since I've been called that."

"You seemed to have survived well without it. Not everyone could, you know."

Lizzie took the compliment, unexpected as it was. And then there was no more time to think because Dilys took her to a different room from the one in which she'd met King Llywelyn last night. This one was adjacent to the quarters reserved for King David, which even his parents hadn't been using in his absence. Theirs had been plenty fine enough. Now that she thought about it, those must have been built originally for Lizzie's mother. As before, the corridors were lined with tapestries, and from somewhere wafted the scent of cooking food that made Lizzie's stomach growl loud enough for Dilys to hear.

"You'll be fed too." Dilys opened the door at the end of the corridor to reveal an airy, rectangular hall with a blazing fire, a polished wood floor, and exposed wood beams that supported the roof.

Light entered through six large windows, three on each side of the hall, all with window seats. The overall effect was welcoming—until the two men in the room (other than the servants laying out a meal on the sideboard) turned to look at her.

Lizzie found herself stiff-legged once more, struggling to cross the floor between them in anything like a natural manner. One of the men was King Llywelyn from the previous night, but the younger man was unknown to her in person—except his face was everywhere, including England's coinage, and had been for the last seven years. This was David, King of England. *The usurper.*

King Llywelyn made a gesture. "Son, I'd like you to meet Elizabeth, the youngest of King Edward's daughters. Her bravery is the reason we know what happened to your mother."

Lizzie's lips were frozen, but somehow she managed to speak through them. "It is good to meet you, sire."

He genuinely bowed. "And you, Elizabeth. Please call me David. I might be standing here, alive, only because of you."

At his kind words, she was overwhelmed by the same rage that had risen up within her when she'd first met Queen Marged. He'd *murdered* her father! *Why was she helping him?* By the light of day, she couldn't even *believe* she'd told his father about Bogo's plan to poison him. *Why was she here at all?*

But her anger faded as quickly as it had come. She knew why she was here: to save her sisters. These people were the only ones who could. The knowledge prompted Lizzie to take a deep breath and get her feet moving again. How the king had got here so quickly, she didn't know, and wasn't hers to question in this moment. It gave her some comfort, looking ahead to what might come next, that her uncle and Bogo were not omnipotent in their knowledge. David certainly wasn't dead! Which meant in this, at least, she wasn't too late.

Then, a dozen other people poured into the hall, men and women, only a few of whom she recognized from the night before. These included Rhys, the Welshman Llywelyn had sent off in the night, Lord Tudur, and Lord Goronwy.

King David's seat was at the head of the table, as it would be. Lizzie chose one almost at the other end, hidden from his view by Dilys, who sat next to her. Llywelyn did not take the seat opposite his son, but sat next to him, at his left hand. A man beautiful enough to rival Bogo sat to David's right, and because he was so handsome, Lizzie thought he might be Ieuan, one of David's chief advisers and brother-in-law. Also present was Humphrey de Bohun. He seemed much less jumpy than he had been the previous night, and she wondered again at the fact King Llywelyn had included her in that conversation and they were including her now.

Nothing happened at first, as everyone held quiet conversations with their neighbors, implying they were waiting for someone else. Lizzie couldn't have guessed who could be more important than King David or who might keep him waiting. But then a young woman arrived and took the empty chair. "Sorry I'm late."

She was smaller than Lizzie, with dark brown hair and blue-gray eyes. Given her placement and the smile on King David's face at the sight of her, this was Lili, the Queen of England.

Lizzie shrunk further into her seat. She hadn't meant to put herself so close to the queen. And then, to her utter horror, Lili smiled at Lizzie too, reached out a hand, and placed it on top of Lizzie's where it rested on the table. "It is lovely to meet you at long last. My husband tells me we have you to thank for this meeting. I know it couldn't have been easy for you to come to us for help, but we will be forever grateful for your courage and sacrifice."

All Lizzie could do was nod her head, rendered speechless by the queen's apparent sincerity and terrifying genuineness. Everyone here had been so kind, in fact, that part of her instinctively refused to believe any of what they said to her could be real.

Then again, they had treated her this well, in just the same way, from the moment she'd arrived at Kings Langley: with respect, but not fundamentally differently from anyone else, even the high lords and ladies around this table. Gwenllian had chosen the dress she was wearing *before* she knew who Lizzie really was.

How did these people ever become leaders of men? According to her grandmother and what her sisters could remember, court life consisted entirely of treachery, intrigue, and plots by individual lords and cabals of lords to raise themselves higher in the king's estimation, or perhaps to replace him entirely.

It was only then, after Dilys poked her, that Lizzie realized she'd been staring at the king and the king had actually addressed her. She blinked, mortified, and there was that smile again. "I wanted to formally welcome my cousin, Elizabeth, to our table."

He then introduced the other people present. It was a large table, and many of the names she didn't catch. But she'd been right about Ieuan. Among others she hadn't recognized were Ieuan's wife, Bronwen; Venny, the captain of the king's guard, though his real name was William Venables, a minor baron from the north; William de Bohun, sitting next to his father; Christopher, the hero of Westminster; Lord Tudur's wife, Angharad; and one man in Templar garb, introduced only as Henri.

Once an attendant priest said grace, people began filling their plates with food, which had appeared on the table while Lizzie had been woolgathering. Lizzie had just taken her first bite when David began to speak. And it seemed everyone else was already aware of Lizzie's story, because King David didn't start with her, instead directing his attention to the Welshman, Rhys. "I would be grateful if you would speak to the situation at Berkhamsted, Rhys. Preferably in French, so all understand." It was a command, though a gentle one and indicated he already knew the details but wanted everyone else to share in that knowledge.

"I speak English too," Lizzie piped up—and then, as everyone's faces turned towards her, she flushed and mumbled into her eggs, "if you prefer."

"Thank you, Lizzie." Lili was the one to speak. "We will keep that in mind." And then, as Rhys began his explanation in French, the queen leaned in to whisper, "Many around this table speak English less well than you."

Lizzie nodded. "Yours is excellent, my lady."

That garnered another smile from Lili, and Lizzie fought down a mix of pleasure to be smiled at and shame that she cared what the Queen of England thought of her. Meanwhile, Rhys arrived at the meat of his story. "The defenses are unchanged, my lord, with two rings of walls, ditches, and moats, plus a final rampart and palisade that encircle the entire exterior. To anyone but us, it remains unassailable." Then he bent his head in Lizzie's direction. "I spoke personally to the mayor of the town, who also runs an inn. He mentioned picking up a young girl on the road who helped him fix the wheel on his cart. He called her *Jonet.*"

Lizzie ducked her head.

The others appeared to take that for the acknowledgment it was, and Rhys continued his story. "The mayor's niece is employed at the castle as a seamstress, and she has been hard at work sewing dresses for the ladies who are newly arrived. They are understood to be Almain's nieces, though nobody could explain their exact relation." He cleared his throat. "The mayor was aware that, around Compline last night, riders had entered the castle with three women who were taken to the keep. He knew nothing more about them than that."

"Was he suspicious at all?" Queen Lili said.

"He didn't want to be, but I think he couldn't help himself." Rhys put up one hand. "This is merely a sense rather than stated fact, but my men and I see the people of Berkhamsted as very proud of their lord, his castle, and their place in the world. That said, the community, as a market town with certain freedoms and rights, is not beholden to the castle in the same way a smaller village might be. They appear loyal to the king." He waggled his head. "All this is from what we could discover overnight. I had to wake the mayor to speak to him."

Just like at a chapter house meeting back at the convent where every nun, even Lizzie herself on the rare occasions she'd bothered to attend, was allowed to voice her opinion, King David genuinely wanted to hear from everyone. When they spoke, he listened, rather than having already decided in advance what he wanted and telling everyone else what that was.

For that reason, as a test of her newfound insight, Lizzie put up a hesitant hand.

David gestured in her direction. "Elizabeth?"

"I agree the people at the castle didn't—" she swallowed before shifting tack, "—nobody I encountered knows what Bogo or—" she stopped one more time to reorient herself, "—my uncle is really planning. They love him. They will want to believe the best of him and will do so until they are forced to believe something else. I don't think we can count on the majority of the residents to side with us."

"How long were you there?" A man named Bevyn asked.

"A day." Lizzie had heard the disbelief in Bevyn's voice and knew defensiveness had crept into hers but soldiered on with an answer. "I listen and overhear."

David gave her a hint of a smile. "And we are so very glad you do, so you will not be censured for it here."

Bevyn raised one shoulder in a half-shrug. "My apologies, my lady. It wasn't what I wanted to hear, and I took my discontent out on you."

Lizzie bent her head, accepting the apology, though still astonished he gave it. It was probably past time she stopped being surprised by what these people did.

David continued. "Thus, we have a problem, and we are here this morning to figure out how to solve it."

"If it is a problem we *can* solve," Queen Lili said softly.

"*If.*" David grunted. "You're not wrong. Mom may have her own ideas."

"You can count on that, son." Llywelyn appeared even more relaxed than the previous night, though Lizzie knew now it was his way of managing anxiety: the more tense others became, the more unwound he seemed. Lizzie rolled her own shoulders, thinking to emulate him.

"You are not giving up your throne to Bogo, *cariad.*" This time, Lili's voice carried a definite warning tone.

David gazed down the table at his wife. "You know my thoughts on that. But you are right I would never give it up willingly to the likes of Bogo de Clare and certainly not because he holds my mother hostage."

"Especially when your mother can take care of herself," Llywelyn said.

"But she has the girls with her, and we can't risk them." David's gaze again fixed on Lizzie's. She hadn't meant to be looking at him. "None of them."

Back at Berkhamsted, and the convent before that, Lizzie had assumed nobody in the royal court would listen to her, treat her well, or want to help her if they knew who she really was. She'd been wrong. Maybe about a great many things. That knowledge gave her as uncomfortable a feeling as she'd had so far, and she'd been plenty uncomfortable.

With a sudden inability to sit at this table a moment longer, she surged to her feet. "I'll do it."

David kept his gaze steady on her face. Everybody else fell silent, watching them.

This time, she looked back—with some defiance. "I can get into the castle. They know me as a servant there. I can—I can—open the gates. I can poison the guards. Whatever you need."

Her words had been sincere, and she was a little irritated to hear them engender chuckles and low laughter around the table. She flushed.

"Thank you, Elizabeth. It is something to consider."

The chuckles stopped.

"Sire, you can't let her. It isn't safe." Tudur's wife, Angharad, protested first. She was younger than her husband, slight of figure, with dark hair and eyes. Lizzie hadn't really met her yet since she'd accompanied her husband to Westminster and back.

"By such courage are plans founded, Angharad." This was from Tudur, whom Lizzie would have expected to express his disbelief at her offer if anyone did.

Angharad turned on him. "She's just a girl!"

Neither David, Llywelyn, nor Lili, the three people who really made the decisions for Kings Langley and the country, had yet added to the conversation beyond David's initial thank you to Lizzie. Slowly, Lizzie regained her seat, realizing they were taking her request seriously, and she needed to give them time to think about it. This truly was a council meeting. As Lizzie sat, Dilys gripped her hand.

"She *is* only a girl, my lord." Venny studied her across the table. "Please don't get me wrong, if she were a boy, I would feel the same way. She's *young*."

"She's a year younger than the king was when he came to Wales," Llywelyn said. "He was a prince's son. She's a king's daughter."

"It seems we have three girls in this," David said, "all of whom have shown themselves so far to be very capable."

"Elizabeth is here at all because she saw the danger taking place at Berkhamsted and came to us." Lili nodded. "I think we should give her a chance."

33

Day Five

Daisy

The fact that her uncle and Bogo insisted all was well with Queen Marged and the girls only served to make Daisy more determined to visit them. What's more, the more her uncle pooh-poohed the idea, the more important it seemed to be. She had also decided there was nothing to be gained from trying to secure more definitive permission from the men. They hadn't actually told her *no*. Better to do what she thought needed doing and let them find out about it later. If they were to be told at all.

Thus, this time well-wrapped against the rain that had begun to fall (in case she ran into her betrothed on the way), Daisy set off across the bailey, her guard, Roger, again in tow. They'd already spent an hour in the church, which was a convenient halfway point to where she really wanted to go. Molly was distracting Isabel, who might, in the end, prove to be something of a problem. So far, she had been reluctant in the extreme to allow Molly any more interactions with Daisy, even in church. And, unlike Roger, she slept in Molly's room.

But that wasn't the most pressing issue in this moment. To distract Roger from asking questions about the direction they were walking, Daisy said lightly, "I was happy to see you again this morning, though a little surprised. Am I your sole duty again today?"

"The captain of the garrison has no other men to call upon to guard you, my lady. None of the foreigners are suitable, and the rest, few enough as they are, are young. Lord Bogo would not countenance as your escort a squire newly arrived from the Continent."

"I imagine not." It truly hadn't occurred to her that Bogo would even bother himself with such things. But if he was uncertain enough about her loyalty to be worried her attention might stray to another, she needed to watch her step—even more than she already had been. The thought made her second-guess this trip to the keep. But then she squared her shoulders. This was not the moment to be timid.

Roger must have seen the motion, because *his* step faltered. "My lady, we are going the wrong way."

"We are not. I am going exactly where I intend."

He didn't quite catch her arm, but he moved closer and lowered his voice. "My lady, I am quite certain Lord Bogo would object to you entering the keep, even more than he would the attentions of a handsome youngster."

"I spoke to him about this last night," she said airily. It was the truth, but not quite all of it.

Roger still looked wary, but he gave way to her certainty, and it was by his authority that they passed without being stopped through the gatehouse that separated the bailey from the old motte. He then held her elbow protectively as she used both hands to raise the hem of her skirts to climb the stairs that led up to the keep.

"Have you heard who is being held in the tower?" she asked him.

"I did not realize anyone was being held here until I saw one of these foreign guards carrying a tray of food across the bailey and up the stairs this morning. It was a great deal of food too."

"Did you speak to anyone else about it?"

"Do you know me that well already?" He looked at her, a little amused. "At first I did some poking around myself, learning only that those within had arrived after dark, and they were more nieces of Earl Edmund." Here he paused, and Daisy sensed he was debating how much to say or whether to speak at all. "I felt the need to know more, so I went to the kitchen to inquire. Cook Agnes gave me a thin-lipped smile and said it was not my concern." He paused. "I gather *you* know who they are."

"I do. That's why we are here." Daisy hesitated, ten steps from the top of the motte. Once at the keep's entrance, they might be overheard, but for now, they were alone. She needed Roger tied to her, and she had very little time in which to do it. It was unfortunate this need had occurred to her only now. She was starting to behave like Lizzie, who perpetually acted before she thought.

"Are you loyal to the king?" He'd told her his life story the day before. His pride in his participation in the defense of David had been palpable. She was hoping it still was.

His eyes widened. "Of course, my lady."

"And to my uncle? And to me?"

"Why would you question me on such a matter?"

"Because what I'm about to tell you may undermine those loyalties."

"My lady—"

She put a hand on his arm to stop his protest. "Do you know who I am?"

"You are Lady Daisy, and you are Earl Edmund's niece."

"Yes, but do you know the identity of my father?"

He frowned. "I'm not sure—"

"My real name is Margaret, and my parents were King Edward and Queen Eleanor of England." She overrode his astonished look, continuing to speak rapidly, "Bogo wants to marry me in order to use me to make a play for the throne. To that end, he has installed a spy in King David's court, who intends to poison him. Maybe he already has." She pointed to the entrance to the keep. "Inside, my uncle holds hostage Marged, the Queen of Wales. She will be used to ensure King Llywelyn does his bidding upon the event of King David's death." She pushed on, knowing the terrible position in which she was putting him but unable to change course now that she'd committed to the endeavor. "That would be their son, and your king.

You are going to have to decide, right now, where your loyalties lie: with my uncle or with the King of England."

"With the king." To his credit, Roger didn't hesitate, which made him either extremely loyal to King David *or* to Uncle Almain, to whom he would run immediately once Daisy was safely back in her room. It was the chance she'd taken.

"If I'd thought through any of this before this moment, I would not have sprung this on you this way. I'm sorry."

"My lady, there is no place I would rather be than at your side."

She had no choice but to trust him, and since by this point he knew everything anyway, it was hardly worthwhile to worry about what she'd done. Thus, with some apparent accord, he knocked on the door to the keep. A foreign guard opened it. He looked surprised when Roger told him Lord Bogo had said Daisy could visit the prisoners, but when he didn't immediately resist or question how true this really might be, Daisy pushed past him and headed up the stairs to the top floor where she understood the queen was being held.

Roger took the steps two at a time to catch up. "We must be careful, my lady," he said once he was close again. "We don't want this tower to end up our prison too."

"It is a risk we have to take. I assure you, I will be careful."

Behind her, Roger gave an unmistakable snort, and she was quite sure he mumbled *you don't know the meaning of the word.*

Daisy really was becoming just like Lizzie.

The guard on duty outside the queen's door was foreign as well, no surprise. As Daisy stopped in front of him, she started to understand a bit more about how Bogo was able to abduct the Queen of Wales without any of the men involved thinking twice about the matter. He had enough of these foreign soldiers to call upon that he hadn't needed to involve Englishmen at all. So far, the only other English soldiers she'd seen besides Roger were the four Bogo had sent to collect her from the convent—and she'd seen none of those since that night. Bogo probably would have sent the mercenaries to St. Margaret's too if he hadn't known in advance that no abbess would consent to giving up her charges to obvious foreigners.

Daisy had explained to Lizzie why her uncle had sent off the regular garrison, but that had been before Bogo had used these mercenaries to abduct the Queen of Wales, an act which it had never occurred to her anyone would consider, much less order. No wonder he hadn't wanted his local people to know about it. Even with Bogo telling her his plan, the thought that she remained woefully unprepared for this kind of intrigue sent a chill down her spine at all the other pieces she might be missing.

This man's French was thick, but comprehensible. "You may not enter. Lord Bogo's orders were clear."

"He gave me permission."

The man glowered. "I was not told."

Daisy stuck her nose in the air. "I spoke to him last night. As I am his betrothed, and I know who resides behind that door, there is no point keeping me out."

At that point, Roger stepped in. While Daisy looked on demurely, he explained to the guard that Lord Bogo had sent them to make sure the women were being treated appropriately to their station.

"They are."

"You can understand, however, Lady Daisy's need to see for herself."

Until two nights ago, Daisy's experience with men had been extremely limited, so she had never batted her eyelashes at anyone. She did so now and was somewhat astounded it actually worked. The guard opened the door to the prisoners' room.

Once inside, however, Daisy stopped abruptly. It was harder than she'd expected to meet these women's gazes. She had no idea what to say. Her uncle had abducted three members of the royal family of England and Wales and had imprisoned them at the top of his keep. There was no getting around that level of treason.

The room they were in was well-appointed enough, as Bogo had said, but he hadn't taken into account that a servant would need to attend to them, as befitted their station. Nor their needs.

Twirling, Daisy snapped her fingers at the guard. He'd already returned to his position on a stool that he'd leaned back against the wall, the front leg lifted off the floor. "You must send for servants to refresh this room immediately."

His lips forming a protest, he dropped back to the ground.

Daisy overrode him before he could say a single word. "It stinks in here. Remove the bedpan at once. I'm shocked that you cared so little for them you allowed them to live in such squalor. From now on, whenever they request it, you will escort them to the latrine rather than forcing them to use the bedpan."

"But—"

"Now!" She stepped back and motioned that he should enter and do the work himself.

His resentment that this wasn't his job rolled off him in waves and was reflected on his face. But he did as she bid, carrying the bedpan gingerly out of the room.

As he passed her in the doorway, she softened her tone. "I will send a maid to attend to these matters in future." Daisy waited until he returned, having dumped the contents of the pan into the latrine located around a curve of the corridor. The keep had once been the very center of the castle, so it was larger than any of the towers in the curtain wall. Though not as modern as Uncle Almain's new square tower, it had been built with a latrine on every level. The waste was channeled inside the walls within a chute to empty into the moat, which was flushed weekly with water from the nearby river to keep it from stinking. The guard had also taken the time to fill the bedpan with water from the pitcher kept in the latrine to flush the latrine shaft.

"Thank you very much. Have they been fed?"

"Not yet." The mercenary was still surly.

Daisy frowned. "I understood food had been sent."

The guard's expression became even more morose, indicating he and his comrades must have eaten the food themselves. There was irony, in that it was only the arrival of the food at the keep that had prompted Roger to ask questions in the first place. His loyalty to her uncle had been undermined before she'd said anything at all.

Roger shot the guard a disdainful look. "I will see to it, my lady."

She canted her head graciously and returned to the room where those same three curious faces were still looking at her. What those faces didn't hold was fear, not even a little. She didn't know whether to be happy about that or merely confused. For her part, she had spent much of last night after she'd supposedly gone to bed pacing about her chamber, angry at her uncle and Bogo and afraid at what the future held for all of them.

Daisy hoped the women realized by now she meant them no harm. Regardless, it was time to speak, so she crossed the room to Queen Marged, who was standing near the single window. When she reached her, Daisy took both of her hands. Marged's were cool and dry, but Daisy's trembled with that same overwhelming fear that had plagued her last night. She spoke in English, knowing that Queen Marged was fluent. "Aunt, I am so sorry my uncle has done this to you. Please tell me, did Lizzie reach you?"

Marged's look was quizzical. "Lizzie?" And then, before Daisy could reply in whatever fashion she was able, such was the fear in her chest that something had happened to her sister, the queen's expression cleared. "You must mean Jonet."

"*Our* Jonet?" This came from the tall, slender, blonde girl, who looked a bit like Lizzie, though with a rounder face, since likely she was better fed. Usually. Daisy was guessing this was Gwenllian.

Daisy was still holding Marged's hands. "You saw her?"

"She came to us as a maid, though we knew immediately she was far too educated to be what she claimed. She was with us when we were attacked."

Daisy recoiled as if she'd been slapped. "She's-she's not—"

"She was alive and well when I left her." The other girl, who had to be Elen, took a step closer. She was shorter than Gwenllian, with red hair that flowed down her back. "We were riding together near the rear of the company. The men took me, but they did not discover her." She paused. "I made sure of it."

Daisy's hands were to her cheeks now, and she was taking in great heaving breaths. She hadn't meant to cry, but she suddenly found herself weeping.

And then, to her utter astonishment, Queen Marged pulled her close. "You called me aunt and Almain is your uncle, so I'm thinking you must be King Edward's Margaret. You and I have the same name, you know, though in different languages."

Daisy nodded into Queen Marged's shoulder. "Please call me Daisy. Everybody at the convent did."

"And I'm Meg. Aunt Meg, if you like. So, Lizzie is Elizabeth … is Mary here too?"

"Molly. Yes." Out came the full story, in English and instinctively whispered so the guards wouldn't be able to hear. With reluctance, she included Bogo's conviction that David was meant to be dead before he reached England's shores. She ended with another apology and, "I don't know what to do now!"

Marged was still holding Daisy in a way she never remembered being held in all her life, not even when her parents had been alive. Maybe her nanny had held her thus, but she didn't remember.

"You have been very brave, and I couldn't be more proud. Between us, we will think of something."

"But your son—

"David—" Queen Marged swallowed hard, "—can take care of himself."

Daisy could feel the woman's tension throughout her whole body and equally her attempt to suppress it. She was far less composed than she was trying to convey to her daughter and niece.

"There's always the window, Mom," Gwenllian said.

"Yes, there is always that, though we have two more to think of now." Queen Marged even managed a little laugh. "It sounds like Lizzie can take care of herself too."

With another wave of astonishment, Daisy realized the *two more* the queen meant were her and Molly. She'd started by calling Marged *aunt*, but that had been really just a courtesy. Somehow, as they'd been talking, and against all expectation, this family had truly become hers.

34

Day Five

Elen

"And we all thought Gwenllian's birthday didn't turn out as well as we would have liked." Elen was trying to make a joke.

Aunt Meg responded, even giving a little cough that might have been a laugh. "Teach me to object to hiking."

She moved to look out the open window with Elen. Truth be told, they had spent most of the day looking out of it, in between taking turns pacing to the door and back, trying to keep themselves moving and not thinking about the danger David was in. What might happen to him was worse than what might be in store for the three of them. Or the five of them, what with Daisy and Molly now to worry about.

It was twelve steps to the door, twelve steps back to the window. Elen thought they were lucky to have that many.

It had rained during the day, but they had kept the window open anyway. Elen hadn't asked how the others felt but, to her, it was a little glimpse of freedom.

"Oh right, blame me!" Gwenllian sprawled backwards on her trundle bed, to stare up at the ceiling. "Though, I guess we only went to St. Albans because Mom was afraid I'd come up with something equally outrageous."

"Instead, someone came up with it for us," Elen said softly.

Gwenllian gave a little moan. "I keep thinking about the people who were with us. I barely knew most of them." She was saying out loud something else Elen had been thinking to herself all day. It was another reason the two of them got along so well.

"You can't dwell on it. What's done is done." Aunt Meg's voice was stony, as if she was trying not to cry. Elen just wrapped her arms around her aunt and hugged her, conveying as best she could that she understood.

Aunt Meg patted her hand. "We'll start with what we're grateful for."

Elen made a face. This was a thing with Aunt Meg, being grateful for what they had, the corollary to *it could have been worse.* Personally, she could have done without a day spent in captivity with nothing to do. Her tablet had been left behind in the field where they'd been abducted. That prompted her to think again about the men who'd died defending them.

So she went along. "We are together."

"We are." Aunt Meg nodded. "Not to mention whole and well."

Gwenllian played her part. "Daisy came to us when she didn't have to, so we would not only know who took us but why."

"Daisy is not supporting Bogo's coup, which is something of a miracle, actually," Aunt Meg said, "and Jonet is really her sister, Elizabeth. Lizzie."

"Which is also a miracle," Gwenllian said. "You *saved* her, Elen, not even knowing who she was. Lizzie will go back to Kings Langley and tell everyone." She paused. "Right?"

"If she doesn't, nobody will know where we are. At the very least, she wants to save her sisters. That's why she came to Kings Langley in the first place," Elen frowned. "Why didn't she say anything about who she was and what she needed when we were with her? She had plenty of opportunity. We would have not gone."

"Since talking to Daisy, I have replayed our conversations a thousand times, wondering if Lizzie gave any hint at any point, and I missed it."

"I don't think so, Mom," Gwenllian said. "We were there too."

"Why didn't she?" Elen said.

Aunt Meg raised a shoulder in a half-shrug. "I can only guess, since she isn't here to ask. It isn't as if there's any love lost between Edward's daughters and us. Maybe we should count ourselves lucky she came at all."

Gwenllian was frowning. "I just can't get out of my head the way she looked when you touched her, Mom. It was like she wanted to murder you."

"So why come at all if she wasn't going to say anything? Or do anything?" Elen said.

"Maybe she was in on it after all," Gwenllian said.

Elen went back to staring out the window. That was a pretty depressing thought, and her only consolation was the behavior of Daisy. When she'd entered the room, she had been hesitant and obviously worried about her reception. The first thing out of her mouth had been an apology.

Not that any of this was *her* fault either. Elen had spent enough time in Earth Two by now to know most of the world was *still* thinking about women in the same way they always had—what in Avalon would be viewed as *medieval*. Well, they were medieval, so you couldn't blame them for that, but this new world was coming whether they liked it or not. And as far as Elen was concerned, everyone had better get on board or get run over. It was only happening, of course, because her cousin was the King of England, which meant Elen herself could mostly do what she liked. Until today.

She didn't like being penned up any more than Daisy and her sisters did.

The light was really starting to fade now. This window faced northwest, so instead of overlooking the rest of the castle, the river, and the town, it was just fields and forest as far as the eye could see. Elen didn't know that she was ever going to get used to the landscape being completely free of telephone poles, tall buildings (other than a castle keep), cars, trains, and airplanes. In this landscape, seeing an airplane *would* be remarkable.

Then she frowned, peering towards the tree line in the far distance, since the trees within two hundred yards of the castle had all been cut down so no army could approach unseen. "Is that a light?"

Aunt Meg turned to look out the window again. She had managed to retain her glasses, bought years ago now at a Walmart in Oregon, but her eyes had changed since then and the prescription wasn't quite right. Aunt Meg never complained about that either. That was the whole point of the grateful game—not complaining about what you couldn't change.

Now, she put her hands on the windowsill and leaned forward, as if those few more inches would bring whatever was in the distance close enough to see. "Gwenllian, come here. Help us look."

"There it is again!" Elen pointed to the same spot where she'd seen the light a moment before, and now she was quite certain it was human made. She watched for a few seconds, by which point Gwenllian was looking over her shoulder. "Could it be—"

"Morse code." That was Aunt Meg again, squinting into the distance. "Once it's full dark it will be easier to see."

"That's probably why they're doing it now, so the guards on the battlement are less likely to notice. How ironic for this Almain person that he employed foreign mercenaries. I bet they don't know Morse Code. They may not even know it exists." Gwenllian had her hand in the cloth of her mother's cloak trying to prevent her from falling out the window without intending to. That would change things for sure.

"Help on the way," Elen read out loud. "Status?"

"Lizzie did go to them." Aunt Meg was practically bouncing with joy. "They know we're here!" Then she swept her gaze around the room. "Next time I wallow in misery, someone please remind me that Future Events Aren't Real. We need a candle. Why didn't I bring my flashlight?"

"'Cause they're from Avalon, Aunt Meg, and we try not to freak out the locals if we don't have to," Elen said with a grin. "Whoever's there should have binoculars, though, right? With good ones they should be able to see us in the window."

"They should. It depends on who has actually come. Let's think." Aunt Meg paused, her hand on the top of her head. Then she turned back to the window. "Elen, give them a thumbs up. Maybe they saw us in the window and that's why they signaled." She strode to the door and banged on it. It didn't have a window, so there was no way for the guards to see inside the room without opening the door. "Excuse me! Please open the door! It's important."

As had happened several times already that day, the guard opened the door, and glared into the room.

Aunt Meg didn't wait for him to ask what they needed. "May we have a candle? Preferably several. It's getting dark."

The guard sighed, but it wasn't a great imposition because the tower had a stash of candles on a shelf. He lit one from the candle currently burning on his table, placed it in a dish, and gave it to her.

Then he handed her a second unlit one. "Let me know if you need more."

"Thank you!"

The guard shut the door.

Aunt Meg practically ran to the window with her candles. "Do you think my hand will be good enough to separate the letters? I've never actually done this myself."

"I can do it." Elen sat on the window sill, the candle in front of her, using a pillow as a shield. She spoke out loud as she sent the message. "E, G, M all well." Elen looked at her aunt. "How do I explain about Daisy?"

"Since they're here, let's assume Lizzie got to them, but we can't confuse them with her real identity if they don't know it. Tell them *E1 daughters captive too.*" Once Elen had sent that, Aunt Meg added, "Ask who's there."

The pause that followed Elen's query indicated that those on the other end were conferring as frantically as Elen and Meg had been. The sky had grown darker in the last few minutes, so if someone *was* standing on the battlement above them, he could be looking towards the light too and know someone was there, even if he wouldn't know who that someone might be. They needed to use this means of communication sparingly.

The next reply was two letters only: *L* and *D.*

It took a moment for Elen to realize what that meant. "Llywelyn *and* David!"

By then, Aunt Meg had deciphered the message too. A moment later, she was bent over at the waist, her arms wrapped around her middle, taking in great heaving breaths that were really sobs of relief.

Elen wanted to comfort her, but didn't dare take her eyes off the forest in case more words came. She had to leave the hugs to Gwenllian, who wrapped her arms around her mom from behind. "He's alive, Mom. It's okay. It's going to be okay."

Then came: *STFN. TTOK.*

Sit tight for now. She looked over at her aunt, who wiped her cheeks with her fingers, getting herself under control. "What's TTOK?"

"*Time travel's okay.* They are telling me to go if we need to." Though her arm was around Gwenllian, Aunt Meg was looking past her into the distance, implying if she looked hard enough, she could see her son or husband within the trees.

No more messages were forthcoming.

"Signal that we understand."

Elen obeyed and then moved the candle out of the window. Although Gwenllian and Aunt Meg were a thousand times happier than they had been, knowing David was alive, Elen herself couldn't help thinking that, if time travel was okay, then the position they were in, which she already thought was pretty dire, might be way worse than they feared.

35

Day Five

Lizzie

The rest of the meeting in David's council chamber had been occupied with specifics, much of which Lizzie didn't entirely hear, since she was focused on the rushing in her ears at what she had committed to. She almost didn't know if she had volunteered because she had assumed they would never take her up on it. Had she been testing them? And if so, did allowing her to do as she'd asked mean they were passing or failing?

It was Lili who saw her confusion and took her aside to explain in a way she could actually hear and understand: "Take a breath, *annwyl bach*. We need to send you in with as much information as we can. Once you enter the castle, you will be cut off from us. All the pieces must be in place before that happens." Then she quoted Proverbs, "The plans of the diligent bring plenty, as surely as haste leads to poverty."

Lizzie thought about quoting back a passage from Matthew about how worrying can't add a single hour to one's life, but she thought that would be petty and not entirely to the point. Lizzie *was* worried, and she was grateful that they were too. Whether they cared one whit about her sisters for their own sakes Lizzie didn't know. Suffice for now that their concern about Bogo's and Almain's plans had them moving as quickly as they could.

And, if she thought about it, perhaps it was a bit of a feat to arrive outside Berkhamsted at dusk with as large a force as they had marshaled. It was certainly the largest army Lizzie had ever seen (having never seen an army before at all), but she overheard one of the men mumbling that the force was too small, particularly when it included the King of England himself.

Lizzie wore the dress she'd had on when she'd left Berkhamsted, all of two—three? (she was losing track)—days before. The men had come to the convent after dark on September 25th. Lizzie had presented herself at Berkhamsted the morning of the 26th. Having spent all day there, she'd left on the morning of the 27th and arrived at Kings Langley the same day. The ambush had been the evening of the 28th. Which made today the evening of the 29th. It was an entire lifetime in four days.

For King David's part, he rode anonymously, with his hood up, in plain (albeit finely woven) clothing. There was nothing to distinguish him from any other baron, including Humphrey de Bohun, his son William, and a host of other noblemen who rode with them. The king could even have been a merchant if not for the sword belted at his waist. King Llywelyn was there too, though he was in full mail armor, neither man considering for a moment being left behind while members of their family were in danger.

David was apparently protected in a manner Lizzie couldn't discern, having overheard (yes, she was still good at it) the queen ask him if he was wearing his *Kevlar*. He said he was, and she rapped on his chest as one might knock on a door, after which she'd nodded, satisfied. Most of the lords and barons present, high and low, had bowed over Lizzie's hand at some point during the course of the day, though there were so many, she struggled to remember their names. William de Bohun had proven to be as handsome as Daisy had told her he was, though not in the same class as Bogo, as well as being blond.

As Lizzie dismounted, having ridden to Berkhamsted behind one of David's men, King David himself appeared in front of her. Lizzie managed an awkward curtsey, which he appeared to tolerate just long enough for her to wish she hadn't curtseyed at all.

"Are you going to kill my uncle?" The question came out on its own accord. Lizzie hadn't even known she was thinking it.

"I sincerely hope not." He was so unlike her grandmother's portrait of him that he wasn't even the same person. To tell the truth, Queen Marged hadn't been either.

Maybe for that reason, she couldn't help continually testing his adherence to his stated principles. It was almost a compulsion by now. "He is your enemy."

"Is he? I prefer to think we are suffering through a difference of opinion."

"He arranged to have you poisoned."

"Apparently. For now, that's hearsay."

"He was very clear it was someone you had with you in France, someone close."

"So you said, and I believe your uncle was sure." David shook his head. "I have trusted every person with me with my life, many times."

"Every person? You have cooks, don't you? And servants?" She paused. "And food tasters?" The old anger reared up inside her.

David didn't appear to notice. "Yes, but those did not come with me to Paris."

"What about a spy at Kings Langley?"

"I don't like that we have one, and we tried to lock down the castle once we learned we needed to, but—" He gave a rueful shake of his head. "At this point, everything is a risk."

"Are you—" Despite her anger, or maybe because of it, she struggled to voice her concerns.

"Taking precautions?" He spread his hands wide. "I never much liked parsnips anyway. I figure if I stick to bread, meat, and cheese—and water from the well rather than wine of a provenance I don't know, I'll be okay." He put a hand on her shoulder. "Are you sure *you* are ready for this?"

"I need to save my sisters."

He took in a breath and, oddly, that settled her a bit too. "Your uncle's capture of them alone would have been enough to require this response, but he made a mistake in abducting my mother." He nodded then, as if she had asked a question when she hadn't. "Yes, even surrounded, perhaps he holds all the cards, because he can murder them. I can't stop him from doing that. I can convince him he shouldn't." His look was very serious indeed, so Lizzie didn't ask him what a *card* was and why the fact that her uncle would be holding all of them was significant. "Your sole job is to get your sisters into the keep. Let us do the rest. I'm not trading my own sister for you."

And to that end, he handed her a plain, leather satchel, buckled closed at the top. It was heavy.

With a wary look she still couldn't help, she unbuckled the strap. Inside was a squat vial and a long coil of rope, knotted every few feet. They were to use it to descend from the tower. "What's in the vial?"

"Poppy juice. As much as we could acquire on short notice."

She stared at him. "I thought you wanted me to get my sisters to the keep and nothing else!"

"I am loath to send you in there with no weapons of any kind. You were the one who suggested poison. I'm not in favor of killing if I can help it, but dosing Almain's men makes sense, if we can. In the past, we've found it an effective tool."

Lizzie blinked. "You've dosed guards in a castle with poppy juice before?"

"Not me personally. And I don't want you to use it if it can't be targeted. We can do this without it."

"Using it could mean I could open the postern gate for you."

"I don't need you to be my Trojan Horse, not that way. Once you are all in the keep, my mother will signal when it's time for us to begin what I am choosing to call *our negotiations*. While you escape from the tower, we will distract your uncle and his men."

"This man says we can leave the postern gate to him." Venny, the captain of David's guard, came up behind Lizzie.

Turning, Lizzie's mouth fell open to see his companion. "Mayor Bill!" Suddenly she found herself wrapped up in a hug. Truly, she didn't know which one of them had moved first.

As they stepped back from one another, Venny gestured. "Sire, this is the Mayor of Berkhamsted, who, as you can see, is already acquainted with the princess." He shot her an amused glance. "He says he knew something was different about you from the start."

Mayor Bill suddenly flushed and bent in a deep bow. "My lady."

"Lizzie," she said.

"You are a princess."

"I was a princess. Now I'm just Lizzie."

Venny laughed. "You have already been spending too much time with our king."

Lizzie let out a little gasp, realizing she had just said very much the same thing to Mayor Bill as both King David and his mother, not to mention Elen, had said to her when they'd met. All of a sudden, she understood. Despite having spent years desperately wishing to place herself above everyone around her, she did genuinely prefer to be known as Lizzie.

Venny turned to the king. "We have surrounded the town and castle completely, sire. Nobody is getting in or out without our say so."

While the king spoke with his captain, Lizzie stepped closer to Mayor Bill. "I'm afraid for you. What if you get caught? What if *we* get caught?"

"Will things be worse than they are right now?"

She thought about that for a moment. "We will be captive too."

"That is true." Mayor Bill lowered his voice. "Sometimes you have to risk something to gain everything."

She looked away for a moment, thinking through the plan. Her whole being was vibrating, much like when she'd jumped from the door-to-nowhere to the old oak tree back at St. Margaret's. She knew this was important. She'd always wanted to feel that something she did *mattered*. Here was her chance. "Then how about we don't get caught?"

36

Day Five

Lizzie

Because of Mayor Bill, Lizzie didn't have the long, lonely walk down the road to the castle she'd been expecting but again rode companionably next to him on his wagon seat.

"Do you think they know yet?" Mayor Bill craned his neck to look up at the battlements.

"No." Lizzie spoke certainly, for her own sake more than because she was actually certain.

"If they don't yet, they will as soon as someone from the castle leaves with the intent to return and doesn't." From the rueful look on his face, he too was speaking matter-of-factly to stem the thudding of his heart.

"Thank you for coming with me. Thank you for helping my sisters."

"As I told the king's captain, I knew there was something special about you the day you helped me with my wagon." He flicked the reins once, not that the horse needed prompting to keep moving. "I'm thinking you are a true princess inside, even if nobody knew it up until now. Don't let anybody ever tell you different."

Moved to hear such words from such an unexpected quarter, Lizzie gripped the seat tightly, thinking again about the task before her. *Get your sisters to the keep*, King David had said, and she had assured him she could do it. But now she was here, staring up at the great towers, she felt herself to be as insignificant as a mouse. How was a mouse to go up against a castle full of soldiers?

Forcing her mind to calm, she told herself this was *her* plan, and it was still the right one. Just because King David had agreed to it didn't make it wrong.

The first time she'd ridden into the castle beside Mayor Bill, it had been morning, and the gate had been left wide open for easy passage. After sunset it was closed. But the guard on the battlement had seen them coming, since they were impossible to miss. He glared down at them from the height. "What do you want?"

"You know me, Hans," Mayor Bill's voice was appropriately exasperated.

"And who's this?"

"J-J-Jonet?" Lizzie found herself saying the name like a question, all of her feigned confidence evaporating, though maybe this was a better mask for Jonet. "I work in the kitchen? You can ask Cook Agnes about me."

"Oh right. I saw you the other day. What are you doing outside the castle after dark?"

"I-I-I had to see my family. I'm back now." This was obvious too, but Lizzie didn't know what else to say.

"Come in." The guard's tone was as exasperated as Mayor Bill's had been.

They again rolled across the bridges and through the gatehouses. Once inside the bailey, she and Mayor Bill gripped hands once. "You're sure you're going to be all right?" he asked her.

"I'm more worried about you. What's your excuse for staying here?"

"I'll be seeing Agnes shortly." He paused. "Shall we see her together?"

"Mayor Bill!" Once again it was the stableman, interrupting their conversation. "What are you doing here? Don't you know there's a war on?"

"There is? With whom?" His face paled, and Lizzie's along with it, fearing the entire castle already knew about the arrival of the king and his army.

"France!"

"I didn't know."

Lizzie was glad Mayor Bill was calm enough to answer. For her part, she was almost dizzy with relief. She was quite sure a war with France would be news to King David too.

"How can you not know? An armada has left Calais and will soon be on the Thames." He puffed out his chest with pride. "The men we sent will be on the front lines of the defense."

This was some story, to the point that Lizzie felt herself believing him and wanting to warn the king. Then she shook herself. It just went to show how easy it was to convince people of anything when their well-being depended on it. Or when their inclinations were to trust what they were told because they trusted the person saying it.

In truth, she had spent her life disdaining the people of Britain for following David. This was a look at the problem from the other side. And, of course as well, this was the very reason her uncle had sent the garrison away in the first place. The fewer people he had to lie to, the better. Those remaining were necessary to the running of the castle or, like Daisy's guardsman, Roger, couldn't be sent away without raising eyebrows.

"Go," Mayor Bill said under his breath. "Tell Cook Agnes I'm here and will see her shortly."

"We can't tell her anything about this, can we?"

He shook his head regretfully. "She can't know."

Lizzie had been glad in the end to time her arrival for darkness, because the main meal would have been served, and most should still be in the hall. Those in the kitchen would be already thinking about tomorrow's breakfast. And, as it turned out, her reception couldn't have been *less* fraught. A few people glanced her way as she entered the kitchen, but otherwise everyone's eyes were on their work, chatting quietly amongst themselves here at the end of the day. They had enough exciting news to jaw over without worrying about what Lizzie had been doing.

Not wanting to call attention to herself, Lizzie sidled around the margins of the room to where Cook Agnes was standing at the top of the cellar steps, staring down them. Lizzie waited a few paces away, wanting to gain her attention while at the same time not wanting to, and shifting from one foot to the other. Agnes continued to stare through another count of ten.

Finally, she noticed Lizzie, gave what might have been a har-rumph, and said, "You're back, then?"

"Yes, Cook Agnes. With Mayor Bill. He says he'll be in later."

"See to your bed. I'll expect you in the kitchen first thing in the morning."

"Yes, Cook Agnes."

And that appeared to be that. Cook Agnes headed down the stairs while Lizzie remained standing at the top. She should have been happy to have been accepted back into the fold so easily. She was certainly glad she hadn't been censured or sent away. And now she had a whole night to manage what needed to be managed.

But something wasn't right with Cook Agnes. The look on her face when she'd first turned to Lizzie had been distraught, as if she'd just learned a loved one had died. And then, as Lizzie stood at the top of the cellar stairs, hesitating, she heard a sob from below, followed by a great heaving breath.

She didn't know what was wrong. It wasn't her place to ask. Somehow, Lizzie found herself descending the stairs anyway, re-calling yet another overheard conversation between the king and one of his men, who'd said, *"We were lucky to arrive home when we did, so we could be here now."* The king had replied, *"Luck? Maybe. But we put ourselves in a situation to be lucky when it counted. Sometimes, you make your own luck."*

Lizzie couldn't help thinking she had the chance to make her own luck now. Sometimes the shortest path wasn't the quickest way to a journey's end. "Cook Agnes? Is something wrong?"

A single candle lit the space. It was enough to see by. Cook Agnes's pose was similar to her earlier attitude, though perhaps more bent over. At the sound of Lizzie's voice, she took in a breath, tipped back her head in a manner Lizzie recognized as an attempt to control tears, and turned around. Her eyes weren't red so much as puffy. "No, child. Go to bed."

Lizzie didn't obey. "Please tell me. Maybe I can help."

"You are a sweet child, but you can't help."

It was another dismissal. Lizzie, however, was a newly discovered princess, not to mention one with a long history of disobeying orders. She took a chance. "Is it about who's in the keep?"

All of a sudden, Cook Agnes's expression transformed from one of sorrow to rage. "He betrays us all!"

Lizzie took an involuntary step backwards. She didn't think Cook Agnes would actually attack her, but her shadow had risen up menacingly behind her on the wall. "Who does?"

And then, just as quickly, the anger was gone, dissolved again into tears. Cook Agnes found a stool, put her head in her hands, and through her sobs, poured out the reason for her grief like water through a sluice gate: she was a *Good Christian*, an Albigensian, and a follower of what Lizzie had been taught was heresy. Cook Agnes was loyal. She loved Uncle Almain for his defense of her religion. It was because of him she had converted. But the story put out about who was in the keep was a lie. Initially she had believed it—because who knew the vagaries of the nobility? She'd wanted to believe it. And yet, doubt had niggled at her all day, to the point that she had chosen to deliver their dinner with her own hand.

The room was well-appointed. The bedpan was clean. But the woman occupying the room was none other than the Queen of Wales. What's more, she and her daughter had burn marks on their wrists that could only have come from ropes. They'd been tied up and were now being held against their will.

If Uncle Almain had lied to her about them, then he could have lied to her about everything else. Right there on the cellar steps, not a quarter of an hour ago, Agnes had lost her faith.

As the story unfolded, Lizzie crouched before her, grateful they were in the cellar and she'd had the foresight to close the door at the top of the stairs before she'd descended them. When Cook Agnes was spent, Lizzie put her hands on the woman's knees, providing comfort but also wanting to gain her attention. "Listen to me. All is not lost. In fact, all really is quite well."

"How can you say that?" Cook Agnes's voice rose in a wail.

Lizzie didn't want anyone else to hear, especially now, so she shushed her. "I didn't go to see my family. Not my father's family anyway."

Cook Agnes bobbed her head. "I know. You saw a man. Are you having his child?"

The supposition was so far beyond anything Lizzie had ever considered that, at first, she didn't even know how to reply other than with a gasping laugh, wondering what King David would say. Likely he would have laughed too.

She settled herself. "No, that isn't it at all, Cook Agnes. You are right that the queen is here against her will, imprisoned by—" she stumbled over the words, almost saying *Uncle Almain*, "—Earl Edmund for his own ends. And I did go to see a man—but that is exactly *why* I went to see him. To get his help. We can fix this. Or at least some of it." She could do nothing about Cook Agnes's loss of faith.

It took a moment for Lizzie's words to penetrate. But then Cook Agnes lifted her head, suspicion entering her face. "What are you talking about?"

Lizzie let the silence extend for a few breaths. She had the sense that truth in this moment was the only way to proceed, but even having revealed herself to David's court, her real identity came slowly. Then again, Cook Agnes had been kind up until now. Maybe she would believe her—and help her again, just like Mayor Bill had. Maybe there was a reason Mayor Bill had sent her to Cook Agnes in the first place, instead of the castle chamberlain, whose job it was to hire staff.

"I came to Berkhamsted that first time following my sisters, Margaret and Mary, whom you know as Daisy and Molly. We are *all* nieces to Earl Edmund. I left to find help for them, so neither would be forced into marriage to Lord Bogo. I did find help, in the form of King Llywelyn and King David, whose forces surround this castle even now."

The latter news barely seemed to penetrate, since Cook Agnes was stuck on the first half of what she'd said. "Your sisters?" She was staring into Lizzie's face. "Who—" As understanding hit, she surged to her feet, prompting Lizzie, who'd been crouched before her, to fall backwards on her rear. "What are you saying? You can't be!"

Looking up at her from the ground, Lizzie cut through Agnes's disbelief. "But I am. My real name is not Jonet, but Elizabeth, though you can call me Lizzie. I am King Edward's youngest daughter. If you help me, we can save my sisters; King David's mother, sister, and cousin; and maybe my uncle too."

Cook Agnes slowly lowered herself back to her seat. "What do you need me to do?"

As Lizzie explained, it occurred to her maybe she'd had it wrong, back in Mayor Bill's cart. A mouse could go where it wanted in a castle, so small nobody noticed it—or if they did, thought nothing of it. Sometimes, maybe, a mouse could be as important as a princess.

37

Day Five

Molly

Molly could hardly believe King David had not only bowed to Lizzie's demand that she return to the castle, but he was on their side. Somehow, Lizzie had convinced him to include Molly and Daisy in his plans to rescue his mother. All the girls had hated him their whole lives, though that hatred hadn't been Molly's guiding principle in the same way it had been Lizzie's. Still, it was more than a little disconcerting to have the man they'd all thought to be their nemesis turn out to be their savior. It was going to take some getting used to.

Molly had no desire to be a warrior, unlike Lizzie, who seemed to have the ability to charge into any fray without hesitation or fear and had thrown herself into this new endeavor with the same fervor in which she did everything else. Bogo had no idea what he'd lost when he'd failed to capture her.

In this moment, when that same courage her sister had displayed was necessary for Molly herself, she didn't know if she had it in her. But she had a job to do, and she was going to do it up to the point it became clear the job couldn't be done.

"Isabel." Molly smiled as sweetly as her pride would allow. "I was wondering if you would sit with me a while."

"If it pleases you, my lady." Though she'd replied in the affirmative, Isabel, as always, looked uncomfortable, as if she might flee Molly's company at any moment. Since it was her job to act as guard to Molly, she was forced to stay, as she had been since they'd met.

Daisy had Roger for a guard, and he had proved more than amenable to any plan Daisy put forward. It might really be that he was going to betray them to their uncle, but he'd had all day to do it, and had not done so. With Lizzie's return to the castle tonight, Roger had agreed to get the three sisters into the keep. He had also promised to dose any guard he could legitimately encounter. They were using a sleeping draught created by Cook Agnes from what Lizzie had brought, augmented by the castle's small supply. The castle physician had been sent away with the garrison and had taken most of his remedies with him, but they had free access to whatever remained. All they'd needed was a key, which Cook Agnes had provided.

Lizzie's decision to include the cook in their plot had been inspired. Never mind her ragged dress, it was as if her little sister had been a caterpillar that had finally shed its cocoon and become the butterfly she was always meant to be.

In turn, Isabel was the least assertive woman Molly had ever met, even at the convent. The question before them now was if they could count on Isabel too. While Molly was determined to give her a choice, she was going to have to decide in the next quarter of an hour whether to include her in the conspiracy, which honestly was her preference, or dose her with poppy.

"How do you know Bogo?" Molly asked. "When we first arrived, Uncle Almain called you Bogo's niece, but I've come to see the way that label is bandied about rather freely at this castle, applied to many women. You aren't really related to Bogo by blood, are you?"

"Not by blood." Isabel took a sip from the goblet Molly put before her. "There is a connection, through the brother of his sister's husband. My mother is that brother's cousin."

In other words, it was a tenuous connection at best. Even the pope wouldn't object to a marriage between relations that far apart.

It would have been impossible not to notice the way Isabel consumed significant quantities of wine, particularly in the evenings. Molly had filled this carafe partially full, deliberately so. It held a single cup for each of them. Molly had a second carafe from which she herself would not be drinking, but which she knew from experience Isabel was perfectly capable of consuming all on her own. It was contaminated with the poppy concoction. Isabel would be drinking it if the conversation didn't go the way Molly wanted it to.

"So then, how did you end up at Berkhamsted?"

"I have known Lord Bogo for some time."

Molly waited. When no more information was forthcoming, she tried again. "Where did you meet him?"

"I was a novice, actually, in Gloucester, where I'm sure you know my lord lived for many years before the death of his brother."

"And you followed him here?" Molly made a gesture. "I apologize, I'm just trying to understand." She didn't say she herself had spent most of her life in convents. It still wasn't common knowledge—or, more importantly, openly discussed, even with Isabel—who Molly really was.

Isabel by now had consumed the entire cup of wine and was looking into it with some longing. "I have been his housekeeper and secretary. He had a vocation to become a priest, but gave it up after his brother's death."

That certainly was a reinterpretation of the situation in the most flattering manner possible. And Molly thought she knew why. "So you gave up yours too?"

"Mine was fleeting, to please my mother. When she died, I had not yet taken my final vows, and I left."

That Molly could understand. She'd had a vocation, but now that she'd left the convent, though she'd told Daisy she wanted to return to Amesbury, after another day away she didn't know if even that was true. She was prepared for the scandal that might ensue if she didn't return. Oddly for Molly, after the events of the last few days, she didn't know if she cared. These were heady heights she was suddenly treading.

"You love him, don't you?"

When Isabel looked down at her hands instead of answering, Molly set the new carafe on the table. She didn't pour it, rather holding the neck as if she was about to. She wasn't so much threatening to deprive Isabel of its contents as wanting to be sure, really sure, this was the only path forward.

"Does he know how you feel?"

Isabel blinked. "N-n-no. I have never said."

Bogo was using Isabel, of that Molly had no doubt. "Would you like another life? Marriage, perhaps, and children?"

Isabel's expression turned confused, and Molly wondered if she'd already consumed more wine than usual this evening. "Why would I want to leave Lord Bogo? He's—" she broke off, her expression lightening, really for the first time in Molly's presence. With it, she was almost pretty, "—quite wonderful."

Molly poured the wine from the new carafe into Isabel's goblet. As the other woman took her first sip, she rose to her feet. "I'll be off to attend Compline with my sister. You don't mind, do you?"

She was already at the door before Isabel could respond, which she did with a wave of one hand, having reached for the carafe with the other. She'd haunted Molly's steps for the past few days, but she'd been asleep before their interlude with Bogo and Uncle Almain the evening before. It looked to Molly as if Isabel would sleep within the hour tonight too. Likely, she would have anyway, but Molly was glad they'd put the poppy, light as it was, in this carafe, to make sure. All they had to do now was escape.

The thought prompted her to scoff under her breath. Earlier she had contemplated the startling things Daisy had been doing and saying, unable to predict any longer what she might do next. Though Molly had always been confidently self-aware, and felt pride at that fact, tonight she could say the same thing about herself.

38

Day Five

Daisy

The bell was tolling for Compline as Roger escorted Daisy and her sisters across the courtyard to the church. As before, this late evening service was attended by a smattering of staff, either the most devout or those who'd had to work during Vespers. Tonight, it was likely Lizzie would be the only kitchen worker, since most of those, like many others within the castle, rose very early in the morning to begin preparations for the day. While Molly had never come to Compline at Berkhamsted before, Daisy herself was a familiar sight by now. She put her nose in the air and paraded forward on Roger's arm, mimicking (not without some irony) the typical manner of Abbess Helen.

Then Uncle Almain appeared out of the stable before they were more than ten steps from the tower. "My dears, what are you doing out so late? You should be in your rooms."

Daisy endeavored to hide her dismay and put on her best innocent look. "It's Compline, Uncle. I've attended every evening up until now. Molly felt moved to join me tonight."

"I wasn't aware." His brow furrowed, and for a moment it looked as if he was warring with himself. "I'm not sure—"

"Please, Uncle." Molly took a step forward. "I have been missing the holy offices so much."

In the face of such apparent sincerity, her uncle could only give way. "Of course."

A wave of relief swept through Daisy, so palpable she worried it could be felt outside her body.

But then her uncle said, "I will come with you."

Daisy had been holding onto Roger's arm, but with his words, her uncle indicated that he should step away. He did so with grace, even as Daisy's innards curdled to have him no longer beside her.

"You are wanted at the gatehouse, Marston."

"On what errand, my lord?"

Rather than answer specifically, Uncle Almain said, "You should gather your things from your quarters on the way. You will be riding to Leeds with Thomas and Aubrey."

If Daisy's stomach had churned earlier, now it was a maelstrom of anxiety. It had tormented her this way so often since they'd left St. Margaret's it was a wonder she'd been able to keep down any food at all. She knew by now that Thomas and Aubrey were two squires who had not gone with the main army, as well as being the young men to whom Bogo would not have wanted escorting her.

With their departure, along with Roger, the castle would be entirely devoid of English soldiers.

Her only consolation was that her uncle did not appear to know that his castle was surrounded. Nor had he noted Lizzie, though, now that Daisy had the wherewithal to look around her a bit, her sister was nowhere in sight.

"Yes, my lord." Roger bowed.

By the time he straightened, her uncle was tugging Daisy away, but she was able to look back and see his questioning eyes. Molly made a gesture of helplessness and apology. In truth, there was nothing any of them could do in this moment. They certainly couldn't tell their uncle he couldn't come with them to Compline.

But then one of her uncle's mercenaries left the main gatehouse and headed towards them, at the same time calling across the bailey, "Pardon me, my lord!" Whatever this new matter was about, it was urgent. Under most circumstances, hailing the lord from such a distance for all to hear just wasn't done.

Uncle Almain stopped, making Daisy stop too. And so did Roger, who sidled somewhat surreptitiously off to one side behind Molly to listen.

Once the soldier reached Uncle Almain, he bowed, though as he came up, Uncle Almain made an impatient gesture with one hand. "What is it?"

He spoke French, as the soldier had done initially. It couldn't be for Daisy and Molly's benefit, so it must be because her uncle didn't actually speak Theodiscus.

"It is Lord Bogo, my lord." The man was far more respectful to Uncle Almain than she'd seen any of these mercenaries be to anyone else. They knew who was paying them, after all. "He is not in the castle."

Uncle Almain's eyes narrowed, but he didn't ask if the man was certain. "Do you know when he left?"

"Nobody has seen him for many hours. After noon, but not long after."

This was an unwanted surprise for Uncle Almain, but equally so for Daisy. It certainly wouldn't please David to know Bogo had escaped their net. *How* Bogo could have known to escape—if that was even why he'd left—was an important question, but perhaps not the most pressing in this moment, given that Bogo was already gone.

And yet, it was possible to be grateful for his absence, since it meant her uncle gave a grunt of dismay. Looking again at Roger, he motioned with his head towards the church. "Stay with the young ladies for now. You can leave after the service. I must see to this."

Without even another glance at Daisy or Molly, he set off back across the bailey beside the soldier.

Roger let out a sharp breath and held out his arm once again to Daisy. "Do not worry. We will get you to the tower. It is clear now that your uncle suspects nothing—at least not in regards to us."

"You will have to leave the castle."

"Rest assured, I will not leave until I'm sure you are safe in the tower."

"But our uncle—"

"He's already forgotten me. I will have to ride away, but I am the last person you should be worrying about in this moment." Then he lowered his voice to a whisper. "The king is here. I can act as your messenger to him."

Molly spoke from behind them. "A messenger we are fortunate to have." But then she paused. "Meanwhile, did either of you see where Lizzie went?"

39

Day Five

Lizzie

Once her uncle had taken Daisy's arm, Lizzie had been the first to sidle away, towards the walkway between the kitchen and the tower. She understood now, thanks to what King Llywelyn had said, that she looked very much like her mother. While the thought pleased her, it made it more important than ever that she not encounter anyone in the castle who would recognize her—especially unawares. Her uncle might even think she was a ghost! Immediately after that thought, he would know exactly who she was. Having come this far, it wouldn't do to ruin everything now.

From the walkway, hidden behind a pillar, Lizzie watched her uncle leave and Roger resume his escort duties. Even though it had been their initial intent to stick together, because separating under these circumstances might be a stupid idea, Lizzie didn't go with them. They'd been surprised by the appearance of her uncle—and the absence of Bogo—and somehow that combination gave her the feeling that she wasn't *meant* to go with them to the church.

Roger was going to have to leave the castle as soon as Compline was over, so they would no longer have his help. Maybe that meant Lizzie herself needed to do more.

It was the poppy juice at issue, really. In addition to Isabel, they had a list of those needing to be dosed, with her uncle and Bogo, obviously, as the most important among them.

Or so they had thought when they'd planned this out. Now, Lizzie was rethinking that plan. She had barely set eyes on her uncle this whole time, but even by torchlight she had seen his face flush when the mercenary had told him of Bogo's absence. He was worried now, and a worried man might not consume as much wine as one who was relaxing by his fire in his quarters. And, of course, Bogo wouldn't be drinking any at all.

"Why were you with them? You're not a lady's maid, you know."

Lizzie almost jumped out of her skin at the voice. As she'd watched her sisters disappear into the church, she'd almost forgotten where she was.

Now she turned to see Cally, the porridge stirrer from the day before, glaring at her. "I don't—

"Cook Agnes might say all is well with you, but I know better." The young woman's chin stuck out. "You think you're better than the rest of us."

"I'm sorry." Lizzie frantically tried to reorient her thoughts. She had so little experience making friends, she didn't know how to repair something she hadn't known was broken. "I meant no offense."

Cally folded her arms across her chest. "Then tell me why you had to leave the castle. Who'd you see? Was it a man? Some of the girls thought so, but I think it was something else."

"Well, I had—"

Cally cut her off, her eyes alight with malice. "I think you're—"

"Leave the poor child alone, Cally." Kate, Lizzie's not-sister, entered the walkway carrying a large tray containing multiple jugs of wine. "Nobody wants to hear what you think."

Lizzie had actually been curious, but now she eagerly stepped closer to Kate, grateful for her protection.

Kate raised the tray. "Since both of you are here, you might as well help me. These are for the soldiers."

Cally frowned. "They get wine?"

"A treat for tonight."

Cally did not even think to question what her master had ordered—whether in person or through Cook Agnes. That it was King David who'd arranged it might not even have mattered to her as she, like most everyone here as far as Lizzie could tell, were loyal subjects of the crown who would be shocked to learn their lord had strayed from his stated allegiance.

Suddenly inspired, Lizzie said, "I'll take two to the keep."

"One of them is for the men at the gatehouse before the stairs. Take the second to those within."

Lizzie could have volunteered to bring the wine to her uncle's rooms, but she had to trust that Cook Agnes had that matter in hand too. It was all the more important now that she stay out of her uncle's way, which was how she'd ended up in the walkway in the first place.

"Go on, then." Cally was dismissive. "Do as you're bid." Then under her breath, she added, "for once." Her attitude was reminiscent of the nuns at St. Margaret's, except for once Lizzie didn't think it was deserved. Regardless, Lizzie was happy to be dismissed, so she grabbed the handles of two jugs and started walking towards the keep. They were heavier than she'd initially expected, full of wine of a rich red color. Tightening her hold, she told herself to be confident and that her errand gave her all the reason necessary to be out so late in the evening.

She arrived at the gatehouse just as one mercenary, who looked hardly older than she, was walking down the steps from the keep to greet two more guards talking in the breezy area underneath the gateway. Feeling somewhat lightheaded at how brazen she had become, Lizzie made a motion with one of the jugs. "For you. Earl Edmund's compliments."

The closest guard wasted no time reaching for the jug she offered, but the second tipped his head to the second jug. "Who's that for?"

"Those in the keep."

By then the third guard had reached them and, having over-heard, replied in Theodiscus, prompting laughter from his companions. Putting up a hand, he said in broken English, "Wait there."

Lizzie found herself shifting from one foot to the other as she edged away, wanting to flee, but fearing to do so. She didn't have long to think, however, since the young man returned within a few moments, carrying three cups. "We'll take one each from that other one first."

Lizzie didn't want to acquiesce, but if this was the guard who was supposed to be guarding the front door to the keep, some of the wine in her jug was intended for him anyway. She didn't feel like she could say no without causing suspicion, so she poured a measure into each cup. The men continued to talk in Theodiscus amongst themselves, to more laughter. In truth, the men sounded well on their way to drunk already.

The instant she finished pouring, Lizzie made for the stairs and was ten steps up by the time the first man had drained his cup and shouted for more. "Girl! Where are you going?"

"Just doing my duty, sir." Lizzie kept going almost at a run, no small feat given the height of the motte and the number of steps to climb. She reached the doorway before any of them replied in English. She didn't really want to know what they had said in Theodiscus.

Only once she was inside did she realize she'd been answering them this whole time in French.

A mistake, but hopefully not a serious one.

She took a few steadying breaths and then climbed the stairs to the top of the tower, where she found the guard, kicked back on his stool—asleep. She didn't want to wake him, but she thought she needed him to drink what she'd brought in a timely fashion, so she carefully set down the jug on the table beside him.

Just as she did so, he snaked out a hand and caught her wrist. "Who are you?" He was speaking in French too.

This time she shook her head, pretending she didn't know what he'd asked, and said in English, "Earl Edmund sent the wine with his thanks."

He looked at her blankly, indicating he hadn't understood her words either, but then he released her wrist and transferred his grip to the handle of the jug. Skipping the use of a cup entirely, he took a long drink right from the brim. And then another one.

Lizzie backed away. She desperately wanted to open the door to the queen's prison, but she couldn't risk it. With one last glance at the guard, who appeared to already have drained half his portion, she fled back down the stairs. Just inside the doorway of the keep, she stopped, unsure what to do next. Should she go to the church? It would mean passing the guards in the gatehouse first by herself and then again with Roger and her sisters.

Deciding she might instead simply wait for them, she hovered by the door up until the moment she couldn't stand not knowing what was happening outside. It wasn't that the timing had to be just right, since they still had some hours until midnight when everything would begin, but she didn't want her sisters to worry about where she was. Admittedly, it might already be too late for that.

Cautiously, she opened the heavy door, reminding herself that she had come to the keep on a legitimate errand and had the same right to leave. These moments of waiting might even have given the guards time to finish the rest of the wine—

—and then she pulled back in horror at the sight of her uncle himself coming up the steps to the keep. He was alone, if that was any consolation, without even his clerk or chamberlain with him. Of course, he'd also sent all of his regular soldiers and companions away.

Twirling, she searched for a place to hide. This entry floor had become an armory, so while there were many trunks and crates, she was afraid of choosing the wrong spot. She had no idea *why* her uncle was coming to the keep, and the last thing she wanted to do was end up exactly where he was looking, next to what he was looking for.

Feeling trapped and helpless, she headed for the stairs. She didn't know what impulse told her that climbing higher would be better than staying on the lower floors, but she followed it anyway, almost blindly, all the while telling herself she was a fool. Her instinct earlier had told her not to stay with her sisters. She couldn't trust it. And yet, she went up the stairs to the next floor anyway.

When the keep had been the center of the castle and the seat of the lord who'd built it, his first grand hall had taken up this entire level. The large room was still set up as a meeting place, but short of secreting herself behind a tapestry or under a table, the hiding places here were no better than the floor beneath.

As Lizzie dithered, the front door creaked open and then slammed shut with a hard thunk, indicating her uncle was now inside the keep. As she pressed herself against the wall of the stairwell, the echo from the floor below—and the silence otherwise—was such that she was able to hear her uncle harumph to himself before saying, "I would have bought more if I'd had the money to do so."

He knew what he meant, of course, but Lizzie could only guess. Was he referring to a desire for more weapons? The thought was fearsome.

But then she had no more time to worry because his footfalls echoed on the wood floor and then in the stairwell. In response, she tiptoed up to the top floor, hoping his heavier footfalls would mask her lighter tread and internally cursing herself for being in this position in the first place.

But then, as she reached the top, she finally remembered she was a servant in an ugly dress and headscarf, one that hid every one of her blonde strands. She had a place here. She didn't need to be afraid.

Reaching out a hand to the floorboards, she swiped at them with three fingers, unsurprised to find them come away dusty. With a quick gesture, she smeared the grime across her forehead and down her nose. Then, knowing every moment counted, she moved out of the stairwell and towards the guard, while at the same time endeavoring to make herself as small and humble as possible. That her uncle hadn't arrived immediately on her heels implied he'd stopped off at the floor below, which made her feel better about not trying to find a hiding place there.

By this time, the guard was on his feet, not apparently affected as of yet by the wine she'd brought. She gestured towards the prison door and said, working hard to mimic Cally's English accent, "I'm here to refresh the room."

An irritated look crossed his face. "I still don't understand you." Nonetheless, he reached for the key, indicating he'd understood what she'd meant, just as before, even if not the words she'd used.

At that point, her uncle's boots sounded again in the stairwell. Lizzie had been hoping to already be in the queen's rooms by the time he arrived, but the guard was having a bit of difficulty getting the door to unlock. More than a little desperately, Lizzie grabbed a bundle of candles from a nearby shelf and clutched them to her chest.

By then, the guard managed to get the door open. As it swung inward, he called into the room in French, "Latrine!"

It was an impressive level of rudeness, overshadowed a heartbeat later by the arrival of Uncle Almain, who burst from the stairwell like a bolt from a crossbow. "What are you doing?"

The guard stiffened to attention. "They needed to use the—"

"Not you, you fool. Her!"

Amazingly, he wasn't referring to Lizzie. He hadn't even noticed her, shrunk as she was against the wall. His finger was pointed at Queen Marged who had come to stand in the doorway, now that it was open.

"I am sure I have no notion of what you are asking, Almain."

"Bogo is gone. Why?"

"How could I possibly know that, Almain? I am your prisoner and have not left this room."

"Don't pretend with me!" Uncle Almain didn't quite grab her arms, but he stopped only a foot away, his anger a halo around him.

Queen Marged just gazed calmly back, seemingly unmoved, and said nothing. Lizzie had never known silence to speak so loudly.

Uncle Almain's hands clenched into fists and the line of his jaw was like granite. Then he spun around on one heel and stalked back the way he'd come. Lizzie kept her head bent and her face turned away, grateful for the candles in her hands. As far as she could tell, he didn't even look at her as he went past, descending the stairs much more quickly than he'd come up them.

The three of them—the guard, Lizzie, and Queen Marged—didn't move until they heard the front door slam closed. Then the queen glanced towards where Lizzie still cowered and, switching to English so the guard wouldn't understand, said, "It's so good to see you again, Jonet. I understand we have a great deal to thank you for."

40

Day Five

David

As Lizzie had ridden away with Mayor Bill, foremost in David's mind had been how grateful he was that chance and courage were still to be found in unlikely places. Lizzie reminded him a bit of the young Humphrey de Bohun, as remembered in his mother's stories of the time before David was born. Lizzie had been raised to hate his entire family, that much was clear. But if David's father and Humphrey could overcome decades of animosity, so too perhaps could David and the daughters of King Edward.

Turning to look at the men who had gathered with him, he furthermore was glad they did not include Elen's parents, left behind in Normandy as support personnel for the insurrection there. He supposed there was irony in that, since here he was, taking steps to put down one of his own in England.

For all that his aunt had orchestrated the evacuation of the entire Jewish population of Paris with aplomb, she would be prostrate with worry right about now. Uncle Ted was a quiet man, but David had seen him worked up a few times, and he would definitely be worked up to know his daughter was caught up in Almain's rebellion. It was only Christopher who'd traveled home with David. These days, he was much less reckless than he used to be, especially since he was missing two of his usual co-conspirators: Robbie Bruce and Huw. Those two had journeyed to Scotland together with James Stewart, not realizing there might be a good reason to stay with David. In addition, Isabelle, daughter of the Master of the Paris Temple and Christopher's newly betrothed, was good in a crisis.

Thus, although initially Christopher had insisted on battering down the front gate of Berkhamsted, he'd soon agreed it would be a mistake. With David's own mother one of the prisoners, David could understand the desire to come at the castle with every weapon in his arsenal. And he had many.

It was William de Bohun, somewhat ironically, who continued to be irate with David for not being more aggressive. "You just sent a thirteen-year-old girl into danger with your eyes open."

"I did." David turned to look at his former squire, wondering how much of William's protective ire was because he knew (having spent time on the internet in Avalon) that in that other world she was destined to become his wife. "It is the right decision. As I recall, *you* were once thirteen and equally reckless." He paused. "In fact, you were exactly her age when I chased you all over the borderlands of Wales, as well as later when her older sister declined to marry you."

William harrumphed.

He had been among those in David's personal court of public opinion, consisting also of David's father, wife, and brother-in-law, who had objected to him coming to Berkhamsted at all. David had expected no less, and he was prepared for more objections when, in a few hours, he insisted on being among those riding under a white flag to discuss the situation with Bogo and Almain. He was going to argue that hardly a month earlier they'd let him walk into far more danger at King Philippe's palace on the Île de la Cité.

Then again, maybe that would be the opposite of making his argument for him. Maybe David was naïve. His father had certainly told him so in no uncertain terms not an hour ago. But he had to believe a quick and peaceful resolution was possible, if everyone could just be reasonable for a single minute.

Regardless, his family would have to agree that by being present himself, he would capture Bogo's and Almain's full attention. David knew he was taking a risk in confronting them, since one of their options was to use David's mother and sister as a bargaining chip. But it would take time for men to retrieve them, and if they were to do so, every resident of the castle would know their lord had betrayed the crown.

Thus, Almain would see it as a last resort.

Far more crucial was the need for everyone to be looking towards the front of the castle as the women descended the tower. At least their window faced nearly the exact opposite direction from the front gate, so nobody looking back towards the keep would see them leaving, even were it full daylight instead of the middle of the night.

Every member of David's own family had faced far worse threats over the course of their sojourn in Earth Two. Part of him felt like Bogo should be no more trouble than a fly buzzing around his head. He might have been only that, if not for the fact that he'd abducted David's mother, sister, and cousin. That said, David had told the truth to Lizzie: they would be here, even without that additional act, in order to save her sisters. It was who they were. It was what *he* did. God help him.

Bogo couldn't be dismissed, unfortunately, not when he had the backing of Edmund of Almain, who was one of the most influential men in England—or had been during King Edward's reign. It was still astounding to David that Almain had chosen to support Bogo's claim to the throne. In the course of a few days, he'd traded a good life for a fleeting chance at power and wealth. David had come to see over the years that a drive for both could do that to a person. It was half the reason he had worked so hard to divest himself of his.

Or maybe, if Lizzie had the story right, this really was just about money, and he made a note to himself to inquire into the finances of all his major lords, and maybe minor ones too. David himself had limited debt, so if he could head off another rebellion simply by providing cold hard cash to one of his barons, it would be worth the expense.

"We have them, my lord!" Mathew, a staunch member of David's guard, not to mention the largest, grinned widely as he came to a halt in front of him and bowed. The bow wasn't very low, it was true, but some things David had learned to accept as the cost of doing business.

Mathew was referring to a party of six men who'd been seen leaving the gatehouse. They'd been allowed to get well away before they were captured. None were foreign, making David think these might be the last of the native English soldiers, sent away now the time for action had come.

After the council meeting at Kings Langley, where Lizzie had reported Almain had sent his men marching to Leeds in case they were needed to repel a French invasion, David had experienced a moment of panic that there actually *was* a French invasion force about to land in Kent. He was concerned enough that he'd communicated first with Carew in London, and then sent messages to all the major ports. The situation with France remained fraught, but David had returned home because his continued presence in Normandy had the capacity to make relations even worse. The people of Normandy had the backing of the CSB, but their negotiations with the King of France had to be managed without David himself looming in the background.

Whether he liked it or not, or ever meant to do so or not, these days David cast a long shadow indeed. He would be stupid not to admit it. It was also a fact he was completely willing to exploit tonight.

"You're in a good mood," David said, more than a little sourly, as he and Mathew set out for where they were holding the captives. For that purpose, they'd taken over a relatively sturdy shed on the outskirts of Berkhamsted, one Lizzie had pointed out before she'd left.

His words and tone made Mathew grin all the wider. "As are we all, sire. The moment we set foot on English soil, everyone let out a huge sigh of relief. Even the Welsh!"

"Only to come home to yet another traitorous Clare."

"He is a Clare." Mathew was philosophical about even that. "This is what they do."

"I still feel like I'm missing a piece of the puzzle." David gave up trying to puncture Mathew's happy balloon.

"Could be because you have spies in your midst, what Lady Elen tells me from her reading can also be referred to as *moles*." He seemed to relish the idea—and maybe the upcoming search for them, once this current matter was resolved.

Upon reaching the shed, Mathew entered fully, but David lounged in the doorway, his arms folded across his chest, staying a full ten paces away as those who watched his back insisted was necessary. The men had been placed in a row on their knees. Mathew paced behind them, and each time he made a noise, at least one of them flinched. They might have been wondering if their heads were about, quite literally, to roll.

"How much did Earl Edmund pay you for your treason?" Even to David, the glint in Mathew's eyes was daunting.

"Nothing! We didn't!" This came from a man on the far end, the youngest of them, and already identified by Venny as the most likely to spill his guts if guts were to be spilled. In truth, none of the men were looking too pleased with themselves. "We were told the French were invading!"

Then a man in the center, middle-aged, with a large beard, looked up for the first time. He'd been focused on the ground in front of him, perhaps steeling himself for abuse. Now, his face paled at the sight of David. "Sire!" He made to rise to his feet, but Mathew put a strong hand on his shoulder and pressed him down again. "I didn't mean to leave them! I swear it! But I was ordered from the castle." He was practically sobbing out his apologies. "I'm sorry."

David straightened in the doorway. "Let him stand and approach."

"Sire!" Mathew was aghast, but at a signal from Ieuan, who stood at David's shoulder, he gave way.

Now that he had the king's attention, the man seemed to find his bearings. He wasn't sobbing anymore, and his breathing slowed. Before he spoke, he bowed respectfully. "Sire. My name is Roger de Marston. I have served Earl Edmund for years. Because of this foul leg," he indicated the left one, "I was sent to guard the princesses, particularly Lady Margaret, whom we call Daisy. I can now be grateful for my weakness, as, once Lord Bogo and Earl Edmund revealed their plans, she spoke of them to me."

"Roger! What is this?" One of the other men, younger than Roger, somewhere in his twenties, was utterly aghast.

Mathew slapped him upside the head. "Quiet unless you have something useful to say."

For his part, Roger squared his shoulders. "I have been loyal to the earl, but I ultimately serve my king and my country. Neither Earl Edmund nor Bogo," here the name came out a sneer and he'd dropped the *lord*, "is king." He looked David full in the face. "My lord, the plan was to poison you and take the throne."

"We do know that, thanks to Lizzie," David said. "Bogo intends to marry Princess Margaret as a means of legitimizing the claim."

From beside David, Ieuan scoffed. "He must know the barons will never support him."

"With you dead, sire," Roger said, "he doesn't need the barons. He needs the people."

"He means to call an election?" Ieuan understood first and began to laugh. "King Llywelyn would win before Bogo! Never mind that he's Welsh."

Roger wasn't laughing. "King Llywelyn wouldn't even stand for election if the consequences were the death of his wife and daughter."

The missing piece chunked solidly into place.

Ieuan spoke Welsh in David's ear. "We should cut him out of the herd."

David made a motion with his hand in Roger's direction. "Come."

As Roger started forward, the youngest knight said, "What about us? Are-are-are you going to kill us?"

David spun around, his frustration peaking. "Why does everyone always assume I'm going to murder them?"

At least he'd spoken in Welsh, so only Ieuan understood. And it was he who answered. "You are so far outside anyone's experience. Many see and believe, but they are always looking for a sign that you are imperfect, that you will fail them too, like every other lord has ultimately failed them."

David rubbed his forehead. "You don't comfort me, but I suppose you didn't mean to, and it isn't your job anyway." He made a gesture. "Get Mathew to stop tormenting them and give them some ale. I just don't want them wandering off."

"Yes, my lord."

David gave him a dark look at the use of the honorific and set off with Roger. "So you believed Daisy." It wasn't so much a question than that David wanted confirmation of what Roger had already said.

"Yes."

"Okay." He gave a low laugh. "Against all expectation, I do too."

"My lord, I must say more. Lord Bogo may no longer be in the castle."

David had been walking fast, and now he came to an abrupt halt. "Not in the castle—"

He was interrupted by the arrival of William, who reined in near the paddock. "The princess did it! She and her sisters are with your mother in the tower. She says Mayor Bill has opened the postern gate. They had another ally, but he was sent out of the castle."

"I was that ally," Roger said immediately. "We have another conspirator too, the castle cook, who perfected the potion."

David swung around to face Roger. "Despite what your companions believe, my hope was to accomplish this rescue with minimal—or no—death."

"Yes, sire. Princess Elizabeth knew your mind. It was to be a light dose, just to make everyone sleepy and groggy when they do wake."

David let out a breath. "You have a rare courage, sir." Luck was with them yet again, though David wouldn't diminish the efforts of these new companions by saying so out loud. Instead, he put a hand on Roger's shoulder. "I can see you did not help Princess Daisy—or me—with an expectation of reward, but you will have a place in my retinue when this is over. If you want it."

"Th-thank you, my lord." He paused. "Are you certain you are well? Some poisons take time to take effect."

Truth be told, David had been a bit concerned about that himself—though admittedly not as concerned as his wife and father. Abraham, who'd accompanied him home from Normandy, had given him a thorough going over before they'd ridden to Berkhamsted. He couldn't find anything wrong. "As far as I know, Roger. The rest we must leave in God's hands."

"But—"

"Never fear." David laughed. "My wife is looking over His shoulder."

As Roger subsided, still looking worried, David turned towards the castle, the towers of which were visible in the distance. "For now, Bogo or no Bogo, we have an insurrection to avert."

He would have liked to have been the one to rescue his mother and sister, but his duties lay elsewhere. Striding back to where his father waited for him, he felt a familiar pounding of his heart. It was time to begin.

41

Day Five

Lizzie

None of them had any idea what had become of Bogo any more than their uncle did. Where Uncle Almain had gone after he'd left the tower was also a mystery, since he hadn't stopped by the church. If he knew Molly and Daisy were missing from their rooms, he hadn't come looking for them here.

Roger was surely gone by now too, though before he'd left he'd given Queen Marged his dagger. He'd also made sure their guard was asleep and the door to their room unlocked, in case the window proved untenable. While there was no escape from the castle down the stairs, they didn't have to be prisoners any longer.

"I don't know if I can do this. It's so dark down there, I can barely see anything." Gwenllian looked out the window dubiously. "My grandfather—"

"You are not your grandfather," Queen Marged said. "I don't want to climb down either, but this is the only way out of this keep for us, and I trust your brother."

"What happened to your grandfather?" Lizzie asked.

Gwenllian turned from the window. "King Henry had imprisoned him in the tower of London, as a hostage for his brother's good behavior. He tried to escape down a rope, but the rope broke, and he fell to his death."

Lizzie found herself blinking at the other girl, thinking about the other partial story she'd heard, about her father ordering King Llywelyn's assassination. Twice. Or maybe three times. "I didn't know that."

"I think there's a great deal we don't know about each other." Queen Marged spoke through gritted teeth because she was working at tying the end of the rope around the big beam above their heads.

Daisy tugged on Lizzie's sleeve, trying to draw her away, probably feeling the need to head off an argument. "Trust is hard for all of us."

"We've all been hurt," Molly said in a low voice, "in one way or another."

"Some more than others." Gwenllian was looking out the window again.

"How have you been hurt?" Lizzie simply couldn't help asking the question. "That was your grandfather, not you. You're a princess."

Gwenllian turned back to her, a look of astonishment on her face. "You've got to be kidding me! Did you forget we are captives of *your* uncle?"

"Gwenllian." Queen Marged's voice held a warning, similar to that which Daisy had used with Lizzie. "We don't need to do this now. We are all in this together."

"Are we?" Gwenllian said. "I didn't know any of them existed before today."

That was more than unbearable. "Whereas I have known about you my whole life."

"Why would you have known anything about me?"

"Because you took my place!" Fury swept through Lizzie at the years of grief and hardship she'd suffered. She made a sweeping gesture that included Queen Marged and Elen. "You all did."

Gwenllian settled with a thump on the windowsill. "That isn't fair."

"But it's true."

"If my father had died at Cilmeri, murdered by men who served your father, I would have been the one to grow up in a convent. And in my case, it wouldn't have been in my own country. It would have been in yours."

That was too much. Gwenllian could have no idea what might have happened, since it *didn't* happen. "Your brother killed my father."

"He did not! He had nothing to do with that! He was as surprised by it as everyone else!"

"You're lying! My grandmother—" All of sudden, Lizzie's throat constricted and tears swelled in the corners of her eyes. She was determined not to cry, but the tears were coming anyway. Daisy was right there to wrap her arms around her, and Lizzie put her face into her sister's shoulder. "Grandmother said."

"Neither the queen nor David murdered our parents, Lizzie. It was Grandmother who lied." Daisy's voice came softly, but it was matter-of-fact for all that. "She was angry and resentful and embittered by her fate. I always regretted the way she passed that anger on to you."

"Why didn't you say something sooner?"

"Would you have listened?"

Lizzie didn't dare look up. She knew she'd humiliated herself, and she was almost as angry about that as how her life had gone. Even worse, Daisy wasn't telling her anything she didn't by now already know.

"We are all family here. We have all been hurt by events outside our control, some more than others," Molly spoke again now, more firmly than before. In a way, the transformation in her these last few days had been greater than in Daisy. "But we don't need to keep a tally, and we certainly don't need to perpetuate that mistake."

Then Lizzie found a hand on her back. It was Gwenllian, rubbing softly. "I'm sorry, Lizzie. I'm sorry about what happened to you. I can't be sorry my father lived. I am sorry you paid the price for it." The hand went away. "All of you."

Lizzie pushed back from Daisy, wiping at her eyes with the backs of her hands, determined not to weep one instant longer.

Queen Marged stepped in. "You have been wronged, and you feel it. We are all sorry for whatever role we played in your relegation, intentional or not." She paused, and Lizzie could feel her gaze, though she didn't meet it. "I'm going to be a mother right now, even if it isn't my place to instruct you. *Cariad,* if you are to be a whole person, you will need to let this go. I realize forgiving us—and my son and husband—benefits us. But you must realize any hatred you feel towards us harms only you."

At the queen's comment, Lizzie's head came up, and she felt a surge of pride. "I do know that."

And in a flash of insight, all of a sudden Lizzie understood why men like her uncle and Bogo—and Gilbert de Clare and Roger Mortimer and Philippe, the King of France—mistook David's kindness for weakness instead of the strength it was. It was men like Bogo who were weak, who filled their cups every morning with envy and greed and told themselves they could never be whole until they stood above other men. It was what Daisy had tried to explain to her, here and in the church a few days ago. Now that Lizzie thought about it, Daisy had tried before then too, but Lizzie hadn't ever had the wherewithal to hear her.

The nuns at St. Margaret's, and even at Amesbury, despite her grandmother's influence, had insisted David hadn't even wanted to be king but had taken the throne because he thought he could serve England and make it better. Looking into David's mother's face, she believed them.

She believed *him*.

Back in the dormitory that first night, Daisy had put her faith in Lizzie, believing she would do *the right thing*. At the time, Lizzie hadn't known what her sister meant. Somehow, despite that fact, she'd followed her sisters to Berkhamsted, sought help at Kings Langley, and volunteered at the king's own council to help. When she'd started, the idea that *the right thing* could have brought her here would have been inconceivable. But it had. And she'd done it.

The right thing.

She could feel her grandmother rearing up from her grave in horror. Lizzie turned on that inner voice and, for once, told it to *shut up*.

"Then you're going to be fine." Queen Marged drew Gwenllian closer with one arm and held out the other to Lizzie. Despite herself, Lizzie went into it. In truth, she had gone out of her way to push away anyone who ever tried to befriend her. In this moment, she could admit she'd done so because it was easier not to care than to lose yet another person she loved.

Soon all the women were standing with their arms around each other, holding on.

The queen kissed Gwenllian's temple and the top of Lizzie's head, as they were the two nearest girls. "We cannot change the past. Events have thrown us around like dolls, the three of you in particular, for far too long. I can't promise that won't happen again, but at least we know more now. At least this part we can do together."

42

Day Six

"My lord! Why have you come with such an army to my doorstep?" Almain gestured broadly to indicate the view behind David.

And well he might ask. David's army had put on an excellent show, moving in force down the road towards the main gatehouse. A thousand torches lit the town, located across a bridge from the castle, and they'd further augmented the image of the size of their army with a hundred campfires lit to the east and west. Finally, they'd rolled up to the front gate with a hastily assembled collection of modern weapons, including the shoulder cannon. David was telling Almain he had the power to lay waste to his castle if he didn't do as David bid.

Almain himself had risen from his bed to peer down from the towers. He didn't look particularly groggy, and there was no sign of Bogo, just as Roger had promised.

"We have a matter that lies between us, Almain. I would ask that you come down to speak to me."

"On what matter, my lord? I cannot imagine what would have prompted such a question—or such a force!" Almain had implied his feelings were hurt. He was so good at the lie that David could feel some of the less experienced men around him wondering if they'd made a mistake.

David held his ground, not yet ready to tell Almain that he knew he held his mother. "Do you really want me to lay the matter plainly before you for all your men to hear? Because if you require it, I will. It is my hope that we can resolve this matter in a few moments of consultation."

Almain held himself still, staring down at David. And then there was a commotion behind him.

* * * * *

"Guys! There's the signal." It had been Elen's turn to keep watch on the forest. "They're ready for us. It's time to go."

But now that it came to it, the six women looked at each other. "Who goes first?" Molly's voice was very small.

"Me." Elen was already halfway out the window. "I can hold the rope at the bottom so it doesn't swing."

"I was going to do it." Gwenllian reached for Elen's arm.

"Too late. Besides, your grandfather, and all that—"

"I'll go last," Aunt Meg said. Daisy was finally managing to call her Meg, even in her head. If they were to be family, it was appropriate.

"You're the most valuable of us!" Lizzie had the adamancy of a new convert. "You and Daisy."

"Don't worry," Gwenllian said in a dry tone. "Mom can always jump and take Daisy with her."

Daisy knew what that meant. After a decade of hearing about Avalon, they all knew what it meant.

Elen hadn't been listening, since she was already gone. Unencumbered by the fancier skirts Daisy and Molly wore, she made it to the bottom quickly to hold the rope steady as she promised, though as before, it was so dark at the base of the motte that she was more of a shape than a girl. Molly went next, after a wide-eyed look at Daisy, who nodded encouragingly. It took her so long to descend, however, that Aunt Meg had time to help Lizzie hitch up her dress, revealing her underdress but also freeing her feet.

By the time Lizzie was on the ground and pressing her back against the wall of the keep beside Elen, two of David's men had come through the postern gate in the outer curtain wall and had swum the moat. One of them relieved Elen of her duty at the bottom of the rope, while the second helped both girls into the water. They could see them better from the starlight reflecting off the surface of the water.

Swimming was a piece of the plan Daisy was not looking forward to. She could swim, barely, having learned one summer at her father's insistence, but had hardly practiced since. She also knew what was in the moats, no matter how often they were flushed.

Gwenllian was next. Like Elen, she still wore her riding clothes, those split skirts Queen Lili had popularized. Right there and then, Daisy resolved to ask for one too.

If they lived through this.

* * * * *

At Berkhamsted's front gate, David put down the binoculars he'd been using to scan the battlements. He didn't need them anyway. "Something's gone wrong."

A man had appeared beside Almain as he stood above the gatehouse and now he whispered urgently in his ear. The traitorous earl glanced once to where David stood with his father and Ieuan—and turned away.

David scrubbed at his hair with both hands. "Doesn't he know we can end this without bloodshed?"

"Sometimes bloodshed is necessary, son," Llywelyn said, his tone both grim and matter-of-fact.

"Maybe, but I've been thinking for a while now that I let it be necessary way too often."

"Almain abducted your mother. There's no way out of this for him without losing everything. It looks like he finally knows it."

David himself had known Almain's posturing about how unfair David was being was a way of stalling, as would be expected if he was a traitor. David hadn't overtly called him on it because he had been fine with the stalling. Almain could take all the time he needed. All eyes had to be on the front of the castle for as long as possible.

They really had managed things perfectly.

But David should have known by now he couldn't control everything.

* * * * *

Even were it daytime, Daisy wouldn't have been able to see Molly and Elen anymore, since they'd made it across the moat and through the postern gate in the curtain wall on the other side. They would have another moat to swim and a rampart to navigate, but none of her uncle's men were defending it, not with David's forces threatening to break down the front gate and surrounding them on every side.

It was only as she reached for the window sill that Daisy herself, the last to go before the queen, became aware that Aunt Meg had been glancing continually between Gwenllian as she descended the rope from the window and the door to their room. Just as the girl's weight came off the rope, a great shout came up from the other side of the keep.

"They know." Aunt Meg leaned out the window and called down to their men below, emphasizing her words with a shooing motion of her arm. "Get them out of here! Now!"

Even as Gwenllian and Lizzie plunged into the water, the man who held the bottom of the rope waved an arm in return. "My lady, I am not leaving without you."

"Mathew—" Aunt Meg's tone was despairing. She glanced towards the door yet again and then gripped Daisy's arm when she was still halfway out the window. "Do you trust me?"

Daisy gazed at the queen. She knew what she was asking. *They could travel to Avalon.* Her breath caught in her throat. She wasn't Lizzie. She wasn't adventurous or careless of tradition. Maybe part of her problem was that she'd always dreamed of a conventional life, with a husband and children. Avalon was so far beyond what she knew or wanted that the thought of going there made her legs shake more than they already were.

And still.

"Yes."

Daisy assumed her uncle would try to send men around the base of the keep, though there was no easy way to do that. That was the whole point of the keep, in fact: there was only one way in, and that was through the front door, which was protected by thirty-foot walls right up to the tower. Her uncle's men could scale it with ropes and ladders, if they could find them in time, but she and the queen might be through the postern gate by then. If only they could hurry.

Meanwhile, upwards of fifty of David's men had decided caution was no longer their friend. They'd forced the rampart and the outer moat and were now standing on the battlement of the stone wall above the postern gate. That still put a moat between them and Daisy, not to mention a fifty-foot tower and its equally high motte, but any of Uncle Almain's men who tried to stop them would be shot full of arrows.

Uncle Almain had hired twenty mercenaries, but twenty couldn't hold off this army, even in a castle as defensible as Berkhamsted, and especially when many of them would still be groggy from poppy juice. David always could have taken Berkhamsted by force. He hadn't done so because he hadn't wanted to risk the lives of his mother and sister.

Meg squeezed her hand. "There still may be time—"

The door to their room was flung wide, opened by one of Uncle Almain's soldiers. He took in the situation with a glance: Daisy with one leg over the sill, half in and half out of the window; and Aunt Meg, shielding Daisy the best she could, the dagger Roger had left them clutched in her fist.

Aunt Meg brandished the dagger at him but spoke to Daisy. "Go! I'll hold him off!"

Daisy didn't have to be told twice.

From the doorway, the soldier shouted, "Stop!"

"Come and make me!" Aunt Meg made the threat, even as she flung one leg over the sill. Daisy aimed to give her room, moving from one knot in the rope to the next as quickly as she could. The instant the top knots were free, Aunt Meg practically threw herself out the window, though not enough to actually fall.

Daisy moved even faster. She was thirty feet below the window, and the queen a mere three, when the soldier appeared above them, his form silhouetted against the light behind him from the candles that lit the room.

The man looked down for the time it took one of David's men on the battlement behind Daisy to loose an arrow at him. It struck him in the shoulder, above the heart. Staggering backwards, he cursed and disappeared.

Then, almost before Daisy could comprehend what had happened, she caught a flash from within the room above her. Light reflected off a blade as someone, whether that man or another, swung his sword at their rope. With their weight upon it, the fibers severed as easily as a hot knife cut butter.

Aunt Meg fell, and Daisy fell with her.

By now, Daisy herself had only twenty feet to fall to the bottom of the keep. If she'd had time to think about it, she would have known that distance wouldn't kill her. All she could do, however, was squeeze her eyes shut and hold onto the rope for dear life.

The fall was interminable and heart-thumpingly fast at the same time, ending with her dropping with a thud into the arms of a man. Her breath was knocked out of her, as his must have been too. Somehow, he maintained his feet.

"I've got you." His arms came around her, and she felt, more than saw, the way he used the momentum of her fall to slide down the slope of the motte.

As they hit the cold water of the moat, she gasped. "The queen—" Daisy struggled in his arms, trying to look over his shoulder to the keep. The base of it was in shadow, however. She could make out movement but no forms.

"Mathew caught her. They're right behind us. Our archers will make sure nobody else follows." He held Daisy with a firm grip, kicking with his feet and keeping their heads above water as best he could. But her clothing had become instantly waterlogged, the dress wrapping around her legs and hindering her movements. Despite their combined best efforts, she went under once and, when she came up, spit out a disgusting amount of moat water.

By then, she had her bearings better and was able to paddle herself the rest of the way to shore. By that point, other men were in the water, trying to help, and many hands reached for her. Even so, her initial rescuer kept hold of her elbow, staying at her side as they straggled up the bank, passed through the postern gate, and navigated the second moat and rampart.

As they were met by more helpers and a blanket came around her shoulders, the man finally let her go enough to sketch something of a bow. "I'm William, by the way. William de Bohun."

"Daisy."

"It's a pleasure to meet you, my lady." He grinned. "Everything's gonna be okay."

43

Day Six

Gwenllian

It was only later, after Almain showed himself to have some honor left, surrendering the castle rather than forcing David to batter down the gates, that the four of them— Gwenllian, Mom, Dad, and David—were able to sit together properly as a family. They'd chosen to stay outside the castle in one of the pavilions they'd brought, rather than sleep in Almain's tower. His rooms there would be cleaned for David later, whether he wanted to stay in them or not, because of the symbolism of it.

Gwenllian and Mom were well wrapped in blankets, having been dried, changed, fed, and hugged by everyone.

"Are you sure you're okay, Gwenllian?" Dad leaned forward to pile another blanket over her knees.

"I'm okay. Honestly, I was more bothered by the wet than the cold." Still, she shivered. "That moat was *disgusting.*"

"I'm still shaken to know how the girls, especially Lizzie, were so utterly neglected all these years. I'm going to have words about her treatment at St. Margaret's." Mom's expression turned grim.

"I should have paid better attention to them too," David said. "Honestly, I never gave them a second thought."

"Like what happened to me in Avalon." The words came out before Gwenllian could stop them. She saw the glance between her parents and guessed her mom must have said something to her dad about this already.

David, however, looked from one to the other. "What are we talking about?"

Mom gestured to Gwenllian. "Tell him."

"The convent where I ended up after Dad died at Cilmeri."

David raised his eyebrows. "Where you didn't end up because Dad *didn't* die at Cilmeri?"

"He did in Avalon."

"That is true."

"Why, Taddy?" The pain of it rose up in her heart, and she not only couldn't stop the words from coming out, she didn't want to. "Why did you go to Cilmeri?"

Between one heartbeat and the next, her father was on his knees before her, gazing up into her face. "It wasn't out of lack of love for you."

"It doesn't look that way to me."

"It wouldn't, I suppose." He let out a breath. "I don't know if you can understand how many ways I was a different person then.

Elinor had died giving birth to you. You were born a girl, which at the time made a difference to the future of Wales. I was grieving the loss of your mother, of everything important to me—every dream, every hope—and that made me reckless. Up until your birth, I hadn't even joined my brother's rebellion."

"You didn't even think of me."

"Maybe you're right. Maybe I didn't—or at least didn't think of you enough. I'm sorry, if that's true." Her father closed his eyes for a moment, and when he opened them, there were tears on his cheeks. She had never seen him cry before. Ever. "When your mom here disappeared, pregnant with your brother, I despaired for my future and the future of Wales. Then I found Elinor and had hope again. In my head, though I can understand if it doesn't look that way to you, when I went to Cilmeri, whether in Avalon or here, I *was* thinking of you. King Edward might ultimately have retreated for a while, maybe even pretended to give up, but he was never going to let Wales be, not unless we were in an impregnable position. I was already past fifty. I had maybe a few more years to live. All I could think was that by going, I could leave a legacy where you *wouldn't* end up in an English convent. I knew in my soul that if I didn't keep fighting, if I didn't go to Cilmeri, upon my death, the convent was inevitable."

Gwenllian didn't reply. She really didn't know what to say. She wanted everything to be okay between her and her father, but it was hard to let this go and it felt a bit like what he'd said was just an excuse.

David had been sitting silently, listening, but now he spoke in a gentle voice, without urgency, which oddly made what he had to say all the more penetrating. "I was there when he came back to Aber for the first time after he almost died, after the battles with Edward's men along the Conwy, after we won." He gave a little laugh. "That was about when I stopped sleeping well. Late one night I passed by your room as he stood over your cradle, looking down on you. Then he picked you up and held you as you slept. He didn't have much time for you during the day, but most nights, you slept on his chest. His example made it easy for me to care for my boys. He loved you then, Gwenllian. You can't doubt he loves you now."

Gwenllian sat a moment, thinking less about the specifics of what her father or David had said, but about Lizzie, and that in the end she was right. Their places had been exchanged. She still wasn't certain her father had really been thinking of her that December day. Or, at least, not enough. Maybe she was just going to have to forgive him for that, the way her mom had told Lizzie she was going to have to forgive Gwenllian. The past couldn't be changed. And unlike Lizzie, Gwenllian *had* been raised with a father who loved her.

She moved forward into his arms. "I'm sorry, Taddy."

"I love you, Gwenny. I'm sorry I ever made you think otherwise."

Gwenllian pulled back, feeling genuinely lighter. They smiled at each other. And then Gwenllian turned a little rueful. "You know, all this would have been different for Lizzie and me if there'd been elections then. Maybe Bogo is a little bit right. Maybe there shouldn't be *any* princesses anymore."

Her comment was followed by dead silence. She couldn't tell if that was because everyone agreed, disagreed, or, more likely, she had inadvertently stumbled on a sensitive topic nobody wanted to talk about.

David did anyway. "You're not wrong, Gwenllian. And nor is Bogo. I should have held an election years ago."

"No, you shouldn't have." Mom spoke immediately. "It would have been a disaster."

"Would it *now*, though? I can think of a whole bunch of very competent people who could do this job great."

"Llywelyn," Mom nudged Dad, who had retreated to his seat, "tell him."

But to Gwenllian's surprise, he didn't. "I've been thinking much the same thing for a while now too. Tell me how you see it, son."

David's expression was one of overwhelming relief at Dad's words, almost as much relief as Gwenllian herself was feeling to have gotten the Cilmeri thing off her chest. "It got me thinking again. I mean, Bogo is a fool, and both he and Almain were deluded if they thought they could abduct my family and then stand for election. Kidnapping is illegal in any universe, so I have no problem arresting them. But that doesn't mean he was wrong about me adhering to my principles."

Mom felt the need to try one more time. "The people aren't educated enough—"

"Of course they aren't. But nor is the typical eighteen-year-old." David laughed. "Or someone who's fifty-five. Who exactly *is* qualified to choose the next President of the United States?" David spread his hands wide. "Nobody! But in the aggregate ..." His voice trailed off as he shrugged. "The system is imperfect and messy and sometimes leads to disaster. I know that. But when are they going to be ready? It resolves a bunch of other problems too, including this possible Edward II situation. He would have to stand for election like everybody else."

"He's only eleven years old," Mom pointed out.

"We don't have an age restriction. At home, I wouldn't qualify to be president for another eight years. Humphrey de Bohun came in the middle of the night to tell you about Edward's existence because the fact that he's eleven doesn't matter. Nobody ever worried if a king was actually *qualified* for the job. Qualification comes with birthright and only birthright. That's why Bogo thought marrying Daisy would solve everything for him."

"A lot of other people don't understand it either," Mom said.

"I can't believe you're defending the monarchy, Mom," Gwenllian said.

Mom wrinkled her nose. "Maybe I can't either."

Now it was David's turn to look rueful. "On top of all that, I have to think of my own sons. I don't want to inflict the crown on Arthur, not without more backing than a bunch of barons pushed to the breaking point by what at the time looked like a host of bad choices, with me as the least evil of them. And does anyone actually think being a prince is a healthy way to grow up? I think one reason I'm sane is because I didn't even know I was one." He put out a hand to his father. "No offense, Dad."

Dad laughed. "None taken, son."

"Seriously, think about England's kings up until now. Working backwards from Edward, whom enough has been said about, his father, Henry III ruled for fifty-six years with a civil war in the middle of it. Henry's father, King John, ruled for seventeen years with a civil war towards the end of it. Not to mention the wars in Wales and everywhere else for both of them. And that's just in the thirteenth century! Before that, Richard ruled for nine years and spent, like, three months in England during his whole reign."

"I think it was closer to six months, and it was because England was viewed as a lesser holding than his lands in France," Mom said, "but your point stands. From the very beginning, starting in 1066 with the conquest of England by William I, it has been nothing but war, rebellion, infighting, and more war."

"Didn't Henry II's own children and wife rebel against him?"

It was a rhetorical question, and Mom took it as such. "What you're saying is that kingship has not served England well up until now."

"Can you legitimately say it has?"

"No." She paused. "Not until you."

"And my reign hasn't exactly been free of warfare, rebellion, and contention, has it?" He threw out his hand in a despairing gesture. "Even now, I apparently have a traitor in my court, one who meant to poison me. We have no idea who that is. Almain isn't talking. Bogo could tell us when we catch up with him."

"If we catch up with him," Dad said.

Mom made a face. "I still don't like it."

David laughed—genuinely Gwenllian thought. "I was elected High King of Britain by all the nations of the CSB, fair and square. I'm not saying I won't keep that."

All of a sudden, Gwenllian felt a rising excitement. Her brother was talking about *real* change. "What about being the Prince of Wales?"

David shrugged. "Dad's the king, Gwenllian. In Wales, I'm just his son." He turned to look at their father. "But think about how many men might want Welsh law to apply upon your death, at the very least to split the kingdom between Padrig and me. Or between the four of us! I don't want any of them pitted against me, like you were against your brothers. I don't want Padrig to entertain for a single second the idea that he might do well to murder me on the way to taking the throne the way Dafydd tried to murder you."

"I don't want that either!" Gwenllian said.

Her parents were suddenly holding hands, having reached across the space between them. They looked at each other, communicating in a way Gwenllian didn't understand and by now knew she never would. Then Mom said, "I guess we should do something about it."

Gwenllian grinned at her brother. "As you always say: what's the point of all this power if we don't use it?"

44

David

David took a good long look at the keep. Daisy stood beside him, with William de Bohun, Christopher, Venny, and the rest of David's guard hovering in the background. For David's purposes, however, it was only the two of them on the battlement, standing together above the postern gate that had proved to be such a sieve in Almain's defenses. Most castles that fell were either surrendered or taken with help from the inside. In the end, all that had been required at Berkhamsted was the determination of Almain's own nieces.

"What do you think?" David asked.

"It was a long fall, more for your mother than for me. I wasn't that far up."

"You were holding onto the rope, though, right?"

"Yes."

David rubbed his chin. "Was my mom?"

"I don't know. I'm sorry I'm so useless."

"Useless is the last thing you are."

"My eyes were squeezed shut. What did your mother say?"

"She didn't see anything but darkness, but it's always dark." He paused. "Mathew says one moment she was all the way up at the window and the next she was in his arms. We can guess how that happened, but you're the one who experienced it."

He hadn't asked the real question in his head, which was: if Mom and Daisy went to Avalon, why didn't they stay? When he'd asked his mom that question, she'd replied fairly unconcernedly. *"How can we ever know? Maybe I didn't go. Maybe my life wasn't in enough danger, as turned out to be true. Maybe the danger to me was actually greater in Avalon. Or maybe it isn't going to work for me anymore."* She'd given David an intent look then. *"That would be okay too, you know."*

"If that's true, we're going to have to be more careful." Dad's arm had come around Mom's shoulders.

"Only as careful as normal people already are. I used to be a normal person. I can be one again."

At the time, David had nodded, though he'd looked away as he did so, unsatisfied by their conclusions. His parents thought it was enough that Mom remained in Earth Two, but David was preoccupied with the larger question.

Now Daisy gave a shake of her head. "I was holding my breath and a little panicked. I can tell you the fall felt like it would never end. I never want to climb out of a window again."

"Here's hoping you don't have to." He glanced at her. "Have you given some thought to what might be next for you and your sisters?"

"We've given it nothing but thought. Though Molly might want a life as a nun, it won't be at St. Margaret's. For now, we would like to stay together. And not in a convent."

"Wherever and however you like. I know my mother would love to have you with her."

Daisy smiled. "Lizzie, Elen, and Gwenllian could prove to be a dangerous threesome!"

"But a potent one, too, don't you think? They did pretty well together here."

"We'll see."

David respected that she wasn't ready to commit. A lifetime of estrangement wasn't going to be overcome in a day. For that reason, he was a little surprised at Daisy's next words, which were,

"Thank you."

"You're welcome." He tipped his head. "It is I who should be thanking you, however."

"You've done that already, and I didn't do it for you." She paused. "Not at first."

"I know. But you did it anyway."

"Are you really going to abdicate the throne?"

He didn't know how she'd heard about his conversation with his parents and Gwenllian, since they had been alone at the time. He supposed he shouldn't have been surprised. This was a royal court.

Rumor abounded, concocted out of nothing sometimes, and this wasn't nothing. "Is that what you would prefer? You could stand for election. You have the lineage more than I do, if you want to get technical about it."

She gazed at him for so long he wasn't sure she was going to answer. Even when she did, it sounded a bit like she was forcing out the words. "No."

"Truly?"

"My grandmother's ghost might haunt me forever for saying this, but England will not be better off without you."

"Abdicating doesn't mean I wouldn't stand for election."

"Oh." She brightened. "That's okay, then."

"Really?"

She laughed. "My lord, my uncle and Bogo deceived themselves from beginning to end. There is no way you won't win."

As she turned away to walk back down the battlement, David realized two things: the first was that, from her easy turn of phrase, she was already spending way too much time with William de Bohun, who was right there to escort her off the battlement; and the second was the way her story and his mother's matched. Mom had thought maybe the time traveling wasn't going to work for her anymore. But another glance up at that keep had David thinking she was entirely wrong. It *had* worked. Mathew was right. No matter how strong he was, he could not have remained standing up on a rain-soaked slope to catch her after a such a fall.

Which meant she and Daisy had traveled to Avalon and returned so quickly nobody, including both of them, realized they'd gone. That wasn't exactly a new situation. Years ago, David himself had fallen from the battlement at Dover, and more recently into a war zone and an ocean, and been sent back in the time it took to breathe in and out a few times. More concerning was *why* they were sent back so quickly. What could be happening in Avalon that the danger there was greater than here? The thought was more than a little troubling.

Ever since his father had acknowledged him as his son, David had been able to see the future and what he had to do next. That wasn't the case any longer. Most of the time, he had no idea where the road they were on was leading him. He certainly hadn't seen Almain and Bogo—or Lizzie and her sisters—coming.

But to know his mother could time travel, even in light of the changes David and his father were planning in England and Wales, might mean they really still were on the right track.

HISTORICAL NOTE

Like David, I hadn't always seen Almain and Bogo—and Lizzie—coming either. But history is not just about the winners. In any clash of cultures, there's another side to the story. In the case of Almain and Bogo, they chose to be resentful of their changed circumstances. For Lizzie and her sisters, David's ascension to the English throne in Earth Two resulted in crushing changes to their lives over which they had no control.

For his part, Bogo de Clare had led an *interesting* life even before David's arrival. He was known in his own time as a *notorious pluralist,* meaning he held many clerical livings, perhaps over thirty. And yet, despite a 1283 order that he commit finally to the priesthood, there is no evidence he was ever ordained. He lived a lavish lifestyle all his life and, according to Wikipedia, "died suddenly in October 1294, his passing noticed by several chroniclers, always unfavourably. The Worcester annalist commented that 'God only knows if his life was worthy of praise, but no-one thought it worthy of imitation' (Ann. mon., 4.517)." In Earth Two, King Edward's death and the changes wrought by David meant he lived a little longer.

For Edward's three daughters, the move to St. Margaret's required each to no longer be known by their given name: Margaret became Daisy; Mary became Molly; and Elizabeth became Lizzie. Pet names were necessary throughout the medieval period simply because the common pool of names was so small. In Daisy's case, the French pronunciation of her name, *Marguerite*, was also the name for the flower the English called *daisy*. Other nicknames for her could have been Peggy, Meg, Mags, or Maggie, just to name a few.

In regards to the discussion of what happened to Gwenllian in Avalon after the death of Llywelyn at Cilmeri, the historical record reports that, when Aber was captured by King Edward, the king ordered baby Gwenllian to be sent to the Gilbertine priory at Sempringham. It is understood by historians that she never learned Welsh, nor even how to properly pronounce her own name. According to the priory records, she was listed as "Wencilian" and signed her own name, "Wentliane." Edward III paid twenty pounds a year to the priory for her upkeep, which ended in 1337 at her death at age fifty-five.

Lizzie, or Princess Elizabeth, on the other hand, was married at the age of fifteen to John of Holland. She appears to have never wanted the marriage and may have rejoiced at his death in 1299. In 1302 she married Humphrey de Bohun (known as William in the *After Cilmeri* series). By all indications, it was a love match. She died in childbirth in 1316 and he in battle in 1322, leading a rebellion against Edward II.

Thank you continuing this journey into the Middle Ages with me!
There will be another book in the *After Cilmeri* series.

www.sarahwoodbury.com

Acknowledgments

First and foremost, I'd like to thank my lovely readers for encouraging me to continue the *After Cilmeri* series. I have always been passionate about these books, and it's wonderful to be able to share my stories with readers who love them too. Thank you also to all my editors, proof-readers, and beta readers. I am grateful for all the ways each and every one of you make the book better.

Thank you to my husband, without whose love and support I would never have tried to make a living as a writer, and thank to my family who has been nothing but encouraging of my writing, despite the fact that I spend half my life in medieval Wales. I couldn't do this without you.

About the Author

With over a million books sold to date, Sarah Woodbury is the author of more than forty novels, all set in medieval Wales. Although an anthropologist by training, and then a full-time homeschooling mom for twenty years, she began writing fiction when the stories in her head overflowed and demanded that she let them out. While her ancestry is Welsh, she only visited Wales for the first time at university. She has been in love with the country, language, and people ever since. She even convinced her husband to give all four of their children Welsh names.

She makes her home in Oregon.

www.ingramcontent.com/pod-product-compliance
Lightning Source LLC
Chambersburg PA
CBHW060849210726
48293CB00006B/1729